Forgotten

Rose of Petrichoria

Book 1

By Katie Hauenstein

For my mother,
who may have forgotten,
but will never be forgotten.

Table of Contents

Part I

Chapter 1

"Mommy? Mommy? Mommy? Mommy…"

I opened one eye to see my daughter's big blue eyes and blonde spiral curls hovering inches over my face. Harmony had a giant smile on her face.

She is much too chipper in the morning.

This is how all my mornings now began since Harmony started sleeping in her "big girl" bed. I had long abandoned the concept of sleeping in. Faking that I was still asleep didn't work. Putting Harmony to bed early didn't work. Putting her to bed late didn't work. Full tummy, warm milk, begging, pleading, crying – nothing worked. At 6:00 a.m. every single morning, Harmony bounded into my room wide awake and ready to face the day.

I turned my head and looked out the window to see a bright sunny day. Glad for the luck of sun on an April morning in Snohomish, Washington, I smiled widely at my little girl.

"Yes, darling. I'm awake."

Harmony threw her tiny arms into the air, then landed on my tummy.

"OMPH! Good morning, little sunshine. How was your sleep?"

Her face got a little sad as she replied, "Daddy was in my dreams again. When is he coming home?"

It had been a year since the accident and the poor child still had a hard time grasping the fact that Daddy wasn't going to be coming home again. I knew the next question would be about Tom.

I pulled my small daughter into a tight embrace as the tears began to fall down her chubby little cheeks. It amazed me how Harmony could go from happy as a clam to down in the dumps. As hard as it was for me, I knew Harmony had it worse. How do you explain Heaven to someone who has no concept of death? How do you explain death to someone who knows nothing of mortality? I decided to nip it in the bud and just answer both of her questions before she presented the second one.

"Oh, honey. Daddy and Tom won't be coming home to us. Remember? They're in Heaven now, and when you go to Heaven, you don't go back home to your family in this world. We'll see them again someday when it is our turn to go to Heaven."

"When? I miss them."

"Not for a long, long time. There are still a lot of things planned for us. We have new places to go and new friends to make. Okay?"

"Okay," Harmony replied. Silence sat between us for a moment as the small child considered everything I had just said to her. "Can we have chocolate chip pancakes for breakfast?"

"Of course!"

The two of us jumped out of bed and raced to the kitchen. I let Harmony win because that's just what mommies do. Harmony grabbed the ingredients she could at her height and gave them to me. I grabbed the Kitchen Aid, griddle, and everything else. Just as we had mixed everything together and poured a few pancakes on the griddle, my phone rang. Quizzically, I looked at the caller ID with a cocked eyebrow; it read "Unknown Number."

The well-wishers are starting early today.

I answered. "Good morning, this is Miriam."

Silence.

"Hello?"

More silence.

"Hellooo?"

Even more silence.

Frustrated, I ended the call. I glanced at the clock and saw it was only 6:15.

Who calls this early in the morning for a prank call? Probably some college kid who's been up all night studying and needed a quick laugh.

Ever since David passed away, I had a variety of people contacting me: banks, hospitals, random businesses we had bills with, insurance, etc. Even though David died a year ago, people were still calling. I couldn't remember how many times over the last year I'd had to say, "I'm sorry, my husband has passed away" and then had to go through each company's insane policy for how to handle it.

Over the last couple weeks, though, I'd started getting these hang-up calls. Once a day at random parts of the day. This was, by

5

far, the earliest one I had received. The phone company didn't help. They said there was nothing they could do about it, so I just lived with it. I understood; it *was* an unknown number.

I shrugged and we continued making the pancakes. A year ago, I wouldn't have let Harmony help. However, I had come to realize I was too much of a perfectionist and control freak. So many missed opportunities with Tom were missed because of it and I decided I was not going to be that way with Harmony. Every moment I cherished and I was glad I abandoned that past self.

We ate our breakfast in relative silence, with the exception of the occasional giggle from a silly face or comment. Of course the words "eat your food" were said many times. Harmony could be so pushy.

After breakfast, I looked at my sticky daughter and smiled. Harmony was my whole world. David blessed me with a life insurance large enough to last us, and he had spent our six short married years together investing wisely. Because of that, I could spend all of my time with Harmony. I had learned enough about investing that I could keep the money working for me.

I took a deep breath. Today was going to be a long day. One year. Exactly one year today. Hopefully, Harmony would be able to understand the things that we would be doing; I hoped we wouldn't spend too much time crying.

"Okay. Let's get you cleaned up and ready to go."

Harmony jumped up and started stripping on the way to the bathroom for her bath. I put the dishes in the sink, and started my way down the hall. Just as I stepped into the bathroom, my phone rang again.

"Hello?"

Silence. Again.

This time, I didn't give whoever it was the time of day. Irritated, I hung up. 7:15.

An hour later? Doesn't this person have a life? How about getting dressed or taking a shower, you weirdo?

Moving on, I gave Harmony her bath and put her in the little black dress with the bright red rose at the waist I had bought for that day. I set out some puzzles and told her to stay put while I showered. Harmony entertained herself very well and never wandered off, so I knew I had nothing to worry about.

Leaving the door open in case Harmony needed me, I walked into the bathroom and looked at myself in the mirror. I still looked young, but my long, black hair had a few stray strands of silver and there were faint laugh lines appearing on my face.

Making sure I got the temperature nice and hot, I got into the shower. As the water hit my face and body, I couldn't help getting lost in my thoughts. For that time, I unleashed the great sorrow in my soul. Life just wasn't fair. I had become a widow at thirty, lost a child at the same time that I lost my husband, and I had miscarried twice. My parents had died long ago and I had never felt more alone than at that moment. Harmony was all I had left. Emma, my mother-in-law, was still involved in our lives, but aside from that, everyone else left.

I couldn't blame them. If I were in their shoes, I wouldn't know what to say either. So I kept to myself, mostly. The only time I was really with other adults was when I went to church. Other than that, I did things Harmony liked to do, which were often the same things I enjoyed, anyway.

I wept as I showered, but got it under control before getting out of the shower. Harmony didn't need to see me that way. After I dried

7

off, I put on my black dress and applied minimal makeup, including the waterproof mascara I had just purchased the day before. More crying was sure to happen today.

When I went in to grab Harmony, I found her dressing up her stuffed animals in clothes for a tea party. As darling as the scene was, I had to interrupt. "Ready to go?"

"Yeah! Where are we going?"

"The flower shop first. After that, we're going to visit Daddy and Tom's places."

"Okay."

Harmony looked a little confused, but whatever her questions were, she kept them to herself. I actually felt relieved, but knew that the day would be difficult for my little girl.

Harmony swooped up her stuffed animals, ran to her room, and threw them in. I didn't even care that she didn't put them away in their appropriate places. It was going to be a difficult day and I wanted it to begin as easily as possible.

We hopped in the car, buckled up, and put on David's favorite music: funk. Harmony knew the words to many of the songs because she had heard them a million times before her dad died, so we both did car karaoke all the way to the flower shop.

The flower shop took way more time than I had anticipated. Mainly because Harmony had a difficult time deciding between all the different colors and types of flowers. We finally settled with a bouquet of blue tulips and white daisies for David; they reminded Harmony of their trips to the local Tulip Festival. For Tom, we bought a dozen green roses. Harmony had said, "Tom would think these are cool! They're like Ninja Turtles or The Hulk!"

As walked out the door, the phone rang again. It read "Unknown Number". I looked at the time; on the fifteen again. I didn't answer and proceeded to put my phone on silent for the rest of the day.

The road trip to the mausoleum was long, but quiet. Having exhausted herself at the flower shop, Harmony fell asleep right away, so I turned the music off. Left with my thoughts for the rest of the two-hour trip, I thought of everything we had been through as a family; as David and I were as a couple. The losses of our two unborn babies, the laughs we shared at the beach with Tom and Harmony, living check-to-check in the beginning, being in a good place later on, all those Sundays and Wednesdays we went to church. How I missed singing with my tenor husband. He had the most gorgeous voice.

We finally made it and I woke up Harmony. She wanted me to carry her. Most of the time, I would have told her that she was a big girl and needed to walk on her own, but today I gladly scooped up my precious, but getting-heavy, girl and held her tight. Harmony had the flowers snuggled between the two of us so it was a bit awkward, but also comforting.

As we got closer to the spot, Harmony started sniffling. Pretty soon the sniffling turned into sobbing. I put her down when we got to David and Tom's plots and Harmony set the flowers into their respected vases. Then, Harmony and I updated David and Tom on everything that had happened in the last year and wept as we declared how much we still loved and missed them. It was difficult to pull away, but we finally did and got back to the car.

Next, we went to the beach. I laid the picnic blanket out on the miraculously dry ground and set out the food while Harmony played with the hermit crabs running around. We ate our lunch with a

9

changed mood of happiness and humor and were soon on our way home.

By the time we got home, it was already nearly bedtime for Harmony. It had been a long day and neither of us really felt like eating. Going against normalcy once again, I let Harmony skip dinner and tucked her in. I did the normal routine of reading a book, singing a song, then praying. On my way out, though, Harmony stopped me.

"Mommy? Can I sleep with you tonight?"

My heart broke for my little one. "Yes. When I'm ready to go to bed, I will come in and get you. I love you. Good night."

"Okay. I love you, too."

I left the door cracked open and headed into the kitchen. I made myself some hot chocolate and put whipped cream on top, then settled onto the loveseat in the living room. David and I used to snuggle there after we put the kids to bed and watch a favorite show or a movie. Tonight, I decided to watch Doctor Who; a favorite for both of us. This one featured the Daleks as the main antagonist. Sometimes I wished I could take a trip in the Doctor's time machine and stop us from getting in the car that fateful day. However, I always came to the conclusion that it would tear up time and space and it probably wouldn't be a great idea. Life the way it was for me was the way it was going to be forever. I sighed at the thought and turned off the television on my way to bed.

Walking back to the room, I remembered my phone was on silent. I felt bad, sure people had been trying to call all day. I turned the volume back on and scrolled through my missed calls. I didn't keep many friends, so there weren't many people on the missed call list. *Betty, Emma, Pastor Marsh, Callie, Unknown Number.* When I saw how many missed calls were from my mysterious caller, I gasped. Precisely one an hour, every hour, on the fifteen.

What in the world is going...

The phone ringing interrupted my thought. The time read 12:15. Scared and angry, I answered the phone.

"Who is this? Why are you calling me so much? I've had this phone tapped. I know where you are and will be sending the police to you!" Of course, my phone wasn't really tapped, and I wasn't even sure if that was the right terminology for what I attempted to convey, but I hoped it would be a deterrent from the seemingly mute person calling again.

However, the caller wasn't mute. That time, he spoke.

"We're going to take you out soon." Click.

Eyes wide and hands shaking, I tossed the phone on the bed and began pacing.

Who is this person and why does he want to take me out? What did he mean by "we?"

I called down to the Police Department and reported the threat. At first, they told me it was probably a prank call, but when I told them about the stalkerish hourly phone calls, they took me seriously and said they would send someone to sit in the front of my house for the rest of the night.

I walked back to my bedroom closet and checked my gun in my safe. Satisfied with its condition, I went out to the living room to watch for the police car. After what seemed like an eternity, it arrived. I waved to the police officer, then headed back to get Harmony.

When I went to Harmony's room, I found her totally sprawled out and asleep. I picked her up and put her in my bed. Exhausted, I plopped onto my bed without removing my day clothes. Before going to sleep, I glanced at the clock. 1:30. Maybe the calls would stop now. That could be a good thing or a bad thing.

Only time would tell.

Chapter 2

I woke up before Harmony the next morning. That was very strange; especially since it was 10:30 in the morning. I checked my phone and saw there were no more phone calls. Sighing in relief, I sat up. Harmony stretched out when I stood. I looked at her curiously.

Is she sick? Maybe she's having a growth spurt?

Just as these questions started running through my mind, Harmony jumped up.

"Mommy! Are we going to MOPS today?"

Slapping my forehead, I said, "Oh no! We slept through it. I'm so sorry, honey."

Harmony didn't even miss a beat. She just shrugged and hopped off the bed and to her room. She showed no sadness about not seeing her friends, no conversation, no giggles. It was weird. I followed her to her room. When I arrived, she was standing in the middle of the room like a little doll; arms at her side, standing straight. "I'm ready to get dressed, Mommy."

"Are you okay, honey? Are you feeling sick?"

"No. I'm okay, Mommy. I just know the next thing is our visit with Nana."

"Oh… okay."

Since when does she keep track of the schedule?

I walked over to my daughter's dresser and picked out a pair of jeans and a pink t-shirt that read "Geek Chic" in sparkly letters. When I turned around, I saw that my daughter hadn't moved a muscle.

Eyebrow raised, I walked over and sank to my knees in front of Harmony. I set the clothes on the floor next to her, grabbed her tiny hands, wiggled her around in a silly little dance, and sang a song I had written for her. Slowly, Harmony loosened up and started singing along. By the end of the song, she was her cute self and ready to play. Her smile returned, which I was definitely happy about.

What a strange morning.

I helped her get dressed and we went into the kitchen for a snack. It was already 11:30 and we were going to eat with Emma at the Evergreen Café. Time just seemed to fly. What felt like ten minutes getting Harmony ready was actually an hour. It was then that I realized I was showered and wearing my blue sundress. I looked over to the mirror and saw my makeup was on, too.

When did I do that?

Though slightly disturbed by the odd moment, I shook it off and rolled my neck to release some tension. Yesterday had been long and my brain was just probably not functioning properly yet. We hurried to put our dishes in the dishwasher, and I grabbed my purse as we headed out the door.

I got Harmony buckled in and gave her an eskimo kiss. Then, I moved around to get into my seat behind the wheel. I turned the radio on, then turned it right back off after I listened to the headlines. Apparently, there had been nothing really new happening since the day before. Driving to the Evergreen Café was unusually easy. I didn't have to wait for any cars or lights; even the normally bumpy roads seemed to have been fixed since my last visit.

I pulled into the restaurant and was happy to find a spot right in front. Because the café was usually packed, that never happened. I parked the car and got Harmony and myself out. Walking into the restaurant, I expected the normal wait time of at least a half hour. However, when I got in, the only person seated in the whole restaurant was Emma. The same look that Harmony had earlier covered her face. She just stared into nothing and sat completely still.

In fact, she didn't even move as Harmony and I approached.

"Nana!" Harmony cried, excitedly.

When Harmony threw her arms around Emma, she became animated and put on a huge smile.

"Well, hello there my little songbird!" Emma greeted Harmony in return. "Hello to you, too, Miriam! I hoped we were still on for today. I tried calling yesterday, but you didn't answer. I hope you were okay. Did you spend the day alone?"

"I'm sorry, Emma, I had muted my phone earlier in the day and forgot to turn the volume back on when we left the mausoleum," I replied as I got Harmony situated in a chair and took a seat myself.

"How was it?" Emma asked.

"Sad. We brought flowers and we wept and talked with them. Afterwards, we had a beach picnic."

"The hermit crabs were silly," interjected Harmony enthusiastically.

"Were they? Did you poke any anemones?" Emma humored her.

"YES! That was *so* fun!"

The waitress brought our menus and some crayons with coloring pages for Harmony. Enthusiastically, Harmony set to filling in the blank pictures and quickly became distracted from the grown-up conversation.

"It was a lovely day for a picnic. David and Tom would have loved that you did that." Emma said, turning her attention back to me.

I just nodded and smiled, then turned my attention to my menu. It was hard for me to talk about David and Tom. I had actually felt a little glad my phone was on silent the day before. I didn't have to say the same things over and over again. "I'm doing okay." "Harmony is doing okay, though we're sad." "No, we don't need anything." Then the variety of stories and reminders would ensue. I just didn't have the energy for that. While people seemed to have forgotten about my parents, no one seemed to have forgotten David and Tom.

It would be nice if people remembered them more than one day a year, though. I hate the calls from people made to make themselves feel better for abandoning us the rest of the year.

Emma was quite likely the best mother-in-law someone could ask for. I appreciated that she remained involved in Harmony's and my life. When everyone else took the easy road of avoidance, Emma threw herself in, despite the fact she dealt with her own pain of losing her son and grandson. I thought that was perhaps the reason she stuck around. Maybe we were the only ones who could understand each other.

At least once a week, we met for lunch and every so often, Emma would come over to my house to watch Harmony while I went to see a grown-up movie. While I looked forward to the day I could share my superhero fangirliness with my daughter, I was fairly certain that Harmony wasn't ready to go see any Marvel or DC Films that were released in the theaters at the time.

Not only did Emma do all of that, she also called to chat every morning. She knew how much I enjoyed that with my own mother before she passed away. Emma and I had become closer than ever in the last year; she had become my best friend.

I shook myself out of my daze and responded, "Yes. They would have loved it."

Emma and I shared empathetic smiles. The waitress came by and began taking orders. I didn't know why we even bothered looking at the menus anymore. We always ordered the same thing. When I ordered for Harmony, she pouted. Being a big girl now, she liked to order for herself.

The three of us did end up talking quite a bit about David and Tom. We shared stories and talked about their characters and personalities. It was refreshing.

"I'm telling you what," I said, "David would be having a fit over the calls I've been getting lately."

"Oh? Are you receiving more calls for him?" Emma replied.

"No. These are strange prank calls."

"Huh. Are you giving your number out at the clubs again? You know I've warned you about that," Emma joked with a wink.

I laughed, "Very funny. I don't think there are any clubs that offer child care. No. These calls are different than that. I had to call the police about them last night."

"Oh my! Tell me about them."

"It started a couple weeks ago. I've been getting hang-up prank calls once a day."

"Why didn't you tell me about this before? Miriam, I would have stayed with you a couple days if I knew you weren't feeling safe."

"Because I *did* feel safe until last night. I promise I would have told you sooner if I felt I was in danger. That's why I'm telling you now."

Emma just nodded and gestured with her hand for me to continue with my explanation.

"Anyway, yesterday, the calls started happening every hour on the fifteens. The first call came in at 6:15 AM! That's why I silenced my phone. I just didn't want to deal with that yesterday, of all days."

"I can't blame you."

"Even then, I only felt irritated, not afraid. It was the last call of the day at 12:15 that scared me. This time, it wasn't a hang-up call. He said something. It was weird. He was British and just spoke matter-of-factly, as if what he said wasn't super creepy."

Kind of cliché that the bad guy was British.

Emma leaned forward on her arms and furrowed her brows. "What did he say?"

"He said 'We're going to take you out soon' and that was it."

"Geez. What did the police say?"

"There wasn't much they could do. The calls have been showing as 'Unknown Number,' so there was no phone number to look up. The phone company was unable to do anything about it as well for the same reason."

"They could have at least sent someone to watch you and Harmony for the night."

We glanced over to Harmony, who had fallen asleep on her paper placemat. She looked so much like David when she slept, except for the long blonde curls sprawled all over the table. Emma smiled. I turned back and responded to Emma.

"They did. But it took *forever* for them to get someone out to the house. Even if Harmony hadn't asked to sleep with me last night, I would have brought her in."

"Have you had any more calls?"

I pulled my phone out of my purse and glanced at it. "Doesn't look like it."

Emma sighed a breath of relief. "Well, good. Maybe those pranksters were just annoyed you hadn't answered your phone all day and wanted to scare you. You know college kids tend to get bored and do some ridiculous things. In college, we would put soap in the fountain every year so it would bubble and foam," she reminisced with a smile on her face and a giggle in her voice.

"Maybe they should try doing their homework," I said under my breath, still quite a bit shaken up.

Emma reached her hand across the table and held mine like a mother would. She noticed I still wore my wedding rings and toyed with them a bit, a sad look on her face.

"Listen, Miriam. I'm sure it's absolutely nothing to worry about, but if you'd like me to, I'll stay the night with you guys tonight."

As I seriously considered her offer, I paused our conversation. In the end, I figured we would be no safer with Emma there than we would be without. "No, I'm sure you're right. It's just hard sometimes to be alone. I just can't lose Harmony, too. I'm not sure how I would live past that."

"You won't lose her. I have a feeling God's not done with you yet."

The waitress brought the bill and Emma paid this time after our normal banter about whose turn it was. Emma woke up Harmony with a tickle, and she laughed and laughed. It was so strange for her to be sleeping so much. I figured it was probably a growth spurt.

Great. Just when we have her wardrobe built up.

We all walked out to the parking lot together and hugged when we got to our cars. I didn't recall seeing Emma's car next to mine when I pulled in.

Maybe I should see my doctor about this.

I got Harmony into the car, then went around and got in myself. Harmony grabbed a book she had stored in the pocket in front of her and started sounding out words.

That learning software is really paying off.

"We're going to go visit with Doctor Smith now, Harmony."

"Okay, Mommy."

Harmony went back to her book as I pulled out and drove off. Again, all we had were green lights and the drive was unusually easy. I got to the clinic and got a spot right up front. Doctor John

20

Smith had been my general practitioner for the last few years. A fantastic doctor, he had really been there for me when David and Tom died. I was lucky that he also had some background in psychology.

I woke up Harmony. She had quickly given up on the book and fallen asleep again.

What in the world?

We walked in and I hoped I would be able to get in to see the doctor.

"Hello, Sonya! Is there any way I can get in to see Doctor Smith this afternoon?" I asked the receptionist.

"Hello, Miriam. Let me check for you," Sonya responded and started clicking away at her keyboard.

Just then, Doctor Smith walked by the doorway. I saw him double-take and walk backward to and through the door. He was a tall, lanky, man with well-coiffed brown hair. I was fairly certain he spent more time doing his hair than I spent doing mine. He flashed me his toothy grin.

"Hello, Miriam," he said with his British accent, "Are you here for a visit with me?" He checked a clipboard he carried. "I don't see you on my schedule."

"I don't have an appointment, but I hoped to get in. I've been having some weird things going on with my mind today."

"Oh. Well, I just had a cancellation if you and Harmony have time to come back now."

"That would be great. Thank you *so* much. I really appreciate it."

"Can I play with the toys in the box?" Harmony begged with giant puppy dog eyes and a pouty lip.

"Of course, Harmony. Come along! Sonya, would you please pull Miriam's file and bring it back when you do?" Doctor Smith said.

When we got to the examination room, I had a seat on the papered table. Doctor Smith found the bin of toys in a cupboard and gave it to Harmony, who was very excited to play with them. As he settled into the spinning, rolling, circular chair, Sonya appeared and handed him my file. He opened it to see when I had come in last.

"It's been some time since you've been in," he noticed.

"Yeah. Things have been great. We've been happy and healthy."

"So if you're happy and healthy, what brings you in today?" he asked, furrowing his brow.

"Like I said, things have been a bit odd today for me. I think I had a blackout this morning. I didn't remember getting showered and dressed. Then I forgot seeing my mother-in-law's car next to mine when we met at the Evergreen Café for lunch."

"I see." He paused and looked at my file. "Wasn't yesterday the anniversary of David and Tom's death?"

"Yeah."

"Is there anything else going on that may be a stress on you?"

"I've been getting these weird calls and Harmony has been sleeping abnormally a lot today."

We looked over at Harmony, who, of course, was wide awake and playing.

Doctor Smith smiled, "Well, she looks plenty awake now. It is probably a growth spurt, but I'll give her a quick check-up if that would put your mind at ease."

"That would be great. Thank you. Harmony, come sit up here with me."

With a frown, she obeyed and Doctor Smith performed a normal well-being check.

"I can tell you that she is perfectly fine. She's probably just tired from your day yesterday. I would wager, that is more-than-likely what is going on with you, too. If it continues, you are welcome to come back in and I'll do further investigation. I won't charge you for your visit today, either," Doctor Smith summarized.

Satisfied and comforted, I thanked the doctor for the unexpected visit and headed to the car with Harmony. I looked at the clock and realized my day was getting away from me. It was a busy, but uneventful rest of the afternoon, filled with boring errands, like grocery shopping, withdrawing cash from the ATM, and picking up packages at the post office. We finally arrived home at 6:30. I put away groceries with the speed of the Flash and began making dinner, while Harmony went to her room to play with her dolls.

I decided to keep it simple with macaroni and cheese and hot dogs, Harmony's favorite. I announced dinner was ready, but Harmony didn't come.

She must be enthralled with her dolls.

I walked back to Harmony's room and slowly opened the door so I could witness her darlingness in her little fantasy world.

Instead, I was shocked to see her standing totally still with a blank stare in the middle of the room, just like she had been that morning.

"Harmony?" I asked, disturbed.

Harmony didn't answer, so I approached her and got down on my knees. Now face-to-face with my little one, I reached out to touch her arms.

"Harmony?"

Harmony switched her stare from into nothingness to straight into my eyes, but didn't respond. Instead of the normal joy I usually saw, I saw nothing. It was as if I was looking into the eyes of a robot.

"Harmony, dinner is ready. I made your favorite, mac n' cheese with hot dogs."

"I like mac n' cheese," Harmony finally said.

"Are you okay, honey?"

"I'm fine," Harmony replied, but she still didn't smile or change the look on her face. She walked around me and down the hall to the dining room table to take her normal seat. There wasn't really any more conversation that night. We ate our dinner, got ready to sleep and I tucked Harmony into bed.

"Good night, honey. I love you," I told her.

"Good night. I love you, too," she responded. Almost as if I had pushed an off button, her eyes slowly closed, and she fell asleep within seconds.

I decided to just retire to my room and read my current book. Being a dystopian fantasy. One of those stories that was extremely far-fetched. That some people actually thought the things I read about could possibly happen astounded me. This one was about a kingdom that came into existence after most of the planet's population was wiped out by an epidemic.

As if the citizens of the United States would ever *give up our democracy...*

As unbelievable as it was, it was a nice escape, and by midnight, I was ready for sleep.

Already in my night clothes, I brushed my teeth and washed my face. When I sat down on my bed and plugged in my phone, I looked at it just to make sure there hadn't been any more calls. To my relief, I had no missed calls, no voicemails, not even a text. I exhaled loudly. I hadn't even realized I held my breath while I checked.

I got under my blankets and laid back in my bed. As I reached over to shut off my lamp, my phone started ringing. Hand hovering over the phone, I looked at my clock and saw it was 12:15 exactly. My phone only read "Unknown Number." I answered.

"Hello?"

After a long silence, I heard, "We're going to take you out today."

Today?!?

Internally, I freaked out. Before they ended the call, I hung up and immediately called the police again. When I informed them about the escalation in threat, they sent someone out again. They told me it would probably be wise to stay at home for the rest of the night and next day and they would have an officer stay there to keep watch. It felt like it took them even longer to arrive than the night before.

Exhausted, I double-checked my door locks and windows, then headed back to bed. I didn't receive any more calls the rest of the night, and I read a bit more to get myself tired again. As I fell asleep, the last thing I thought was –

Who is trying to take me out?

Chapter 3

The next morning, Harmony didn't wake me up again. I looked at the clock and it read 11:00.

What in the world is up with this child?

I wasn't really upset. It had been a very long couple days and we both obviously needed the rest. I got up and involuntarily stretched. My whole body felt stiff and awkward as I made my way across the hall to check on Harmony.

When I opened the door, I was horrified at the sight. Although Harmony still lay asleep in her bed, her room was trashed. The drawers and closet were opened, and clothes, books, and toys littered her floor. However, Harmony just laid there in exactly the same position she was in when I tucked her in last night. I walked across the room and checked the window, which was still locked and not broken. There was no sign of entry at all.

Then, I rushed over to Harmony and startled her awake. "Harmony!"

"Mommy?" Harmony looked around her room with big eyes, clearly as surprised to see it the way it was as me. Someone had come into my daughter's room and fury filled me. For what reason they went only into Harmony's room, I didn't know. Telling

27

Harmony to stay put, I went to my room, opened my gun safe, grabbed the gun out of it and searched the rest of the house for an intruder. Satisfied after a thorough search, I went back to my room and put my gun away.

I went to Harmony's room to look in and was even more shocked than before; the room was pristine. It looked as if nothing had happened in there and Harmony no longer stood where I left her. I walked down the hall and saw my little one sitting in the dining room.

"How did you clean your room so fast?" I asked.

Harmony just shrugged and said, "I was bored, so I put all my toys away and put the clothes in the laundry basket."

Seeing as though my search of the house couldn't have taken longer than ten minutes, it still seemed like she cleaned the room awfully fast to me.

"Why didn't you stay in your room like I asked you?"

"I saw you go to your room and thought it was okay."

"Okay," I drawled warily with an eyebrow raised. "Sit right here. I need to go talk to the police officer sitting out front."

Trying to maintain my composure, I walked out the front door, locking it behind me. With as much dignity as possible, I approached the police car parked in front of my house. Inside, I found a sleeping police officer. I could see his short dark brown hair beneath his uniform hat that had fallen slightly over his eyes. So as to not surprise him too much – I didn't want to get shot or something – I knocked gently on the window of the car. The officer shook his head to become conscious and turned red with embarrassment when he rolled the window down.

"Ma'am," he greeted.

"Is it normal for you to fall asleep while guarding a house?" I asked sarcastically.

"No, Ma'am. I'm awfully sorry."

"While you were sleeping, someone broke into my child's room and tore it apart."

His face sunk and blue eyes widened at the news.

"Unfortunately, while I searched the rest of the house, she cleaned up the crime scene, so there is no evidence of your incompetence. I promise you, though, I will be personally going in to the precinct to put in a formal complaint today."

"I'm glad you're safe, Ma'am. Again, I'm very sorry for falling asleep. There is no good excuse for it."

"No, there isn't. You can go now. You're obviously not up to the task of keeping my daughter and me safe."

Without saying a word, the officer rolled his window up, started up his car, and drove off. I turned back to the house and went inside. Harmony sat in the dining room, but had gone back to her room at some point to change into day clothes. It was then that I realized I still wore my pajamas. I shrugged it off. It didn't really matter to me what a sleepy police officer thought of me.

"Why did you leave the dining room when I asked you to stay here?" I asked.

"I thought you'd be happy that I got myself all dressed."

Pinching the bridge of my nose, I said, "I really need you to work on listening better. When I tell you to do something, there is a reason for it. We're going to take a trip to the police station today, Harmony, so we're going to eat really quickly, I'm going to get dressed, and then we'll go."

"Okay, Mommy," Harmony yawned.

Wanting to get going quickly, I threw together a quick lunch, since we slept through breakfast, of chicken nuggets and broccoli covered in cheese. Harmony poked her food with her fork.

"What's the matter, honey?" I asked.

"I don't really like chicken," she said.

"Since when?" I scoffed. "You've been having chicken nuggets since you could start having solid foods."

Harmony just shrugged. Assuming that she must be entering a new phase of civil disobedience, I just finished up my lunch. I got up and brought my dish to the sink. Just about to give her one more chance to eat her food, I saw that Harmony had eaten everything.

Taken aback, I said, "I thought you didn't like chicken."

Harmony giggled, "Silly Mommy! Chicken is my favorite!"

Something was definitely not right. I pressed my lips together, then said, "I don't know what's going on with you lately, but you can talk to me about whatever you're feeling. You don't have to lie or mess around." I sounded harsher than I intended.

Harmony looked genuinely confused and, nearly in tears, said, "I'm not lying, Mommy. I love chicken."

After a long pause, I said, "Okay. You can just talk to me when you're ready. I'm going to go get into my jeans and a t-shirt and we'll drive to the police station."

Harmony's expression suddenly went from sad to amused as she said, "Mommy, you already have your jeans and t-shirt on."

Sure enough, when I looked down at myself, I was fully clothed in my jeans and white t-shirt. I had my pink high-tops on. My hair up in a ponytail. I put my fingers to my lips and pink lipstick transferred to my fingers. My eyes widened.

Am I going crazy? No. I heard once that if you question whether or not you're crazy, you're probably not. But was that true or just something I heard on some TV show? How am I dressed right now?

I barraged myself with questions for which I had no answers.

I did a quick head roll to pull myself together and began to rationalize everything to myself.

This is no big deal. I saw Doctor Smith yesterday and he said it was stress. I'm dealing with tons of stress: the anniversary of David and Tom's death, the calls, the odd things Harmony has been doing, the threats. Now I find out the police officer who should have been guarding my home last night fell asleep doing it. Yeah. Stress. That explains it.

Even to myself, I wasn't convincing. On the way out the door, I laughed, a little crazily, with Harmony about it. When I turned to lock the door, Harmony took off skipping.

"Harmony! Get back here!" I called and took off after her just as she rounded the corner. When I caught up, Harmony stood in front of the neighborhood playground with pleading eyes.

"Harmony. You cannot take off like that! You terrified me!" I scolded.

"Can I please play for a while on the playground? Please, please, pleeeeeeease?" Harmony begged.

With a sigh, I replied "Okay. But only for a few minutes. We need to get going."

Harmony squealed with glee, opened the gate to the playground, and ran in. I gradually made my way to the playground and closed the gate behind me. There were two reasons I was alright with letting Harmony play a while. First, it gave me time to cool down and clear my head before heading down to the police station. Second, it had been a crazy last couple days and Harmony deserved a little time to run and play. Harmony had essentially been stuck in the car for two days straight.

I sat on the bench and thought about how it had been a part of every stage of David and my lives. Ever since we married and bought the house around the corner, we had been coming to this bench. Tom was so cute as a little toddler in the baby swing, and after we had Harmony, Tom played so well with her. He had pushed her in the same swing she was now on and helped her climb and go down the slide. When Harmony was scared to do the merry-go-round, he had started spinning it slowly and worked it faster over several days. He was such a good big brother.

David and I would sit and watch the kids play when he came home from work. After a long day of work, it was nice for him to sit and decompress that way. One time, David told me that sitting on the bench watching the children play was his favorite part of his day because it was a good reminder of what was truly important in his life.

As Harmony sat on the big-girl swing, I remembered Tom trying to teach her even though she was too young to really understand. He eventually gave up and just pushed her himself. Now, here she was swinging all by herself; she was so cute how she whooped every time the swing started zooming forward and giggled when it went back.

While I watched, I noticed a tall man in a black suit on the other side of the playground watching as well.

How long has he been there? I don't remember him being here when we arrived.

32

I had never seen him in the neighborhood before. Then, I realized he wasn't watching Harmony; he was watching me. We made eye contact and he gave me a knowing smile.

We're going to take you out today.

I remembered the latest threat.

Could this be him?

Terrified, but trying not to show it, I approached Harmony, who was at the top of the slide, and said, "Okay, honey. It's time to go now."

"Aw! Just a few minutes more?" Harmony pleaded.

"No, honey, we need to go. Now."

Harmony slid down and held my hand. I tried to nonchalantly leave the playground.

Maybe I'm just being paranoid. I'll bet those college kids who've been prank calling me are just trying to scare me because they think it's funny.

When we got to the sidewalk, I noticed the man began following us. I turned to look ahead and the street corner to my house seemed much further away than it should be. Picking up the pace, I walked toward the far-away corner; the man picked up his pace as well. I went faster, almost to a jog.

"Mommy! You're going too fast!" Harmony complained.

We didn't seem to be getting any closer to the turn no matter how fast we went.

I need to get to the car.

Turning around, I saw the man had almost caught up with us. I scooped Harmony into my arms and began running. I glanced to the side and saw that I passed the same house over and over again. On the other side of the street, I saw the same trees passing over and over again. I looked ahead and could no longer see the corner. Just a straight line of sidewalk.

Up ahead, I finally saw change in my path, but it did not lead into another neighborhood; there was no corner that would take me to my house. What I saw was a white hallway. I quickly changed direction and ran toward the house we kept passing.

This isn't possible. That's my house. But – I never turned – and my car is gone!

There was no time to try to figure it out; the man was gaining on me.

Without thinking, I slammed the door open and closed and locked it. As I set Harmony down, I realized that I had locked the door when I left. I brought my hands to my face and slid them down.

What is going on here? I've completely lost it. That has to be it. Maybe he drugged me somehow in the last week.

I rushed down the hall to my gun safe and pulled the gun out.

"Mommy? Are you okay?" Harmony asked, following me into my room.

"Everything is going to be fine. I'm going to lock the door. Don't open it for anyone except me. Do you understand?"

"Yes, Mommy," she responded.

At that moment, Harmony's face went blank and she started staring forward. I had to leave to protect us, but as I left the room,

Harmony still stood in the middle of it. Reluctantly, I left my little girl standing like that and locked my bedroom door.

I made my way to the front door and looked through the peephole; he wasn't there. I exhaled loudly then realized the door was no longer locked.

How did he get in? He's in the house. Where is he?

There was no spare key for him to find; I didn't hear him trying to break in; the door hadn't been kicked in. At that point, though, it didn't matter how he got in. The important thing was that he did, and I was the only one to protect my daughter and myself.

I slowly started making my way through the house. Completely paranoid, when I went to the kitchen, I not only opened the pantry, but every cupboard in the room. Stranger things had happened that day, I wouldn't put it past him to be able to hide in one. Over in the living room, I looked behind the television, couches, and chairs.

So far, so good.

The linen closet in the hall was empty as well. I made my way to Harmony's room. When I opened the door, I couldn't believe what I saw; the room was a disaster again.

That's impossible. Harmony has been with me the whole time.

Gingerly, I stepped through the toys and clothes and began checking her closet and even the drawers.

Under the bed. He has to be under the bed. It's the only place in the house I haven't checked that he could possibly be.

As quietly as possible, I made my way to the bed and lowered myself to the floor. I felt like I was starring in a horror movie and everyone in the audience screamed at me not to look under the bed. Hands shaking, I paused to regain my composure; they had to be

35

steady if I ended up having to use the gun. Taking a deep breath, I lifted the blanket and looked under the bed.

He's not here! Why would he unlock the front door, but not come in?

Then, a horrifying thought occurred to me.

If he can unlock the front door, he can get into my bedroom!

I jumped up and raced across the hall to my room, which now had an open door. Harmony stood in the middle of the room; not moving with a blank stare. The only difference between when I had left her and now was the flowy white dress she now wore. In front of Harmony, the man bent on one knee, looking into her eyes.

I cocked my gun and pointed it at the intruder, "Get away from my daughter."

As the man stood up, he raised his hands in the air, but said nothing. He had a smug look on his face.

"How dare you change her clothes?! Who do you think you are?"

No response.

"You talk to me! I'm sick of your harassment and threats! What kind of drug have you given me and how did you do it?"

The man smiled with what appeared to be pity. However, he still said nothing.

"I deserve to know! Who are you working for and why are you trying to kill my daughter and me?"

To this, the man tilted his head back and began to laugh. It wasn't a maniacal or cruel laugh, but almost mirthful; as if I had just told a hilarious joke.

"Stop laughing! There is nothing funny here. I will shoot this gun if you try anything and I'm growing tired of your arrogance!"

The man put his hands down and slowly began walking toward me. I glanced at Harmony, who remained as still as a statue. Looking back at the man, I saw that he was only a couple feet away. He put his hand in the breast pocket of his suit.

Up to that point in my life, I had never had to use my gun in defense before. In fact, I hadn't even been to a range since David and Tom had died. Could I live with taking a life? If it meant saving Harmony, I would have to.

I closed my eyes and squeezed the trigger.

Chapter 4

In that moment, time stood still for me. I couldn't open my eyes as I flashed back to a moment in time I shared with David. The gun I just shot had just been purchased a little over an hour before and we were standing at my gun safe. It was a big decision for me to buy a gun. Only recently had I felt the need for it while he was away. The house two doors down had been burglarized and I wanted to be prepared should something happen while David traveled for business.

I put the pink-handled Walther PK380 gun in the safe for the first time and locked it. David gently put his index finger under my chin and turned my head so we were looking straight into each other's eyes. I knew he was about to give me advice from the look he gave, but I had been momentarily distracted by the deep blue color they were. I always felt at peace looking in those eyes; like I escaped into the sea of his soul.

He took a deep breath and said something I would never forget and had considered before I pulled the trigger on the strange man.

"Miriam, this gun is not only yours by right as an American citizen, but it is a major responsibility. Before you ever pull the trigger to shoot an attacker, remember that it is something you can never take back and it will change your life forever. There will be lawyers and police reports and possibly even news reporters. However, the most important thing to protect is your soul. So when you are looking that person in the eye, keep that in mind."

I had been surprised at the advice; at how fatherly he sounded. A lot of women would have been offended at his tone; they may have thought he was being condescending. But that was not how I felt; I knew that he said it out of genuine concern and desire to protect me even if he wasn't home.

Little did I know at the time that the moment would arrive; the moment I would have to think it. David wasn't just away on a business trip; he was dead. Harmony was catatonic across the room for some unknown reason, I was drugged, and a stranger stood before me to make good on his promise to take me out.

Everything had been considered. What it came down to was that if I died, Harmony would be left all alone; her dad, mom, and brother gone. I couldn't do that to her. After all consideration, I pulled the trigger.

BANG

In the relatively small space of my bedroom, the sound was deafening. My ears rang and hands shook from the impact of the recoil. Despite all the strange things that had just happened, I was positive I didn't miss; he had been standing right in front of me. For another couple minutes, I kept my eyes closed, breathing deeply and rapidly, not wanting to face the gory dead body I knew I would see once I opened them.

I can't believe I just did that. But we're safe now. He can't hurt us if he's dead.

Reluctantly, I opened my eyes, but saw no dead body. Instead, I saw the man still standing in front of me, smiling at me. Terrified, I stumbled back and fell on my rear.

"How is that possible?! Who are you? What are you?" I asked as I tossed the gun unsafely onto my bed.

The man put his hand back into his breast pocket. I knew that he would just do whatever he planned. If I couldn't shoot him point-blank, then nothing really could be done to help my circumstances. I held my breath.

He paused and pulled out what looked like a picture frame. As he looked at it, I exhaled loudly and gawked at the situation. He had no weapon; I just shot at an unarmed man. Horrified with myself and scared stiff at what this man was getting at, I brought my hands to my face and began sobbing. I had reached the point that I had enough.

"Please. I can't take the madness around me anymore. Just do what you're going to do and stop messing with my head!"

Holding out the picture to me, he gestured for me to take it. Shaking even harder, I reached out and took the framed picture from his hand. It was a portrait; a picture of me, but not me. I was much younger in the picture with a tiara of gold jeweled with emeralds. Instead of a necklace, I wore a broach that matched my tiara and the dress was a deep green, made of some expensive material. The color of my green eyes seemed brighter and my black hair seemed darker.

Feeling so confused, I looked up from the picture. Making himself at eye level with me, I saw that the man had gone to his knees. His face began to shift and change until he became recognizable. He was Doctor Smith. I dropped the photo to the floor and pulled my folded knees in front of me, wrapping my arms around them.

"This world is not your own, Miriam," he said, lowering himself again to my level.

"Doctor Smith? What have you done to me?!"

"You can call me John."

"Whatever you want to be called is completely irrelevant right now, *John.*"

"It isn't. It's important to me that we are on a first name basis, that you will recognize me."

"Okay then. *John,* what have you done to me?"

"Saved you."

"That's a leap. You may have been there for me when David and Tom died, but I don't remember you *saving* me. This is certainly not saving me. You're literally driving me mad and have somehow made Harmony catatonic."

"I've done no such thing to either one of you."

"I'm not stupid! Look at her," I said, pointing in the direction Harmony should have been; but she wasn't.

"Where is she?" I screamed as I jumped to my feet and began searching my room. John just sat in the middle of the room, patiently waiting for me to come back. Not finding her in my bedroom, I opened the door to the hall to search the rest of the house. Behind the door, a blinding light resided where the rest of my home should have been. I slammed the door shut and turned to face John again. When I did, my bedroom had disappeared, being replaced by white space and a table with two chairs.

John gestured for me to have a seat. Feeling utterly defeated, I sat down and put my head in my hands. I wished I could pull myself together to be stronger, more defiant, but, overwhelmed at the nonsense of everything that had happened so far in my day, that would not be happening.

This must have been how Alice felt when she was lost in the woods of Wonderland.

"Where is my Harmony? I can't lose her, too."

John tilted his head with a look of empathy spreading across his face. He clearly knew what was going on, but wouldn't say it. As if trying to figure out what to say, he looked down at his folded hands on the table. There was a long silence as I stared John down, knowing that repetition of my question got me nowhere. As silly as this seemed, I had been told that my stare could bring anyone down and it was my last resort; in all the nonsense of the day, I figured I would give it a shot.

John looked up and stared right back into my eyes. Unlike David, his eyes were brown; they didn't seem cruel, as I expected them to be. I concluded that he must be psychotic and had brought me into his psychosis somehow.

John finally responded to my question. "Miriam, Harmony is no longer here."

"I can see that. Where is she now?"

"I don't know." He shrugged. "She has found somewhere to be, though."

"That is not a satisfactory answer! I demand to know where she is right NOW!"

"I can't give you an answer I don't have, Miriam. I'm not the one in charge here, believe it or not."

"You're not making any sense at all. You are going to make major bank selling this drug, by the way. I think I'm officially crazy."

John laughed. "Miriam, I have not drugged you, at least not in the way you're thinking. I've saved you."

He leaned in now, on his elbows. "This will all become clear in time," he said.

I turned my head and saw that the picture now propped up on the table. Pointing to it, I said, "What is this about? I have never worn a dress as nice as that, much less a tiara. And I've never been that thin."

Again, John laughed. What he found so humorous, I had no idea. I wasn't trying to be funny; I was trying to get answers.

"I assure you that it is, indeed, you," he said with a smile.

"Okay, so you're really good with some photo editing software."

John just shook his head. I ran my fingers through my hair starting at my face and working back to just above my ears and held my head there.

How am I going to get out of this?

I thought to myself, but startled when my thoughts echoed out loud in the room for both John and me to hear.

"Don't worry, Miriam. We will be taking you out soon," John said. Then, he disappeared; so did the table and chairs. Left standing in the middle of the whiteness, I looked around to try to settle myself into my new surroundings. Looking up, I saw the same bright light I had seen when I opened my bedroom door. Everywhere else around me, there was nothing. Since there was no floor, I didn't even know how I was standing.

"Miriam."

44

I heard my name behind me with an impossible familiar voice, followed by two more voices synchronously speaking.

"Mommy."

I turned around to see my whole family; David, Tom, and Harmony all stood there. Harmony spoke first with excitement.

"Mommy, I found Daddy and Tom! Are you so happy?"

Wide-eyed with confusion, I nodded and approached my family while beginning to weep with joy. If I had to be stuck in this psychosis, at least it would be with my family. I strode straight up to David and gently brushed his cheek with my hand.

"David? Is that really you?" I asked hopefully.

"Yes. It's me," he replied as he gently brought my hand down and pulled me into a kiss. I held him tight; I felt that if I let go, he would vanish and I would wake up from all of this being a strange dream. I felt tugging on my dress.

Great. Now I'm in a dress. When did that happen?

Looking down, I saw Tom holding on to the end of my pink sundress. He had a giant, toothy grin and blond curly hair. I dropped down to my knees and pulled him into a tight embrace with tears in my eyes.

Jokingly, Tom said, "Mommy, I can't breathe!"

We all laughed with him and I turned to hug Harmony, too. Harmony decided to copy her big brother and said the same thing, which made everyone laugh harder. David came down, too and our whole family hugged each other.

"I've missed you all so *much*," I said. "I don't know how all this is possible, but I don't really care at this point. If this is a dream, let me sleep. I don't know how I could possibly live my life without all of you again."

"I don't know how we're here either," David said. "But I agree. I'm just glad we're together again."

"Let's play Duck, Duck, Goose," Harmony suggested. Though it was odd timing, we all decided to acquiesce to her request. Harmony declared that she would be it and circled everyone several times before making Tom the Goose. She would get his seat and he would do the same thing; he chose Harmony and took her seat. That's how it went the whole time. Tom and Harmony just kept selecting each other while David and I took in the joy of our children playing together again.

The game eventually transformed into a game of tag between Tom and Harmony. I moved over to David and sat next to him, putting my head on his shoulder and holding his hand. Somehow, we went from sitting on the floor to sitting on a white bench. Not caring that my thoughts would be broadcasted to everyone, I thought
–

This is perfect. I could live like this forever. I never want this to end.

I had the terrible feeling, though, that this wouldn't last forever. I knew David and Tom were not really there; they were gone and never returning. Whether or not Harmony was actually there, I didn't know. I didn't care that I experienced some kind of hallucination; I was happy.

At the peak of my joy, I saw John appear.

"It's coming close to time," John said.

David and I stood up together. "Time for what?" David demanded protectively.

"Time to take your wife out," John responded nonchalantly.

"I guarantee you that you will not be doing anything of the sort today."

"*I* guarantee you that I will."

John snapped his finger and David disappeared.

"No!" I screamed and began crying immediately. "Bring him back!"

"I can't, Miriam. He is gone forever now."

Tom and Harmony ran over to me. "What's going on, Mom?" Tom asked.

"I'm not sure, honey," I said, trying to be as calm as possible for my children.

Harmony walked right up to John. "Please don't take my mommy. We love her."

John snapped his finger and Tom disappeared; he snapped again and Harmony disappeared.

"It's all for the best, Miriam."

I was beside myself in agony, reliving the tragedy of losing my family again. "How could you do this to me? What kind of game are you playing here?"

"I am playing no game," John said. "We simply thought you might want to visit with your family one more time before we take you out."

"How did you even do that? Where are they now?"

"Technically, you did it yourself. We just guided you into it. As to where they are now, I have no idea. They have found somewhere to be, though, and you can be sure they are together and happy."

I sat back down on the bench.

"Why are you doing all this? Why not just kill me now? Why do you have to torture me before doing it?"

John sat next to me and looked me in the eyes. "We are not going to kill you. We are going to take you out. We have saved you."

I frowned in confusion.

"It will all make sense in time. I promise," John said. "We haven't done it yet because things are not quite ready for you."

"What things?"

"I would rather not say here. I would rather you wait and trust me."

"Trust you?! You've been tormenting me with hang-up calls for weeks, threatened me, and have taken my family from me. How can I possibly trust you?"

"I'm sorry about those calls. We were having a hard time communicating with you so deep into it."

"Into what?"

"It will all make sense in time."

I stood up, angry. "Stop saying that! I don't want things to make sense in time; I want things to make sense now!"

"I can't give you answers now. It would not be safe. We are *so* close to taking you out; you just need to be patient a little longer."

"I haven't been patient and I have no intention of being patient."

I tried to pull myself together again.

I've had to do this quite a few times today.

I closed my eyes and tried to cement my new memories of David, Tom, and Harmony into my brain. I didn't trust John, but I did believe him that my family was now gone forever. I would never see David's blue eyes or my children's curly hair. There would be no more games or cuddling. We would never sit on the bench at the park. I was pretty sure I would never see Emma again, either.

John put a hand on my shoulders. "I'm sorry that this is so difficult for you. We never expected it to be this long or for you to go so deep. We really only thought it would be a couple months."

I stopped trying to make sense of what he was saying.

It will all make sense in time.

John smiled, having heard the thought broadcast. I still believed he was psychotic and I had no idea what he had done to me, but I was sure I was doomed. My life as I knew it was over.

John disappeared again, leaving me sitting alone. "We're ready for you now, Miriam," I heard John's voice, but didn't see him anywhere. I stood and looked around.

My feet began to dangle. It felt like I was floating. A bright spotlight shone on me; I had to cover my eyes. Slowly, I started being pulled up toward the blinding light. Not knowing where it would lead, I lowered my hands and closed my eyes instead. When I reached the light above me, I felt cold, as cold as ice. A few moments later, the light flashed brighter for a moment, then everything went dark.

49

Chapter 5

For a moment, I thought I stared at the light again. I could only see white.

Am I dead?

"Ow!" I pinched myself. It definitely hurt, so I was pretty sure I wasn't dead. Hearing a rhythmic beeping, I looked over to see some kind of monitor. Based on the IV on my wrist and tubes in my nose, my guess was that it tracked my breathing and heart rate.

I must have passed out or something.

I decided I would just lay there for a moment and stare at the white above me.

I'm not uncomfortable.

I shifted a little more and realized I laid in a bed; a white bed. I turned onto my side and brought the white blankets closer to my chin so I could cuddle in the softness.

As I looked around the rest of the room, I noticed that *everything* was white, not that there was much else to the room. There was a stool by the bed, an open wardrobe filled with white dresses, a couch, a plush chair, a small table, and a door that I figured led into a bathroom.

Everything in there is probably white, too.

It didn't escape my notice that there were no windows, books, television, or computer in the room.

I reflected on the strangeness of everything that had happened before. Doctor John Smith was some kind of villain and my world literally disappeared before my eyes. By some mystery, I spent some time with David, Tom, and Harmony, even though David and Tom had been dead for a year. Next thing I knew, I flew toward a light and fainted.

I'm nuts. That's it. Something happened that finally threw me over the edge of my sanity and I'm in some kind of asylum. That's why everything is straight-jacket white.

I was desperately trying to figure out what was going on.

Fairly certain that I was being monitored, I stayed laying that way for some time. I wasn't quite ready to face my new reality yet. A tear fell from my eye, then another, and I soon began sobbing into my white pillow. I turned onto my side and clasped the pillow against my eyes as I cried loudly, my body shaking in my sadness. My entire life had just been ripped away and replaced with whatever I faced now.

I remembered being a child and crying into Mother's lap when I felt sad; she would stroke my hair and say motherly things like, "it will be okay" and "Mama's here." Even though she had been gone for some time, I missed her at that moment. She had a way of bringing peace to the worst situations.

Even though the pillow was now thoroughly drenched, I used it to wipe the tears from my eyes before sitting up. When I finally did, I realized the bed was tall enough that my feet dangled over the side.

As I sat up, the door to the room slid open and John walked in. I widened my eyes in fear and the beeping on the monitor increased.

"John," I whispered.

John smiled. "Good. I am glad you recognize me, though I am a little surprised. You've only ever seen me once in – Doctor Watson's office." He hesitated over the name, and frowned a little. "I am sorry for how rude I was then. It was uncalled for."

I frowned. "Who is Doctor Watson?"

He looked up, surprised. "You recognize me, but not Doctor Watson's name?"

"Of course, I recognize you. Is this some kind of a sick joke, John?"

"No. No, of course not."

Forgetting that I was hooked up, I dropped myself to the floor and tried to move. "Get these out of me now!" I yelled.

John quickly came over and carefully removed the IV and breathing tubes, though I wasn't sure why he obeyed my command so instantaneously. When he finished, I grabbed his wrist. "Where is Harmony? You tell me right now!" As I got more upset, I felt weak and dropped back onto the edge of the bed.

"I am not entirely sure what is going on here, but I will figure it out," John said, obviously concerned.

I wonder how long I've been out. It feels like at least a couple days.

"What are these clothes you put me in?"

I was dressed much differently than the sundress I wore before I went out. I wore a dress seemingly identical to the other ones in the open wardrobe. Long sleeves became wider as they descended the arms, ending with an oversized bell. With embroidered empire waists, the skirts stretched out long enough to barely sweep the floor as I walked; the material was light and flowy.

Well, this is kind of a nice dress for a crazy person.

The fact that I was insane was something I started to accept.

"*I* did not dress you. Your father insisted –"

When he referenced my father, I slapped him and he stepped back. "How dare you bring up my father? It's bad enough he and my mother died *years* ago, but now you have to bring them into this – this – whatever this is?! Tell me right now what is going on, John!"

John held out his hands. "Alright. We will figure this out together. May I sit on the stool?"

I pursed my lips. "Fine. I'll play your game, for now. I don't know how a gun didn't work on you, but I assure you, I will get my answers, and I won't let you hurt me anymore."

I felt my hair, which was up in a loose bun and wondered how they were able to do that while I was unconscious. My hands and feet were well-manicured and pedicured as well.

That's odd. I can't remember the last time I was able to get my hands and feet done.

"How about you tell me who you think I am?" John asked.

I barely heard his question as I continued examining myself. I was thin, much thinner than I had ever been even before I had Tom and Harmony. My face was smooth with no signs of forming wrinkles.

"What have you done to my body? I don't remember authorizing any surgeries. I certainly can't afford liposuction or face lifts."

"I want to help you get answers, Miriam, but you have to help me, too. Who do you think I am?"

I sighed. "Fine. You're Doctor John Smith and have been my doctor now for several years."

"Who are you?"

"Miriam Dutch."

"Hmm…" John opened what appeared to be some kind of tablet and began taking notes. "What is the date?"

"April 12, 2016. Obama is president," I responded, anticipating the next question.

"President," he murmured as he wrote it on his pad.

"What is your birthdate?"

"August 31, 1985."

There was silence as he scribbled it onto the strange tablet; it took quite a long time. Being the geek I am, I decided to ask about it.

"What kind of tablet is that? I always love new gadgets."

He looked up at me like he was trying to remember something for an exam. He had his "aha" moment.

"It is only a simple tablet called a Note-Taker. It takes what I write and uploads it to the flow directly."

"Cool. Can I see it?"

"Sorry, no. Privacy laws dictate that I cannot show anyone the screen."

"Oh."

"Who is in your immediate family?"

"Really?"

"Humor me, Miriam."

"It's just Harmony and me now."

"Now?"

I swallowed hard. He was really going to make me relive it. "Yes. My husband, David, and son, Tom, died in a car accident a little over a year ago."

"Will you tell me about it?"

I looked down at my hands. "I would rather not."

"It will really help me help you."

I rolled my eyes and sighed at the cliché. "If you insist.

"It was early in the morning and the rain poured on the freeway on our way to the airport; we were going on our family vacation. David was so focused on the road while Tom slept peacefully behind him and Harmony slept behind me. It had been so long since we had done anything all together and we thought this last minute trip was a brilliant idea.

"We were going to Kona. I was so excited to bring him there because it was my favorite place in the world. It was one of the things that had drawn me to him; his eyes were the color of those blue waters." I went silent for a moment, then shook and stepped off the rabbit trail.

"Anyway, I was feeling tense because of how bad the weather was. Both of the children were sound asleep and I stared out the windshield at the star storm of rain pelting it.

"David noticed my tension and began to sing our song, *Fly Me to the Moon*, to calm me down. It was working. He nearly made it to the end of the chorus, when he was interrupted by the sound of a semi honking its horn. As it careened toward us in our lane, he swerved to miss the truck, but fishtailed and the giant truck hit the car on the driver's side. The car was pushed until the truck stopped, then we continued down the road in terrifying acrobatics.

"The next thing I knew, I woke up in a hospital bed. Looking to my right, I saw Harmony curled up on a little couch. Looking to my left, my mother-in-law sat holding my hand, head on the side of the bed sound asleep.

"I don't want to talk about that anymore."

"That is quite alright, Miriam. It sounds like it was a difficult time for you. I think I have enough for now. It is evening. Are you hungry?"

"Not really," I lied. There was no way John was going to get me to ingest any of the food in the place. My stomach growled.

John laughed. "Miriam, I assure you. You are safe. I will have something sent for you. The bathroom is behind that door," he pointed to the other side of the room at the door I had already assumed was the bathroom door. "When you are done eating, take a shower and get some sleep. Hopefully, I will have some answers for you in the morning."

With that, John got up and strode out of the cell. I ran after him, but the door slid shut in my face and I couldn't find any way to open it. Huffing, I turned around and decided to explore my tiny cell – I would not call it a room.

As I made my way across the cell, I allowed my toes to linger a little on the downy carpet. The first thing I examined was the open wardrobe. I ran my hands through the seven dresses hanging in it; they were, indeed, identical.

I squished my feet over to the couch, which had the coffee table in front of it and the chair next to it. With another huff, I plopped myself on the soft cushion.

At least everything is soft. Just the way I like it.

I kicked up my pretty, little feet, nails painted rose red, onto the coffee table and leaned my head back against the couch. Breathing in and out slowly, I closed my eyes and tried to regain my composure. Again. If I could remain calm and collected, I might be able to convince them I wasn't crazy. I would be there no longer than a week and then I would have my little Harmony back in my arms. Having me there had to be some kind of a mistake.

I'm sure Harmony is safe with Emma.

Then, I accidentally nodded off.

I startled myself awake, not knowing how long I had been that way. Blinking the sleep out of my eyes, I looked at the coffee table to find that, at some point while I slept, someone had brought me food. It was some sort of broth with vegetables in it with a glass of water. Because my stomach growled again, I decided to brave the food. It didn't taste like it was poisoned or laced with anything, so I ate it with gusto.

Taking a deep breath, I decided I would make my way to check out the bathroom and take a shower. I felt stiff again when I stood up, so I did a few stretches.

I wonder how long I was out that time.

Shuffling along the plush carpet, I walked over to what I had been told was the bathroom door. When I went to turn the knob, I noticed that there wasn't one. I tried pushing the door, but it wouldn't budge. Looking all over the frame, I finally saw a button. I pushed it and the door slid open. I glanced behind me at the door to the room to see if I had missed a similar button over there, but there wasn't one.

I turned around and gaped as I entered into the bathroom.

I don't even have a bathroom like this in my home. These are the bathrooms in this asylum?!

My previous assumption that everything was white in there was true, but there was so much more to it than that. A giant walk-in shower was in one corner of the room with a large jet tub in the corner next to it. The toilet was pristine, as well, with a no-slam lid and auto-flusher. The tile on the floor was so clean, I was sure I could eat off it, though I would never want to do that.

The sink was made from some kind of white marble and the mirror had a beautiful white wooden frame with flowers carved into it. Then, my eyes landed on my reflection. I blinked and rubbed my eyes to make sure I saw correctly.

This has to be some kind of trick.

The face I saw in the mirror was not the same one I saw recently, at least, not exactly. It was definitely me; the features were all correct; my eyes were the same, maybe the green was a little deeper. The shock of it all was my age.

I'm so young! At least, I look like I'm young.

I knew I had been changed somehow by how my face felt, but knowing it didn't prepare me for what I saw. Gone were the wrinkles and blemishes from years of acne and the sunshine in Texas.

Reaching back, I took down my bun, which I figured had roughly a million bobbi pins in it. I dug my fingers into it and shook it down. My hair was stark black with no grays and landed at the small of my back. Seeing my slim waist was even more shocking than feeling it.

What did he do to me? Better question – what is he going to do with me now?

At that point, I started to get terrified of my predicament. Backing away from the mirror, I exited the bathroom. Eyes wide with fright, I made my way back to the bed. Bringing the blankets back up to my chin, I lay on my side. Knowing that I was no safer in the bed than I was anywhere else in the room, I closed my eyes as I began to cry and tried to figure out my situation again.

I'm not crazy. I can see that now. Something strange is definitely going on here. Did I have plastic surgery done and I just don't remember it? No. I wouldn't have plastic surgery. Then why do I look so young? Why is my hair so long? And why am I so thin? Is Doctor Smith really some kind of bad guy? Did he really drug me and do this to me? Where is my Harmony? I need my precious Harmony.

In the midst of all these questions and tears, I fell back to sleep.

Chapter 6

When I woke up, I kept my eyes closed; I hoped that everything I experienced was just a dream. When I opened my eyes, I wanted to see my little nightstand with a touch lamp and my cell phone on it. I wanted Harmony to rush in and wake me up. I peeked open one eye and, unsurprisingly, disappointment swept through me.

Ugh. What is going on here?

I rolled onto my back, wondering about the time. As I looked down to my stomach, I felt the rumbling.

Ugh. I just ate. Why am I hungry again already?

Despite knowing it would disturb me a bit, I bit my lower lip, got up, and walked to the bathroom. It was time. Avoiding the mirror, I did what I needed to do, then decided I would take a shower.

No knobs.

There were no obvious buttons either. Giving up on the idea of a shower, I pressed my lips tightly together, blocked sight of the mirror with my hand, and walked into the living area.

As I sat down, I heard the door slide open. John came in and looked very surprised to see me awake. Because he carried a tray of food, I decided that rather than go nuts on him, I would take the approach of kindness. Dad always said, "You'll catch more flies with honey than vinegar." I was never sure why I would want to catch flies.

"Have you figured anything out yet?" I asked.

He closed the door behind him and set the tray in front of me. The food on the plate was unlike anything I had seen in a hospital. A grilled chicken breast seasoned with garlic complimented a generous portion of broccoli. To the upper left of my plate, a bowl of corn chowder wafted tendrils of steam, and to the upper right, a large glass of apple juice had my taste buds salivating in anticipation.

"This is certainly a step up from last night. Is it lunch time?" I asked.

John chuckled and said, "No. It is dinner. You slept all day. And you have some more solid food because you held the soup down well last night."

"Oh. Will I ever be able to walk around outside my room or get a room with a window?"

"Eventually."

"Do you think I might be able to get a clock in here? It's really frustrating to not know what time it is."

He smiled and said, "I don't see why not."

An awkward pause ensued as both of us tried to sense the proper way to proceed.

"Miriam, about the mirror – "

"Yes. Tell me about what I saw, please," I asked as if I simply requested a weather report.

"You were not meant to see yourself – yet."

"Because I look like I'm at least ten years younger than I ought to be?" I took a bite of chicken.

"Something like that."

"Plastic surgery?"

"No."

"Liposuction?"

"No."

"Then what?"

"I do not think you are ready for that knowledge – yet."

"John, I'm quite confused on what is going on here," I said between bites of my chicken.

Oh my goodness. This is the tenderest chicken I've ever had.

"I understand."

I set my fork down and looked John in the eye. "You're not going to tell me anything are you?"

"Not much yet, Miriam."

"Of course not," I responded, frustrated. There was a bit more silence between us as I finished my chicken.

After sniffing the chowder, I decided to skip it. As I ate my broccoli, I tried to stay focused on my food. It was the best hospital food I ever had and the apple juice tasted like it had been freshly made.

When I finished, John asked, "Was it to your liking?"

"Yes. Did you do anything to it?"

He laughed heartily. "No. That is a good sign."

"Of what?"

"That you are still you up here," he said tapping the side of his head.

"Can you tell me about your experience before waking up in here?"

I raised an eyebrow. Doctor Smith had been there; or at least, I thought he had been. Hesitatingly, I answered, "I'm beginning to think it was some kind of dream. You don't appear to be as villainous as you were."

He looked at me expectantly.

Sighing, I explained, "I had a couple weeks of prank hang-up calls, which eventually lead to me getting two calls with someone saying 'We're going to take you out.' I had reported the threats to the police, so a police officer guarded my home the night before. There ended up being a break-in because he fell asleep. I informed him that I would be filing a complaint with the department.

"I was ready to go, but couldn't remember getting ready. I left the house to go to the police department to report him, but Harmony took off around the corner. I locked the door and chased after her. I followed her to the park and allowed her to play for a while. A few minutes into the play time, I noticed I was being stalked by – you – though I didn't recognize you immediately."

I paused as I observed how calm and collected John was as he wrote down what I had just said.

I continued, "I got Harmony down from the slide and began walking home. You followed. The corner I needed to turn appeared to get further and further away, no matter how fast I ran. I got so fast, I had to pick up Harmony and carry her. Pretty soon, I couldn't see the corner anymore; all I could see was a long stretch of sidewalk. I passed the same house and the same trees over and over again until I saw that the sidewalk was going to become a white hallway. Then, I turned into the house and recognized it as my own, even though it was impossible."

I took a deep breath, trying to maintain my composure as I relived my last moments before waking up in the white room.

"We made it inside before you caught us and I locked the front door. I took Harmony back to my room, locked that door, and searched around the house for any intruder. I didn't find any, though I saw the front door had been unlocked. I rushed back to my room to find it open and Harmony in the middle of the room, not moving and dressed in white. You and I exchanged words, and you kept giving me answers that made no sense. Harmony disappeared.

"You showed me a picture of myself like this," I gestured to my face. "You disappeared. Then I spent some time with David, Tom, and Harmony. You made them disappear, then I got brought up into a blinding light. That's when I woke up here."

John nodded as he furiously wrote down everything. "I see – "

Trying to remain calm, I asked, "Just for peace of mind, Harmony is okay, right? I figured you sent her to stay with my mother-in-law while I was here."

John's face paled. "I'm sorry, but I cannot talk about that with you right now."

Anger shot through me. I said, "What do you mean you can't talk to me about it? She's my daughter. I deserve to know!" All calm had fled, leaving a trembling shell of myself in its place.

"I understand, Miriam, but – "

"She is only four years old! She needs to be with family! Please at least tell me that she is okay!"

John stood up and slowly backed his way to the door, but didn't respond.

"Did something happen to her? Did she die? Is that how I lost my mind? Please tell me!"

With that, John sped up and quickly got out and slid the door shut. Beside myself, I screamed. "I know you're monitoring me! I'm a mother! I deserve to know about my daughter!"

Staying calm got me nowhere. I didn't care that I now showed that I could, indeed, be insane. I threw my tray across the room at the door. Bits of broccoli and golden apple juice melded with the chowder to ooze down the pristine plaster. I felt oddly happy to see color on the wall. With a growl, I made my way to the bathroom.

"Come on, shower! Turn on!" I screamed at the shower, despite the fact that it was not sentient. Much to my surprise, water started pouring from the shower head. I sighed and began sobbing. Again. Taking deep breaths to calm myself, I got out of the white dress and looked at my unfamiliar reflection in the mirror. Aside from my eyes being puffy from crying, I still looked like I did earlier.

"Who are you?" I asked the reflection as I stepped into the scalding spray.

Chapter 7

Over the next few days, I became more comfortable with John. I still hated him for not telling me anything about Harmony and I still suspected him responsible for my current circumstances. However, after even more incessant begging about Harmony, John still had no answers. I began to believe him when he said he didn't know where she was. He genuinely seemed to wish he could answer and even said he would if he knew anything. I concluded that if I ever wanted to see my little one again, I would have to convince him to let me leave; the only way that would happen was if I cooperated.

Each day, John brought my meals and started bringing his own so we could eat together. I would share stories with him about my childhood, David, my kids, and pretty much anything else John wanted to know about. I didn't really mind. I didn't have anything to hide.

One day, after I had told a story about the time I went to Disneyland with Dad, and he didn't realize Splash Mountain actually had water and was truly shocked when he got drenched, we laughed so hard, our sides hurt. As our laughter died down, John abruptly changed the subject and asked how I had met David.

"Oh. In college," I began. "Before him, I'd never dated anyone, so I was surprised when he was actually interested in me. He was so smart. So handsome. Blonde short-trimmed hair, blue eyes, square jaw. Oh! And a gentleman! He even opened doors for me – " I was quiet for a minute as I pictured my beloved husband and my heart ached for him. I also realized I was suddenly talking to John as if he was my best girlfriend and it felt weird. Calming myself, I told him how David and I met.

"I was sitting in the university library staring out the window, mindlessly watching the rain slam down into the miniature ponds it created all over the parking lot and lawn. I was wondering why I had come to Washington, where I knew no one, for college rather than staying in Texas.

"Of course, I knew what I thought about when I made my decision. I needed a change; a fresh start. I had been in ministry training nearby in Dallas, but after three years, discovered that wasn't where I belonged. I went back home to live with my parents to try to figure things out the year before, but six months into that, they both died in a plane crash on their way back from an anniversary trip.

"They were all I had left; I had no siblings or grandparents or aunts or uncles or cousins. We never had problems with each other. They were more than my parents. They were my best friends. They encouraged me to pursue my dream of making music. So there I was, sitting in the library, trying to not only wrap my brain around music theory, but also to make them proud.

"Thinking about them brought a tear to my eye and I rubbed it. After I did it, my eye stung a bit, so I kept it closed. When I looked at my hand, I saw black eyeliner, mascara, and eyeshadow smeared all over my index finger.

"Stumbling and frustrated, I threw all my stuff in my shoulder bag and jumped out of my chair to go to the bathroom to wash out my eye. Unfortunately, I displayed grace beautifully when I turned to leave the table and my foot caught the leg of my chair; I fell flat on my face.

"I started to push myself up onto my elbows. My nose was killing me. I rubbed it with my un-made-up hand. The last thing I needed was black smeared across my nose, too. Looking at that one, I saw blood streaked across my other index finger. I started repeating a mantra in my head as I struggled to get up.

'I'm not going to cry. I'm not going to cry. I'm not going to cry.'

"Not wanting to deal with it or see who stared at me, I slowly eased myself back to the ground and pressed my forehead on the heels of my hands. Suddenly I heard someone asking me if I was alright and offering me a tissue.

"I glanced up from my hands to see him standing there looking gorgeous. Nodding, I started to pick myself up again, trying to not get blood or cosmetics all over the library carpet. I sat on my knees, accepted the tissue, and tilted my head forward to stop the bleeding. I thanked him and looked around the room. Miraculously, there were only a few other people in the library, and either they hadn't seen my slick ballet moves, or they were graciously not making me feel more embarrassed than I already was.

"He told me I was welcome and I snuck another peek to see him staring at me. I said I wished I could say it was unusual for me to be so clumsy. Luckily, my nose stopped bleeding rather quickly and I pushed myself from my knees into a squat to get myself back up. Unluckily, I didn't realize my feet had fallen asleep while I sat there and I fell back on my butt when I tried to stand.

"I tilted my head back and looked at the ceiling and started laughing at myself. Loudly. In the library. Really, at this point, there was no saving face. I could hear he laughed, too, but he clearly laughed with me and not at me. I shook my legs out to wake them up, then awkwardly pulled myself up with my wrists on the table. We both ended up on our feet at the same time.

"When we eventually stopped laughing, I said, 'I'm Miriam. I would shake your hand, but I'm afraid that would just be another misstep for me.' I looked down at my hands and thought about how my face must look right now. 'I'm such a mess,' I laughed.

"'David,' he responded. 'Let me help you with your bag.' Knight-In-Shining-Armor that he was, he bent down, put everything back into my bag, and slung it over his shoulder. 'I'll hang on to this while you get yourself cleaned up.' He offered me his arm and escorted me to the door of the Women's Room.

"When I walked in, I was horrified at my reflection. I looked like I had just gotten the snot beaten out of me. I cleaned up my face with the soap from the wall and pulled out my tiny emergency mascara and lip gloss from my jeans pocket.

"Feeling satisfied with my recovery, I stepped out of the bathroom. David was sitting on the bench by the door, looking down at his hands and bobbing his knee. It almost seemed like he was nervous, but I reconsidered that observation. Considering the show I just put on, it would be absurd.

"I walked over and extended my hand to him. 'I think it's safe to shake your hand now.' Laughing, he accepted the handshake and stood up.

"Clearing his throat and giving me a slight smirk, he said, 'Maybe it would be safest for me to escort you to your car. Wouldn't want you to take another spill.'

'I'm afraid I walked here this morning. It wasn't pouring when I left the dorms.'

'Then I suppose it's a good thing I *did* drive this morning and rescued you from yourself a few minutes ago. I'll drive you home.'

'Yes, I was most definitely in Damsel-In-Distress mode. I would appreciate a ride. Thanks.'

"He happened to not only have his car with him, but it was parked right out front. He ran to the passenger door and opened it for me before putting my bag in the backseat and hopping into the driver's seat. I told him which dorm I was housed in and off we went.

'It's a good thing you saw me fall in there. Again, thanks for that,' I said to him.

"He scratched the back of his head, 'To be honest, I saw you before that happened and was trying to work up the nerve to go over to say hello. When you fell, my nerves went away and all I could think was that I had to help out this beautiful girl.' He glanced at me and gave me a wink.

"I tried to suppress the blushing, but failed miserably. I hadn't really tried even making friends since being up in Washington, but after my glorious display of clumsiness, David still seemed interested. Figuring I really didn't have anything else to lose, my pride was already broken, I went for it. 'You know, rather than go straight to my dorm, would you mind stopping somewhere to eat? I've been in that library all day and I'm starving.'

'Are you asking me on a date?' he asked me with a snarky grin.

'The answer to that question depends on your answer to mine.'

"Smiling, he said, 'I know just the place.' He took me to what became our favorite restaurant and the rest is history."

"Amazing," John said. "Your memories are stunning to me and you are quite the story-teller, Miriam."

"Thank you. I'm not really sure what you mean by that comment about my memories, but I have a feeling if I ask, you'll just tell me I'm not ready to hear it yet."

John laughed. "You are probably right."

"I know you keep telling me you don't know where Harmony is, but I had a thought. Do you think you could contact my mother-in-law, Emma? If I could find out if she has her, it would really set my mind at ease."

"Emma?" he asked, somewhat surprised at her name. He tried to recover. "I don't know if she will know anything about Harmony, but I can certainly try finding out. If I can find her, would you be interested in seeing her?"

"Yes! Oh yes! I would love to see her! You could really do that?"

"I can certainly try."

John smiled as he stood up, said his goodbye, and left.

I was very excited for the visit.

Maybe she'll know where Harmony is.

Chapter 8

I looked at the clock. It was a few minutes past the time John had said he would be bringing Emma to visit. I wiped the sweat from my clammy palms on my shaking legs. I had spent the whole morning sitting on the sofa, essentially staring at the door. I was too excited to do any different. When the door slid open, I shot up out of my chair. Emma walked in and immediately started tearing up. I ran to her and embraced her and began crying, too.

"Thank God you're here," I said. My heart raced with excitement over seeing her. I pulled away from her and saw her trembling lower lip. It was the same look she would give me after David passed away and she was trying to be strong for me.

"Please, have a seat," I said and gestured toward the solitary chair in the room. Emma didn't move.

"What's wrong, Emma? Is there something you need to tell me?" I asked, concerned.

Is something wrong with Harmony? Or Emma?

Emma looked down and tried to breathe through her crying. I held her hand. "Ella," she said. "I'm Ella. Remember?"

"What?"

"Ella, hon. Not Emma."

I blinked my eyes a few times at this, unsure if I had her name wrong because of whatever was going on with my brain. Deciding it was not the most important thing to focus on, I moved on to my main concern. "Is something wrong with Harmony?" I asked with bated breath.

Emma furrowed her brow in confusion. "Who?"

I took a step back. "What do you mean, 'who?' Harmony. My daughter. Your granddaughter."

Emma's face paled and she turned and knocked on the door. "I'm ready."

"Emma, what's going on? You know Harmony. Sweet little girl with David's blonde hair and blue eyes."

Emma knocked a little harder and the door slid open. Before she left, she turned to look at me. "I'm sorry. I just can't do this." With that, she bolted.

I sunk to my knees and put my face in my hands. I felt like I had been crying for days; it was evident by my swollen eyes that I had been.

Why wouldn't Emma know who Harmony is? Have they done something to her?

I stood to my feet and said without shouting, "Whoever is watching, I'm not in the mood for lunch right now or dinner tonight. I'm just going to shower and go to sleep." I did exactly that. I showered, went to bed, and stayed there for the rest of the day. When I laid down, the lights shut off on their own, or that was what I perceived, at least.

When John said he could bring Emma to see me, this was not the visit I had imagined. I thought I would find out that Harmony was alright and that I would get some of the motherly advice Emma was always ready to give.

She looked so hurt and confused. I don't understand. She didn't know who I was talking about when I mentioned David or Harmony. She probably wouldn't have known who I was talking about if I had talked about Tom either. Is there something wrong with me? I'm ready for some answers and I will be getting them tomorrow.

At that thought, I closed my eyes, determined not to cry before I went to sleep.

I failed miserably at that attempt.

Chapter 9

I didn't sleep at all that night; I didn't even toss and turn. When the morning lights automatically came on, I still laid on my back staring at the ceiling, trying to keep my eyes open. Every time I closed my eyes, I saw the horror on Emma's face. When I mentioned David and Harmony, she looked at me like I was Hannibal Lecter crazy. The way she backed off was almost like she thought I was going to lunge at her and take a bite. She was *terrified* of me.

Turning onto my side, I felt like crying, but I was out of tears. I had cried so many times over the last few days, I couldn't do it anymore. Instead, I took a deep breath and hopped out of bed. Glancing at the clock, I could see it was just about time for John to arrive.

Sure he knew more than he let on, and angry about it, I was done playing his game and ready for some answers.

I walked into the bathroom and looked at myself in the mirror. It was bizarre how green my eyes were. The eyes I knew were a green/brown hazel, but these eyes were purely green. I took down my ponytail and brushed my long hair. I brought it all over my left shoulder and put it in a braid. While my hair had always been dark, it had never been this long. Definitely a change, but I liked it. I was starting to get used to my new reflection.

As I contemplated again how it was possible that I looked like this, I heard the door to my room slide open. I turned my head to see John coming in with breakfast for two, as usual, and moved to join him in the main room.

"Good morning, Miriam," John greeted me with *way* more glee than normal, which said something. "Did you sleep well?"

I turned the rest of my body, chucked a hip out, and crossed my arms. "Are you serious? Are you really asking me that question?"

As if he hadn't seen my body language or heard the tone I used, he said, "If you're having difficulty sleeping, maybe we could get you a new pillow or mattress. Perhaps you just need some sound. The sound of rain hitting the roof always helps me sleep."

"You cannot be for real right now!" I threw my pillow at his perfectly coiffed hair. "How can you come traipsing in here acting as if yesterday was a perfectly normal day?"

He sat down and gestured for me to do the same, but I stood my ground. He sighed. "Look, Miriam. I realize that Emma's visit yesterday did not exactly go the way you wanted it to, but if you put yourself in her shoes, maybe you could understand her reaction to you."

"How can I put myself in her shoes?" I asked incredulously. "To do that, I would have to know what in the world is going on. I would have to know why I'm even here to begin with."

John nodded and continued his assertions about Emma. "With some people, it is difficult for them to see a loved one in the hospital. I think, perhaps, that was what happened."

I sat down on the couch next to his chair and leaned towards him. "Do you think I'm an idiot? We've talked about how I have a degree, so you must know that I'm smart. Here's what I want: I want straight talk. I want answers. And I want to be spoken to as an adult rather than a child. I don't need things sugar coated or censored. I need the absolute, undiluted truth."

"I know you need answers. And you will get your answers – today."

I wasn't expecting that response. I thought there would be more of an argument about it. "Really?"

"Yes, really. But I need you to understand how today is going to work."

Curious about what he was going to say, I sat back in my chair and crossed my arms and legs. He hesitated again, so I gestured for him to continue.

"I can tell you this right now: there has never been anyone with your condition before. Because you are the first, I have needed to observe and interview you to find out what is happening in your brain and figure out how I should go about getting you out of here."

"I'm the first? How? I'm not anything special and I haven't been to any exotic places recently. Well, I've never been anywhere truly exotic, but that's beside the point. I understand where you're coming from, and I know I haven't been the best patient, but, to be honest, I'm terrified. I don't know if I'm losing my mind or if there is something wrong physically in my head, but I do know that things do not seem right to me here."

"You are the first because your condition is the result of a combination of a disease and technology that was not available when the illness was an epidemic. I completely understand that things don't seem right to you. Based on our conversations, it makes sense that it would not."

Throwing my hands in the air, I said, "See? Cryptic responses like that are the biggest red flags I've ever seen!"

John lifted both hands face down in a "calm down" gesture and smiled a little. "I know it seems that way, but you will understand with time."

"What did you just say?"

Questioningly, he said, "You'll understand with time?"

"Why did you say that?

"Because it's true."

"No. That's too coincidental." Abruptly, I stood up and started pacing the room.

How is it that he is now saying the exact same thing that he said before I woke up here? Did that really happen after all?

"Miriam, what's wrong?"

Should I tell him?

"Miriam?"

Yes.

"In that dream, you said those exact words numerous times right before I woke up here. How is it that you know them?"

"Oh. It makes sense that you would have heard me saying that," he mused, halfway present with me.

"You really did say that? That wasn't just in my head?"

"Well... it's complicated."

"Try me."

"Yes, I did say that. Your mind must have interpreted me being there because I *was* here with you."

I have no idea what he is talking about.

As if reading my mind, John said, "I know it does not make sense right now. But it will make sense… You will eventually grasp it."

I chuckled a little at his rephrasing himself. He smiled. "Okay. I'll just wait for the answers. Go ahead and tell me about the process," I conceded.

John took a deep breath. "There are three steps. Right now, we are doing the first one, so you are already nearly a third of the way through the process. What I am doing is trying to prepare you for what is coming without directly telling you what's going on.

"Second, I will tell you what is going on. Finally, we send you home. You will need to have weekly appointments with us during your transition, but you will be free to go."

I sighed in relief.

Home. I can't wait to get home and hold Harmony.

"You should also prepare yourself for the truth. I can just about guarantee that it will be nothing you have considered and hard for you to hear."

Harmony is dead.

That was the worst thing I could imagine hearing. It would explain my mental breakdown and why Emma couldn't visit me for very long. I had figured this was the case sometime the previous night while I stared at the ceiling. I nodded in response. However, that didn't fit into the category of nothing I had considered.

"Do you need a moment, Miriam?"

"Yes," I responded absentmindedly. "Could you come back in around an hour?"

Sitting back and tilting my head toward the ceiling, I thought about what he had said as he left the room.

"Your mind must have interpreted me being there because I was here with you." How can that possibly make sense with time? Probably the same way seeing my dead husband and son, then seeing all of my family snapped away will make sense with time.

I closed my eyes. The only thing I thought could help me prepare was a little shut-eye. Exhausted from having little sleep the previous night, I fell asleep quickly.

I look across the blue water of Kailua-Kona and take a deep breath.

"This is so beautiful," I remark, tilting my head to face the warm sun.

"Yes, it is."

I turn my head and see David looking at me. "This can't be real. You and I never came here together," I muse.

"I know. But I'm here now."

"I'm scared, David. I'm all alone and no one seems to understand me."

"It makes sense that you'd be scared. You don't know what's going on. I'd be scared, too."

"Do you know what's going on?"

"Nope. I'm in your head. Remember? You're dreaming right now."

"Oh, right." I turn back to look at the ocean.

David steps closer to me and lifts my chin delicately so that I am looking at him. A tear fills his eye just at the moment one fills mine. "I love you. I promise you that everything will be okay. I'm not saying everything will be easy, but it will work itself out."

I smile. "I love you, too. Thank you for being here now."

David brings his face to mine and gently brushes his lips against mine, then kisses me the same way he did on our wedding day. He pulls me close to him by the hips and laughs in the kiss. He is so full of joy.

When he ends the kiss, I realize that we are now wearing our wedding clothing. That dress was the prettiest one I had ever seen. I look back up to say something about how dapper he looks in his tux, but he is gone.

I turn to look back at the ocean, but it is different. The island is different, too. I can see all around the island, so I know I am no longer on the Big Island of Hawaii. Rather than sand between my toes, there are pebbles. No longer is the water calm and blue; it is as grey as the overcast sky that appears and the waves crash hard on the shore. The wind blows my long hair all over my face and I move my hands to get it out of my face.

When my sight is clear, the ocean is gone, as are the pebbles and the wind. All I can see is white. Just white. Like before I woke up in my strange new world.

A small table with a picture frame appears before me. I pick it up and look at it; it is a family photo of all four of us. I smile, but then the photo starts transforming. The photo is now a picture of me as a teenager with my parents, but it is the me I now see in the mirror. Just like the other photo I had seen, I am wearing a green dress, brooch, and tiara. My parents are wearing regal clothing as well.

What?

Chapter 10

I woke up to the sound of the door sliding open. As promised, he came back after an hour. I stayed seated as he made his way over to sit next to me on the sofa; I had a feeling I was going to want to be sitting down for whatever he had to say.

"This is the part where you start giving me answers," I muttered. I really could not stand the man and all his games.

John leaned on his knees with his elbows and folded his hands in front of him. "First, my name is Doctor John Quincy, not John Smith. I understand that you have a troubling memory of me. I can assure you I have never done anything to harm you and I certainly had no intention to confuse you."

Slightly confused by the change in name, I said, "Alright. I was probably having some kind of meltdown and had some hallucinations or a vivid dream or something, right?

"I am thinking that was a vivid dream, all things considered."

I took a moment to breathe, then asked, "Where is Harmony? Is she dead?"

John took a deep breath and puffed up his cheeks as he slowly released the air. "That is a complicated question, Miriam."

"So you've said."

"To answer that question, I need to explain everything. The truth is going to be a hard thing to hear. Are you sure you are ready?"

"I've been ready for a while now." I began to get irritated with the run around.

"I will try to explain it in a nutshell, but it will still be a long explanation. To begin, we are not in the year 2016, and Barack Obama is not the President."

How much time have I lost? "What year *is* it?"

"2255."

I gasped. "Who is the President?"

As if it matters! How is this even possible? Is he being honest? There's no way!

"I will get to that later. Around two hundred years ago, a mad man created a virus, commonly referred to as 'The Daze,' that grew into an epidemic. To be fair, the original purpose of it was to expand only his mind so he could maintain more knowledge; it was not meant to pass on to other people.

"Rather than expand the mind in a positive manner, it made it so people would randomly go into a dream state. It triggered the fear portion of the brain, so I suppose it was more of a nightmare state. When the nightmares began, people would continue to wander about. The man took no blame for his mistake and instead founded an organization, claiming he worked on a cure, when, in fact, he did not.

"The Daze was around for so long, that it eventually just became a part of normal life. People would abruptly act out their nightmares, many times ending up dying because of it. Jumping in front of cars to escape unseen horrors, stabbing themselves or others, things like that. Sometimes, people committed suicide because they couldn't handle the insanity any longer.

"If neither of those killed the victim, The Daze itself eventually would. At its peak, The Daze would completely take over the mind, blocking the basic instinct to survive. The person would stop seeking shelter in adverse weather, they wouldn't eat or drink for nutrition. They would die from the natural elements, starvation, or dehydration. The Daze morphed into a contagious disease that transferred through touch.

"Eventually, the vaccine cure, the first of its kind, was released to the public. By that time, most of the world's population was gone. Many more still died after the cure released because they were not lucid enough to seek it out and everyone they knew was already dead. Mass graves in the form of bonfires happened all over the world; there wasn't enough land to bury everyone. Those who did not accept the vaccine cure died of lung failure from the smoke of the burning diseased.

"While everyone was now cured, chaos still broke loose. Power was up for grabs because most of the world's leaders were dead and most of our infrastructure was failing or had already failed. Here in the Northwest of this continent, the man who helped release the vaccine cure collected quite the following.

"Aside from that, he helped bring organization to the chaos. He was eventually crowned King so he would be able to reconstitute normalcy and bring prosperity to the land. He appointed Nobility to provinces and each province also elected Delegates to represent them on the Arborian Council. Other countries followed suit and more monarchies were created. Life returned to a semblance of normality and the people are now happy."

I stared blankly at him, wondering if he was being sincere with me. He had said *I* was a good story-teller, but what I had just heard was a whopper.

As calmly as possible, I said, "Alright. I am going to suspend logic for a moment and say I believe everything you just said. Question: People are happy with a monarchy? They gave up their right to vote? I find it difficult to believe that Americans would so quickly give up that freedom."

"It is true that there is unrest among a small part of the population, but it is not due to having a monarchy. Because our rulers are good, and there are elected Delegates of each province, the people are content with the way things are. It is impossible to make everyone content. There would be unhappy people no matter what type of government we have."

I scoffed and pinched the bridge of my nose. "Well, this is all very interesting, but what does it have to do with Harmony?"

"I am getting there. As I said, it is going to be a lengthy explanation even though I am trying to shorten it for you. You were injected with a mutated version of The Daze through the treachery of a man named Darrel Watson. You had stopped him from releasing it by warning the Guard outside the lab and telling them to seal and air-clean the place before allowing anyone in to rescue you. You made it clear there was no other way to stop the release, that the man was dead, and that you needed to be quarantined to prevent spread of the mutated virus. After we took care of you, the building was burned to the ground, just to be safe.

"Luckily, we were able to put you in a cryogenic chamber and finally found the cure about a week ago. Unluckily, there was a complication with your time in there that we are still trying to figure out. You seem to have memories of a life back in 2016; complete with family and friends. You even have stories of specific memories."

At this, John reached out and took my hand.

"Miriam, the reason why the answer to your question about Harmony is complicated is that Harmony has never really existed outside of your mind. David, Tom, and Harmony were never alive, so they cannot be dead."

My heart beat fast and I started hyperventilating. I couldn't believe what my ears were hearing. It made sense with everything I had been experiencing, but it was still unbelievable.

Being in the future? Alright. The government and boundaries have been completely changed? Okay. My family never existed? No.

"Why can't I remember anything about this? And how do I know you're telling me the truth?"

"I don't really know yet why you can't remember anything about your real life. My theory is that your imaginative memories have replaced your real ones."

Becoming overwhelmed, I took a deep breath and asked, "How long was I out?"

"It has been … Well, it's been ten years. There is something else," John hesitated before deciding to continue. "You are a direct descendant of the first King."

"Really?" That was all I could say. I was still trying to accept the fact that the life I knew never happened and I lived in the future. Then it hit me. What was he trying to tell me? "Wait a minute. If he is my ancestor, that would make me – " I couldn't say it.

John finished my thought. "Royalty. Yes. More precisely, the Princess of this kingdom: Arboria."

"Princess? As in, someday I'll be the Queen of this country?"

"Kingdom. Yes. You will be coronated Crown Princess the day after your twenty-first birthday."

I'm not even twenty-one yet?

"When is that?"

He didn't respond.

"Doctor Quincy, when is my twenty-first birthday?"

"In one week."

"My coronation is in a week?!"

"No. You will be coronated the day *after* your birthday. Your coronation is in a week and a day."

"Are you saying that I am not the heir until next week?"

"Sweet tree blossoms, no; of course not. You *are* the heir right now. Your coronation is into your new role as Crown Princess. It is a tradition acknowledging your readiness to rule, should the need arise."

The room started spinning again, so I bent over and put my head between my knees to prevent passing out and to wrap my brain around everything I had just learned. He had been right: the truth was hard to hear. I wasn't sure which truth I had more of a hard time with. That the family I loved and cherished never really existed or that I was to be coronated Crown Princess of a kingdom two hundred years from where my memories lay. Democracy no longer exists here.

If I'm not already Crown Princess, that must mean…

"If I'm not coronated yet, that must mean my parents are still alive, right?"

John smiled. "Yes. In fact, they are awaiting my call to let them know you're ready to come home. I told them you would probably need at least tonight here. There is a Welcoming Ball tomorrow that was scheduled before we knew about your condition. The public knows nothing about your memory loss. It would be devastating should they find out. Perhaps you'd like to stay here and let things soak in before you're thrown to the wolves?"

My head shot straight up. While I wasn't crazy about my circumstances, I had no desire to be in the white room anymore. "No. No. No, I am not staying here any longer than I have to. I will gladly go home today. Now even."

I could tell that John was surprised by my response.

"I need to learn as much as possible about the culture and societal expectations before I have to go to a freaking ball tomorrow and declare my readiness to rule in a few short days," I explained.

John nodded. "Very well, I will contact your father immediately. Miriam, I need you to know that while you are able to go home, I will still need to meet with you once a week until I deem you prepared to live life normally."

"Yes, I understand. You already told me that. There is nothing wrong with my short term memory, Doctor Quincy."

John stood up to leave. "Yes, Your Highness," he said with a slight bow. That was going to be hard to get used to.

Who am I kidding? This whole life is going to be hard to get used to.

Part II

Chapter 11

I paced the floor of my room, waiting on my dad to arrive. *My dad. The King.*

About an hour ago, I had received a package that contained an emerald green sun dress with brown flats. It was nice to see a color besides white. I threw off the white patient dress and pulled the green dress over my head. The short sleeves hung off my shoulders, which I thought looked lovely.

Harmony would love being a Princess. All the dresses and parties. I miss her. David would tell me how pretty I look. Tom beg me to change into some pants so I could get on the floor and play with him.

Finally, the door slid open and John walked in. "I am here to escort you down to the waiting area to your father and mother, Your Highness."

"Please don't call me that. I'm not ready for it," I said, exasperated.

"Alright, Miriam. But you should know that it is a societal norm for people to call you that and bow or curtsy. It is just one of the things you will have to get used to."

I huffed a little, but followed John out the door. Directly across from my room an elevator stood open and waiting for us to enter. As we walked in, I looked above the doors and saw that we were on the thirty-fifth floor.

"There's a private elevator for the floor I was on?"

"Yes. You are also on the top floor of the building, which is also private. It was for security purposes."

That took me aback. "Is my life in danger?"

"Not any more than any other Royal, I'm sure. As I told you, there are a small number of citizens who are dissatisfied with some things going on, so there is always a chance of a random rebel attack. Don't worry, though. The Royal Arborian Guard is the best in the world. You are in perfectly safe hands."

"Can't say I blame them," I muttered under my breath, not loud enough for John to hear. I wasn't sure if *I* liked that our country had a monarchy. I would just have to be patient and wait until my time came to change things. There was plenty I could do in the meantime. I had an entire country's history that I had to relearn, after all.

"Where is Arboria located? Are we in the area Washington State once was?" After I asked the question, I realized he probably didn't know what I was talking about. Sure enough, he crooked his eyebrow and looked at me like I had two heads.

"I'm not sure where or what Washington State was, but I can tell you that Arboria consists of the Northwestern portion of what used to be the United States. There are many trees of many different varieties, thus the name the kingdom was given."

My heart raced again as the elevator got closer to the first floor. I hated to hope. Just because my brain was right about John with his appearance, personality, and voice, it didn't mean that it was right about my parents. The King and Queen could look completely different than I remembered my parents. I wondered how old they were and what they looked like.

Do I look more like him or her? Are they honorable people? How nervous should I be right now? What am I getting myself into? Nothing. I'm not getting myself into anything I haven't already decided on, as far as I know. Not that there was much choice, my being the only heir to the Crown.

"What would have happened if I hadn't survived the cryogenic freeze? Who would have reigned after my parents?"

John looked up like he was really having to think about it – like he was dissecting my family tree.

"I am not really sure, to be honest. I am not originally from Arboria and it never occurred to me that you would not survive, so it was not something I worried myself with. I would imagine it probably would have been your cousin, Duchess Elleouise of Maple."

"Elleouise. Ella. Emma! My cousin? She's my cousin? No wonder she was terrified when she met with me! I treated her like my mother-in-law. I hope that kind of thing doesn't happen all the time."

John smirked and looked pleased that I had figured that out on my own. "These are new waters for you, Miriam. We are all treading the waters right with you. That is why we are still going to see each other once a week."

As slow as the ride felt, we finally reached the bottom floor. The elevator rested for a moment before dinging and opening. John put his hand in the center of my back and guided me down the hall toward the door to the lobby. Before opening the door, John moved his hands to my arms and turned me so I looked at him. It was uncomfortable, but his expression told me he was trying to ease my nerves and anxieties, so I let him do it.

"One step at a time. There are no press here; there are not even other family members or friends out there. The only people you will see are your father and your mother. Take a deep breath."

Tears began welling up in my eyes. "What if I don't recognize them? I would think that would hurt them. It would hurt me if Harmony didn't..." When I said her name, I couldn't complete my thought. A burning pain that swelled from my heart to my eyes brought me into a full sob.

"Your parents have been counseled about your delicate condition. It might hurt if you don't recognize them, but they will understand and will be there for you during this transition."

Pulling myself away from John, I took a few deep, albeit shaky, breaths and slowly faced the door. With trembling hands, I tapped the button on the door frame and the door slid open. At first, I didn't see anyone waiting, but after I took a few steps and looked around, I saw them. My parents. My fears were fruitless because I *did* recognize them. Though in my memories, they weren't wearing crowns or capes – Mom didn't wear gowns, and Dad wore a military uniform rather than the suit he now wore – they *looked* the same.

All three of us froze and stared, they at me and I at them. Hope and fear were displayed all over their faces. I could see that they wanted more than anything in this moment to have me recognize them, and I did. A smile slowly formed on my face and they mirrored my expression. At the same time, we ran to each other in a giant mess of kisses, tears, and embraces. I might have lost my husband and children, but at least my parents were alive again; and they were very real.

Chapter 12

Because of my lengthened stay indoors, without even one window, the sunlight blinded me, even though it was covered with clouds. Trees grew everywhere I looked and I breathed in their comforting fragrance. Ahead of a long black vehicle with tinted windows looked like a limo. I supposed it was our transportation, but there were no wheels on it. Nevertheless, Father opened the door to the backseat and Mother got in. I raised my eyebrows at him and he simply smiled and gestured for me to enter. After we were all in and buckled, I heard some chatter from the driver's seat. Something about assigned altitude.

Next thing I knew, the car rose off the ground. My hands flew to my sides to steady myself and Father smiled hugely, very entertained by my surprise.

"I keep forgetting that you don't remember this time. There were no hovers yet in 2016, were there?"

At first, I wondered how he knew my memories were from 2016, then I remembered John telling me he had appraised them of my mental situation. I shook my head and stared out the window. "No. We had a variety of vehicles with wheels that ran on roads on the ground," I said quietly as I took in my surroundings.

Nature and man seemed to balance each other out in my new world. Rather than cut down trees, these people, my people, built around them. More trees had been planted, too. They were probably planted where buildings burned down and on the roads that had clearly been removed.

It was like looking at a futuristic village of elves. When we passed the Space Needle, I knew we were in Seattle.

"What happened to the Space Needle?" I asked. It was a bit different than I knew it.

"You remember it?" Father asked hopefully.

"Not like this. It looks like they had to rebuild it part way up."

"After the fires, they rebuilt it with a stronger metal and made it higher up. It's now the tallest building in the world. It is painted that way so it blends in with the trees." The stem of the building had been painted brown and the top was painted a green identical to the trees surrounding it. "You will see it emanate a green light at night. The light that it emits illuminates the whole city just enough and is a symbol to anyone in the kingdom who sees it that everything is alight in the capital. How do you remember it?"

"It was tall, not as tall as that, and white. The top was the same shape, but didn't rotate on the outside. It rotated on the inside. You could see everything from there. It must have been before whatever fires you were referring to."

"It sounds like you have some fond memories of it."

"Yes. David and I used to go up to the top and look at the world around us. It was how we collected ourselves and brought our lives into perspective when we had a big decision or a big change. We went there after both miscarriages." Knowing I had said too much, I pressed my lips together and looked at my hands.

Mother took my hands and lifted my chin so I could see her eyes. Hers were a beautiful emerald green, the same as mine, and they were full of compassion and love. Mine were full of tears at the reminder that I had two more children I lost several years earlier.

"Miriam," she said with kindness, "I can't begin to understand everything you've experienced. Having a miscarriage is difficult. I had one before you were born and one after. Both were only 11 weeks along, but I loved them *so* much. I want you to know that your father and I are here not only for you to support you in your transition, but for whatever you remember going through. Regardless of whether it happened in your false life or your real life. That life in your dreams was very real for you and any emotions you feel about it are real and natural."

If we hadn't been buckled down, I would have hugged her. She always did know the right things to say. I put my hand out and touched her cheek. "You're exactly how I remember you; both of you are. In my false life, I lost you shortly before pursuing higher education. David and I had two miscarriages, but also two living children, Tom and Harmony. A year ago, I lost David and Tom in a car accident. A few days ago, I lost my little Harmony when I woke up here. She was all I had left, really."

I stopped to take a shaky breath. "I have been through a lot, but *I* want *you* to know that when I saw you and your faces matched my memory, I felt like I started to get my life back. I miss them terribly, especially Harmony since her loss is so fresh, but I feel like I'm getting a second chance at life."

Now both my parents were crying with me and I could tell they felt just as burdened by the seatbelts as I did.

"Approaching the Evergreen Palace, Your Majesty," the driver called back.

It was aptly named. Just like all the other buildings, the Evergreen Palace was woven with the trees. A wall encircled the largest tree, which sat at the center of the grove. Every tower, spire, wall, and gate shimmered a glistening white in the sunlight. The bright stonework stood in stark contrast with the evergreens it danced with. My mouth dropped open.

"This is the most beautiful place I've ever seen," I said with my still shaky voice.

The driver lowered the limo when he heard confirmation it was safe, and greeted the guard as we entered the gate.

"How do you keep people from simply flying their cars in? Why bother with a gate at all?"

"There is an EMP field surrounding the palace. Should someone decide to do something stupid and try to come in from above, it shuts down the electricity in their hover and they crash past the palace," Father responded.

I nodded and mouthed "oh" as we continued down the driveway. "I know that the majority of people don't know about my memory issue," I said. "Who does know?"

Mother answered this time. "Let's see. The doctors and nurses who worked with you at the hospital, our service-specialists, your tutor, Duke Peter and Duchess Elleouise of Maple, your two Guards, and us, of course."

"Ella. Is she alright? I'm pretty sure I really freaked her out when she came to see me."

"Yes, she is doing better and is very excited to see you. She was your best friend before your infection with The Daze."

I smiled, "She was my mother-in-law in my false life, Emma. Maybe this transition won't be so difficult after all. I don't suppose I was dating someone named David, was I?"

"No. We didn't know anyone by that name," Mother said.

By the time we got to the palace, it was dark. When we got out of the car, I stretched and yawned. "What time is it?" I asked, still yawning."

"Around 9:00, dear," Father replied. "It's been a long day and you have a longer day tomorrow. Let's go to bed a little early, hmm?"

"That sounds like a great plan. I could use a nice, warm bed about now."

As we stepped out of the car, the clouds were dumping rain on us.

"The buildings and cars might be different, but it is still as rainy as ever here in Seattle."

"Seattle? Oh, right. 2016." Father paused. "After The Daze epidemic, when borders were being redrawn and new governments were being established, most cities were renamed, too. Seattle was renamed Petrichoria."

"I've always liked that word. 'Petrichor.' The scent of rain on dry ground."

Father smiled at that and kissed the top of my head as he put his arm around me and drew me to his side. Mother took my other hand and we walked into the palace. Though I fully expected everything to be white and match the exterior of the palace, the interior was much different. It had the feeling of a giant cabin in the woods. The walls were painted the same color brown as the trees sprinkled throughout the room, and any furniture was either green or ivory.

The green lighting inside was much like the Space Needle as Father had described it, and after closer inspection, I discovered it was, indeed, coming from there. I imagined the lights were probably normal during the day, if they needed to be on at all. The ceiling was a clear, glass dome and I could see the sky's heavy release of rain hit the glass roof. I closed my eyes and took a deep breath through my nose.

"Petrichor," I whispered, so quietly neither parent heard me. It was like the scent seeped in through the trees. Because the palace was built around trees, I had assumed it would be cold because of gaps. However, I was pleasantly surprised to find it warm.

"I'll take you to your room and help you get settled in," Mother said.

I gave Father a hug and we went separate ways. The walk to my room was quiet and long.

"What is this room?" I asked Mother about the giant room that stretched higher than the top floor.

"We call this the Core. This tree that the stairs are built on is the center of Evergreen Palace. Each floor branches off into hallways."

"It's beautiful," I said, mesmerized by the water hitting the glass ceiling again. As we climbed past the fourth floor, I noticed a tall man with combed back, medium length blond hair, a square jaw, and narrow eyes watching me. I stopped and met his haunting gaze. When I did, he smiled sideways and tipped his head like a cowboy from Texas.

"Come along, Miriam," Mother said when she realized I had stopped moving.

"Right," I said, knowing it made no sense with her command.

"Who was that?" I asked as we approached the branch off the fifth floor that led to my room. "Did I know him? He seemed interested in my being here."

Mother smiled. "You don't know him yet. Tomorrow, you will meet him at the Welcoming Ball. Your father will explain more before the event. Did you find him handsome?"

"Uh – yes. Didn't you see him? He was like a Texan god!"

She laughed at what I said, probably knowing where Texas used to be because she was Royalty and needed to know the history of other places aside from Arboria. Or perhaps Texas was still around. I could not imagine *them* giving up the rights of a constitutional republic.

When we arrived on the top floor and turned to the left, I was out of breath from climbing five stories. Mother wasn't winded at all and I figured I would get used to the stairs in time. That's when I saw him. Of all the people from my false life to be my personal guard. "No. Not him," I whined, pointing at him.

Obviously confused, Mother and the Guard exchanged glances. The Guard actually looked a little hurt by my complaint. "But, honey, I haven't even introduced him to you," she said.

"Doesn't matter," I said shaking my head. "I recognize him."

"Tree blossoms, Miriam. You only met him one time before your freeze and he was a teenager, then."

"No. Not from here. From there. He was the officer who was *supposed* to be watching my house when it was broken into."

"But in hindsight, that was probably just your mind getting ready to come out of the cryogenic chamber, right? Besides, you also thought Doctor Quincy was a villain."

I thought about that for a minute while holding my left arm with my right hand. I supposed that could have been what happened, but we could have been broken into, as well.

I looked at the short, stocky man in his decorated forest green dress uniform; he was only a couple inches taller than me – and I was only 5'5". His dark hair fell from under his beret and his kind blue eyes seemed genuinely confused.

Poor guy. I'm an idiot. This guy is not the man from my false life. He's just doing his job.

I looked at him and softened my expression – certain there had probably been a scowl on my face.

"I'm sorry, Sir," I started. "Life is kind of confusing for me right now. I'm afraid you may have to have some patience with me. What is your name?"

"Frank, Your Highness," he replied. "Rest assured, I come from a long line of Royal Arborian Guards and have worked hard to earn the privilege of serving as your personal Guard. It is my honor to protect and to serve you and I hope to prove my worth in time."

"I'm sure you will." Hoping no permanent damage had been done, I smiled to reassure him.

Mother opened the door and I stepped in. Unlike the rest of the palace, my room was painted a dark red. The furnishing and blankets on the bed were all brown. Several vases of white roses were placed around the room on the various tabletops. Some genus of rose even climbed the pillars of the four poster bed. Naturally, there was a slim evergreen tree near the center of the room.

"It's lovely," I said. "Why are there so many roses?"

"You've always been loved by the people. Ever since you were a child, you've been referred to as the 'Rose of Petrichoria.' You used to have a big obsession with them when you were small and were well known for it. Wait until you see the scepter that has been crafted for you. You will love it."

"Scepter?"

"Every King and Queen of Arboria has had a scepter made for him or her. It acts as a reminder to your people and yourself of the vows you will make on Crowning Coronation Day. You'll begin training tomorrow. For now, my little rose bud, get yourself a bath and go to bed. I'll lay out a nightgown for you and make sure it isn't white," she said with a wink.

I laughed. Clearly, they had heard about my distaste of the interior design of my room at the hospital. After hugging and saying our good nights, I headed into my bathroom. The maid must have prepared the bath ahead of time. It was still hot and had red rose petals floating on the surface of the water. As I stepped in, I could feel and smell the rose-scented bath oils that had been put in the water.

Despite the fact they were everywhere, for some reason, the roses were not overwhelming. Actually, they were calming – the sight and scent of them. After I got out and put on the lovely green nightgown Mother had laid out for me, I settled into bed and closed my eyes. I was home – and I thought maybe I would get some good sleep that night.

Chapter 13

I was wrong. It was no fault of anybody, except – technically – myself. If I hadn't somehow given myself that disease, none of this would be going on. I would remember everyone I supposedly love and I never would have lived that false life that felt so real to me. I missed David. I turned over on my right side and stroked the pillow next to me.

I'm not even really a widow. Why can't I just let this go?

I closed my eyes to try to sleep again, but all I could see was David's smiling face. All I could feel was his warm hand cupping my cheek. All I could hear were the sweet nothings he used to say to me. All I could smell was the cologne I had bought him for Christmas. All I could taste was his familiar kiss.

Closing my eyes, I tried to recreate our wedding day in my mind to help me get some sleep.

I couldn't believe the day had finally come. The day I would become Mrs. David Dutch.

I was a little sad that Mom and Dad weren't here for my big day, but I knew they had to be watching me. They would have loved David. He was smart, charming, and handsome, but mostly, he loved me. I mean he really loved me. Aside from seeing the love Dad showed Mom, I had never known anyone to love as deeply or cherish as much as David did me.

Though it was true my parents weren't able to be here, David's family was; and he had a huge family. I'm pretty sure most, if not all, his family was there, though I wouldn't really know anything about who was there until I walked down the aisle.

I stood up from my chair and looked at myself in the giant floor-length mirror. This was my dream dress. I couldn't believe the deal I got when I purchased it. It was as if the universe wanted me to have it. The ball gown had delicate lace around the bodice and intricate beading in floral patterns covered the bell of the gown. The long sleeves were lace and began to bell out at the elbows, ending at my hands. The heart-shaped neckline was even there; the perfect dress and I didn't even have to get it hand-made.

I heard a knock at the door and opened it. At first, I didn't see anyone, but then I looked down and saw him. My little Tom. He had David's blue eyes and blond hair. When we had found out I was pregnant three years ago, I was terrified. I never thought I would be the girl who got knocked up by her boyfriend. A million things had raced through my mind. What if David didn't want the baby? What if he didn't want me anymore? What would his parents think? What am I going to do?

But David was so good about it. We told his parents, who were shocked, but graciously took us into their home so they could help with the baby when he came. It was important to them that David and I both finished our degrees and by that point, they had grown very attached to me. Without them, I'm not sure David and I would have made it through.

Tom's big blue eyes got even bigger as he took in my appearance. In his sweet little voice, he said, "Mama, you look like a princess!"

I giggled, lowered myself to him and pulled him in for a big hug. When I pulled away to look at him, I said, "And you look like a little prince in your tuxedo." I straightened his bowtie and asked, "Are you ready? Do you have the rings?"

He nodded excitedly and pulled the rings out of his pockets. Since I didn't have parents to give me away, David and I decided to include Tom as more than a ring-bearer; he would walk me down the aisle. I looked at our bands in his little hands, then helped him put them back in his pocket. Standing up, I put my hand out for him to take it and he did.

We walked hand-in-hand to the sanctuary; I could feel him still staring at me in awe. The ushers stood by the wooden double doors waiting for the cue to open them. My heart raced. Though I knew the photographers would be taking lots of pictures, I desperately wanted to remember every moment myself. I knew it was probably wishful thinking. Between the adrenaline and the tight dress, I already felt light-headed, sure that I lost brain cells every moment the dress was on. Resigning myself to a long day in it, I took a deep breath and decided to simply enjoy every moment.

Debussy's Claire de Lune started and the ushers opened the doors. When everyone stood, I gasped as I saw how many family and friends had made it. Overwhelming love seemed to consume the room and I felt it from every person in attendance. Even the previously occupied small children stopped what they were doing to see. For a moment, I froze and couldn't go anywhere. Then my eyes landed on David.

I took a deep breath and walked down the aisle to him. I took his hand with my unoccupied one and he held Tom's other hand. The day wasn't only creating a marriage relationship between the two of us, but a permanent family relationship with Tom as well. I glanced down at him and he was beaming. I looked back up to David and smiled a huge smile.

The reminiscing made my sleeplessness worse. I abruptly stood up and did a couple jumps to try to shake myself out of it; maybe exercising would make me tired enough to sleep. After a few minutes, I threw myself back on the bed, more awake than I was before the workout. Glancing over, I saw the holographic clock next to my bed read 11:00.

It's not too late. Maybe if I go for a short walk or do a couple laps on the stairs, I can make myself tired and then I'll be able to go to sleep.

When I walked over to my walk-in closet and opened the door, I felt dumbstruck at what I saw. The loveliest clothes, shoes, and accessories lined the walls of the closet – which was the size of my master bedroom in my false life. I was only trying to find a robe and I had no idea how things were organized. I stepped in and ran my hands along the dresses, shirts, pants, skirts, and cloaks; the materials were so soft and I found myself wondering what types were in there. I turned around to look along the other side and that's when I saw the robe; it was hanging behind the door, of course. More like a kimono, it was made of green satin and long enough to hit the floor when I put it on.

Nicely covered, I stepped out into the hallway.

I wonder where I should go? I haven't even had a tour yet. I guess I'll just walk around and maybe my subconscious will take me somewhere relaxing.

"Is everything alright, Your Highness?" Frank startled me out of my thoughts. I had forgotten I now had a Guard. At my jump, he quickly apologized, "I didn't mean to startle you, Your Highness. I'm so sorry."

"It's okay. You're just doing your job." I took a deep breath to slow my heart beat. "Do you ever get to sleep?"

He chuckled. "Yes, I do. There will be a different Guard here in the morning, Your Highness."

"Please, call me Miriam. I'm not used to 'Your Highness' yet and I'm not sure I ever will be."

"I can do that in private, but in public, I will still need to call you 'Your Highness.' It's a faux pas to call you anything else, except 'Princess.'"

"Princess is fine. Thank you."

"So – is everything alright? What are you doing awake at this hour?"

I rubbed my left arm with my right hand. "Just having difficulties adjusting. I'm sure I'll be fine. I was just going to go for a walk to try to make myself sleepy."

"I'll accompany you, Miriam."

"It's really alright. I'm sure I'm fine on my own."

"It's my job. If I didn't follow, I could lose it."

"Alright, then. But I'd like to have some quiet time, if you don't mind."

"Anything you want."

I turned right out of my door toward the spiral staircase of the Core, what they called the giant central room of the palace. The green lighting from the Space Needle made it feel eerie, but also strangely calming. When I got to the second floor, I noticed an amber light emanating from a room at the end of one of its branches.

Wondering what was there, I strolled down the hall to the room. Walking through an open, large wooden archway, I realized what I had found: the Scepter Room. The scepters of the Kings and Queens of Arboria lined one and a half walls and were behind glass. Each couple's scepters shared a case. They were all beautiful and were made of everything from steel to titanium. Every scepter had some sort of embellishment on the staff and a colored transparent stone on top.

Feeling done with the Scepter Room, I left and walked back out to the Core – Frank trailing at a reasonable distance behind me – and continued my way down the staircase to the main floor. Stopping, I looked around at the different directions I could go.

"The palace is so big," I said to Frank as he continued his pace to stand next to me.

He chuckled. "Yes. It is quite daunting if you do not know your way around. You will get used to it."

I looked over at him. "Mother mentioned that you and I have met before. I'm sorry I don't remember."

Shrugging, he said, "It's alright. It was long ago. Your father tricked you into keeping me occupied while he had a meeting with my father, who is the High General."

"Oh? Where does that fall in the ranking of the Royal Arborian Guard?"

"Second in command. He is only second to your father, whose title is the Commander in Chief of the Guard."

"Oh," was all I said as I continued to consider all my options of destinations. Deciding on a glass hallway, I walked over and into it. Frank stood outside as I made my way down the hall. The forest outside was beautiful, especially with the torrential downpour and whistling wind.

Pretty soon, the hallway ended at a glass door. When I got into the room, I was in awe at the sight.

Rows of a wide variety of roses filled the room. Other greenery surrounded them and I realized they weren't in rows; it was a maze and I happily entered it. Something in my soul told me that this place was mine. Not just because I was the Rose of Petrichoria, but because it *felt* like it.

Turning corner after corner, I smelled each type of rose and tried to memorize their color. I finally made it to the center of the maze, where a bench-swing hanging beneath a white gazebo seemed to beg me to rest upon it. When I approached the swing, I realized it was more of a sofa with plush cushions and pillows than a bench. The same climbing roses that were on my bed also entwined the gazebo and beautiful blue-white roses surrounded me on all sides. I took the steps to the sofa-swing and sat on it.

Yes. This feels right.

I gently rocked back and forth and looked up to see a full moon shining onto the rose garden windows; it was the only source of light, but it was enough to see what I needed to see. I leaned my head back and soaked in its light as if it were a hot sun.

"Rose?"

I shot up off the sofa at the sound of the familiar voice. I fell down the steps, luckily landing on my rear-end – and I could feel I didn't break anything. I put my hands to my eyes and pressed the heels of my hands on them.

It can't be. It simply can't. He isn't real, so he can't be here. When I remove my hands, he won't be there and I can move on.

I was too afraid to look; to hope. But he rushed to my aid just like he did in my false life when I met him.

"Are you alright?"

"Yes," I lied. I was physically fine, but I was breaking inside.

I opened my eyes and my assumption seemed correct. David was still there. The square shape of his face, his blonde hair, his nose, mouth, everything was just as I knew him.

"My name isn't Rose. It's Miriam."

We sat there in silence staring at each other for what seemed like forever until he finally broke the silence.

"Do you remember me?"

"I don't know. You remind me of someone I used to know, but it can't be."

He stood up and helped me up, eyes never leaving mine. That's when I noticed the color of them in the moonlight. His eyes weren't the Kona-blue I remembered, but chocolate brown.

"Who is it I remind you of?"

"I can't say. I'm sorry."

I looked down at my hands, which were fidgeting. I knew how important it was for me not to tell anyone about my secret: that I had no memory of this world. I wished I could tell him.

He gently tilted my head up by my chin. "Miriam, I know – I know about your memory. Please tell me."

A tear escaped my eye and my heart broke. Mother said I wasn't seeing anyone named David before, but maybe she just didn't know. This man seemed so familiar with me.

"My late husband, David. He died about a year ago."

His eyes furrowed with compassion and he held my face with his hands.

"Miriam, I'm not David, but I'm glad you had someone during that time you were away. I missed you so much."

"Were we – "

"Yes. We were together." He traced my face with his index finger as he said this to me. He was clearly older than me by quite a few years, but I guess that was to be expected. Even though I was frozen, the world kept on going without me.

My mouth fell open and I whispered, "If you're not David, who are you?"

A little bit of sadness filled his eyes as he told me, "Peter."

I *knew* he wasn't David, but he looked *just* like him. I put my shaking hands on his face to ensure that he was real and to see if it felt the same; it did. I looked into his eyes, and even though they weren't the blue I knew so well, I could see his love for me in them. I told myself it didn't matter. He *had* to be the same; he just *had* to be. Everyone else I had met that matched appearances with the people in my false life were similar, if not the same, so he *had* to be, too.

Next thing I knew, he was gently pressing his lips against mine, his left hand moving back up to cup my face. I kissed him back, hoping maybe this was like a fairytale; maybe I was cursed, and only the kiss of my true love would break the spell, bringing my memory back. Our mouths moved in a rhythm that was different than David, but familiar to my new body. His lips took a path from my lips to my cheek, from my cheek to my ear, and from my ear to my neck. I tilted my head back and his right hand kept me standing as I

117

swooned. Tears of joy streamed down my cheeks. Finally, something good was happening to me.

"Peter?"

"Hmm?" He hummed, not stopping his kisses.

"Did anyone know we were together? Why didn't Father and Mother tell me?"

At this, he froze. Slowly he released me and took a step backward. "It's complicated," He said scratching the back of his neck; a nervous tick if I had ever seen one.

"What is complicated? Is it because I'm Royalty? If so, I'll make it work. I'll talk to Father. Maybe he can – "

"It's not that; I'm Nobility."

"Then what?"

"I can't."

"But you just said you're Noble."

"I am." He pressed his lips together and an emotion I had never seen on that face appeared. Perhaps it was regret.

"I'm not eligible."

"But why?" My tears of joy were quickly turning into tears of sorrow. It wasn't fair. I had finally found him and I couldn't have him.

After a pause, he quietly said, "You have to understand. You were gone for ten years. I waited as long as I could, the people became insistent when I turned twenty-seven and you still hadn't awoken. There had to be an heir for my bloodline and there came a point when I couldn't say no anymore. I had to."

"You're married?"

"Yes."

I slapped him. Hard.

"If you're married, what are you doing here? Why kiss me? Why make me think there's a chance?"

"We could still be together."

I slapped him again. Just as hard. On the other side.

"How dare you? I am a person. I am a woman. I am your Princess! One day I'll be your Queen. I will *not*, however, be your mistress."

"Please, Miriam – "

"And kissing me? Sharing an intimate moment with me because you *knew* I wouldn't remember you? It's shameful. You're lucky I'm feeling merciful right now and I won't tell Father what you did. He'd ruin you."

"*Rose –*"

"No. I think you'd better leave before I kick your family jewels, which are apparently more important to you than the love we shared."

I looked away from him and felt him walking away.

"Oh, and Peter?"

He turned slightly to acknowledge he was listening and I looked him in the eyes.

"You're nothing like David. It's a shame you share his appearance."

He turned slowly and made a silent exit.

Waiting a few minutes to make sure he was gone, I collapsed back down on the sofa and rocked for a few minutes, still crying. How things could get worse for me, I didn't know. After a while, I yawned between sobs and made my way back to my room. Though my eyes were swollen with tears and my face was flushed, Frank respectfully said nothing.

"Are you alright?" I stopped my ascent of the stairs and looked to see the blonde man from earlier speaking to me with concern in his eyes.

"Do I know you?" I croaked.

"Not yet. I see you look upset, though, and thought to ask."

"I am alright. Simply tired."

"Good." He said it, but his face told me he didn't believe me at all.

"Good night, Sir."

"Good night."

After the interaction, Frank's silence seemed magnified. I was sure he probably saw Peter's exit and put two and two together. When we got back to the room, I turned to him and placed my hand on his shoulder.

"Thank you. You're definitely doing a good job proving your worth."

He sighed in relief. "I didn't realize he was in there, Miriam. I should have cleared the room."

I brought my hand down and crossed my arms.

"So, you know about our history, then?"

"Everyone who was an employee at the palace at the time of your freeze knows. I know because my father knew."

"Great," I said sarcastically. "I expect you to have discretion and keep this to yourself."

"Of course, Miriam. What happens in your life is private and I would never sully it by gossiping about it," he said sincerely, almost like he was taking a vow.

I nodded and went into my room. Not bothering to remove my robe, I went straight to my bed of roses, laid down, and turned onto my left side. I was becoming good at falling asleep while crying.

Chapter 14

At around 5:00 the next morning, I was woken by a hologram that had appeared out of a small, flat box in a little nook in the corner of the room. Father spoke.

"Good people of Arboria, this day, I bring you news of great joy. Early last night, my daughter, Princess Miriam, returned home from her long sleep. Here, at the palace, we will be having a ball to welcome her home.

"While not everyone can attend, I do hope you will share in our celebration this evening. I have arranged a concert in the capital of each province for you to enjoy.

"I would also like for you to be aware that the Princes arrived for the King's Test this morning. They are quite excited for it to begin in two days' time.

"Have a glorious day. I am proud to be in your service."

At that, the hologram shut down. Laying back, I tried to go back to sleep, but I had no such luck. After a few minutes, I heard the sound of my door opening and closing. I turned to see a woman slightly younger than me. She looked at me with wide brown doe eyes. For some reason, her random appearance didn't surprise me; it felt normal.

"Who are *you*?" I asked.

She tucked a loose blonde strand of hair behind her ear and looked down. "Adele, Your Highness. I am your lady-in-waiting. I am here to help you get ready for the day. And His Majesty wanted me to assure you I know about your memory problem."

She walked over and handed me a note with his signature. I would know it anywhere – it was as indiscernible as a doctor's.

"Oh." I hadn't realized this sort of servitude was going on. It seemed archaic for a world such as this one; like bringing a dinosaur to a dog show.

"I'm sorry," I said. "No one informed me that someone was coming."

"No need to be sorry, Your Highness. I am sure you are experiencing a lot of new things."

"This may seem like kind of an odd question to you, but I would really like to know … How did you come by getting this job? People don't get born into servitude, do they?

Luckily, she didn't seem offended and laughed. "No, Your Highness. We are not in the medieval times. The people working here are the very best of our society. They spend a lot of time and energy training, learning, earning certifications, and becoming renowned to even be *considered* for a job. It is the best there is. We get our healthcare, food, and shelter taken care of, *and* we get a nice paycheck, too. Does that ease your mind?"

I sighed in relief. "Yes, it does. Thank you for being patient with me and giving me that explanation. I hope I didn't offend you."

"No, Your Highness, I am not offended at all."

"Please, you can call me Miriam. We're obviously going to be spending a lot of time together, so we'd best be on a first-name basis."

"How about I call you Miriam in private? It is considered inappropriate to call you simply by your first name in public."

I smiled. "How about 'Princess' in public?"

"I can do that."

"Sounds like a deal."

This crusade to have people call me by my name is not going to work. Might as well roll with it.

"Does everyone normally wake up at 5:00 in the morning or is today special because of the ball and celebrations?"

She laughed. "It is because of the ball and celebrations. Also, His Majesty wanted to be sure you had as much time as possible with your tutor today. You will need to start getting ready for the ball at 4:00, so you had an early wake-up time today. No worries. Most days you get to sleep as long as you want, but I would advise not sleeping past ten. It could give the wrong impression."

"Right. Thank you for the advice. I'll remember that. But doesn't the ball start at 7:00?"

"Yes. It will take that long to get you ready."

Lord, have mercy.

I stood up and joined her by the closet door. She quirked her eyebrow.

"Are you in your robe, Miriam?"

I looked down and realized I still had it on. I was so upset when I came back last night that I didn't even think to remove it before climbing into bed.

"I love satin. It was so soft, I didn't want to remove it," I lied. I felt like I was doing a lot of lying lately, but I supposed I should get used it. I would soon be lying to the whole kingdom – hopefully not for long. I hadn't given up hope that my memories would return.

Smiling, she said, "Well, I will let your seamstress know. Perhaps she and I can design some nightgowns and dresses in satin for you."

"I would really like that."

We stepped into the ginormous walk-in closet to decide on my attire. I hadn't noticed last night, but most of the wardrobe was some shade of green, ivory, or brown.

"Why is everything essentially the same color?"

"They are our kingdom's colors. You will notice that the King and Queen also wear these colors. You *do* have some dark red colors, but only because of your nickname."

"Nickname? You mean the Rose of Petrichoria?"

"Yes and no. Because of that title the people have given you, some of your friends and family simply call you Rose. Or the media may refer to you as Princess Rose."

"Oh, I see." Good thing she told me that or I may have been confused if someone called me "Rose" at the ball. Peter had used the nickname the night before, and it *had* confused me, though I didn't think he would be sharing anything with anyone about our run-in.

"I think we will go with something simple," she said as the pulled down a silk, emerald green, halter-topped sundress. I glanced out the window and saw the day was sunny. But I was too distracted by her label of this as a *simple* dress to say anything about the crazy weather.

"*Simple?*" I asked. "That has to be the most expensive dress I've ever laid eyes on!"

Adele smiled and blushed – I guessed she took it as a compliment. I let her believe that. It *was* a lovely choice, and I wished I would have meant it as a compliment.

I was a little embarrassed at first about undressing in front of someone, even if she was a woman, but I figured I might as well get used to it. I knew I could do it myself, but I wasn't about to put her out of a job. If I was her human doll, so be it.

"Sit down here," she said as she pointed to the chair at the vanity. It was turned around so I wouldn't be able to see the mirror.

"I like for people to see the full transformation after I have finished," she explained.

"Alright. I'll go with it," I replied.

I sat down and silence settled for a while. Then I couldn't take it anymore. It was just too awkward to have someone touching my hair and face and not interact with her.

"Adele, do you have family?" I asked.

"Yes. I am married, though we do not have children yet."

"Is he handsome?"

She crooked up one side of her mouth in a half-smile. "I was the envy of Petrichoria. Most women who know him wished he would fall in love with them, but he only has love for me."

127

"That's lovely. It's nice during the beginning of a marriage. So much love, the problems and quirks you discover don't really matter at all."

She gave me a confused look, then she had her moment of realization. "I may be stepping out of line, Miriam, but would you tell me about your husband?"

"Of course. We met in college and married about three years after we graduated. He was a few inches taller than me, blonde, and had the most *amazing* blue eyes. We had a happy life. Even when the world seemed to be falling apart, he would hold it together. He was the strength in our marriage. Protector, lover, comforter.

"We had two children, Tom and Harmony. They were both blue-eyed with blonde hair. They looked so much like their father, though I did hear that Harmony looked like me every once in a while.

"He died about a year ago, he and Tom, in a car accident. Harmony was never able to accept that David and Tom wouldn't come home. And, of course, I lost Harmony when I woke up." I sighed. "Sorry. That was more than you asked for."

"Do not be sorry. Sometimes it helps to talk about something with someone who is not a shrink."

I laughed. "Glad to hear that the word 'shrink' is still used like that. Some things *don't* change."

We both started laughing and she had to stop doing my hair for a moment because she was moving too much. We finally calmed down and I wiped a tear from my eye. Luckily, she hadn't done make-up yet.

Another time of silence happened as she quietly finished my hair. I felt tugging and pinning, but she managed to not hurt me as she yanked on my hair.

As she stepped around in front of me, she said, "There. Perfect. Your hair is so easy to work with. It is long and wavy. Very nice."

"Thank you."

"Now for your face." She looked at my face pensively – like an artist looking at a blank canvas. She pulled out her giant trunk of makeup, which was surprisingly organized, and got started. It was quiet again because I couldn't move my face.

After what felt like forever, she pulled the mascara brush away from my eye and smiled. "I think you'll be happy with this. Stand up."

I did.

"Walk over to your full mirror and look."

I started walking and she said, "Wait! I almost forgot!"

She ran into the closet and came out with a pair of ivory ballet flats. "Shoes," she said as she bent down to help me put them on. "*Now* you can go to the mirror."

I finished the short trek to the mirror and was stunned at what I saw. Aside from being young, I still wasn't used to that, I was beautiful. Though I never thought I was *ugly*, I never imagined looking like this.

The colors of the dress and shoes went well with my skin tone, and the make-up was complimentary to my features. Even though my hair was gorgeous, it was on a whole different level. Parts of it were braided and other parts were left straight; the parts that were straight were twisted with the braids into an intricate woven bun. Little ruby roses accented the bun in several places.

She looked nervous, probably because of the expression of shock that appeared on my face.

Not turning away from the mirror, I told her, "I have never been so beautiful. Thank you *so* much."

Her eyes filled with tears and she brought her hands up to cover them. She took shaky breaths. Concerned, I walked over to her.

"Are you okay?" I asked.

"It's just," she started. "It's just I hoped for this. When I was told about everything you have gone through and are going through, my heart broke for you. I wanted to help brighten your day the only way I know how and I can see that I did."

"Yes, of course you did. You are very good at what you do. You are clearly the right woman for the job." It was true. Not only that she was the right person for the job, but she also somehow made me forget the events of last night, being in the hospital, the horrors of losing Harmony, and my nervousness about being the Princess of a kingdom I knew nothing about.

"I have to get going, Miriam. It was a privilege to meet you and I look forward to many styling sessions in the future – including today at 4:00 for the ball. If you think you are beautiful now, wait until you see yourself ready for the ball."

"Bye," I said as she walked out the door, gaping at myself in front of my mirror.

Now what? I know I need to eat and go to the tutor, but I have no idea where to go.

As if on cue, I heard a knock at the door. "Come in," I yelled, not thinking there was anything else to be nervous about.

However, Ella walked through the door. Her eyes were down and her fingers fidgeted. "Hi. You look lovely."

At first, I was tongue-tied, but after a brief pause, I simply responded, "Hello. Thank you."

Another awkward silence fell upon the room. Finally, she looked up to my staring eyes and spoke.

"Miriam, about what happened at the hospital –"

"I don't want to talk about the hospital or my time there."

"I understand, but I realize now that I acted very selfishly. I was consumed with anxiety and fear and didn't even think about what you were going through. It was terrible of me to just run out on you."

I nodded. "I forgive you and I understand. It must be difficult seeing me this way. Knowing I have no real memories of you."

"Who did you think I was when I visited?"

"You. But you around twenty years older and my mother-in-law."

Her jaw dropped. "Twenty years older?"

I laughed. "I swear I feel just like Dorothy returning from Oz." I mimicked her pointing. "You were there. And you were there. And you were there."

She laughed, too. "You used to make me watch movies from twentieth and twenty-first centuries because they fascinated you. 'The Wizard of Oz' was one of our favorites."

I smiled at that. It was nice to have Emma, I mean, Ella, back. Sure, she wasn't my mother-in-law, but she was my best friend and it felt like it. That feeling of never being apart, but having been separated for many years.

"So, why are you here?" I asked.

"Oh! Uncle Aaron and Auntie Amoura asked that I help you around the castle until you get familiar with it again. Here's your schedule." She handed a small paper to me that I hadn't noticed in her moving fingers. It was crumpled, but still legible.

6:00 – Breakfast

6:30 - Tutoring

12:00 - Lunch

12:30 - Tutoring

4:00 - Preparation for ball

7:00 - Ball

I wrinkled my nose. "That is a lot of tutoring. I hope he lets me take a break or two during the time I'm with him. Although, I guess I do need a lot of help, so I probably shouldn't gripe."

Ella made a face I couldn't decipher. "Hmm."

"What?"

"Uh – nothing."

"No. Really. What is it?"

"It's just that – never mind."

"Ella, what is it?" I asked as I touched her shoulder to let her know she could tell me whatever it was.

Did I offend her or something?

"Well, before, you know, you used to study a lot. Even after you finished your private tutoring, I would always find you in the palace library reading some book. I knew your memory had been screwed up, but I had no idea it changed you, too."

"Hmm, indeed. I didn't realize it either. No one has said anything besides you. Maybe I'm only different in a few ways."

"Maybe." Awkward silence. "Let's go to breakfast."

When we left the room, I saw Frank was gone and a new Guard was there, just as Frank told me would happen. This one was tall with blue eyes and blonde hair beneath his beret.

"What is your name?" I asked him.

He looked at Ella and shifted on his feet. "Louis, Your Highness."

"Louis, we're going to be together a lot. I'd appreciate it if you called me 'Miriam' in private and 'Princess' in public."

I knew the way the conversation would go, so I just got to the end of it.

He looked at Ella again and I did this time, too. She wore a frozen look of shock on her face.

"Do you have something you'd like to say, Ella?" I asked her.

"You never talked to the Guards before."

"Well, I do now. They're people, and it seems ridiculous to have them around all the time and not know their names."

I turned back to Louis. "Do we have a deal?"

He gave me a crooked smile and answered me, "Anything that pleases you, Princess."

Chapter 15

Letting go of our disagreement, Ella and I locked arms as if we were best friends. She probably did it out of an old habit; it should have felt like a new thing to me, but it didn't. It was as if my body still had the muscle memory; as if it remembered this life even if I didn't.

As we strolled to the dining room, I tried to memorize the way. It seemed like if I could figure out each hall from the main room, I would be able to figure it out.

I smiled as we walked; this really was a happy thing and nothing was going to ruin it for me.

We entered a room just off the Core on the second floor. Louis opened the double doors for us, but waited in the hall. When we entered, I saw why he didn't come in: there were already Guards everywhere.

As I looked around the room, my focus shifted to the giant table before me. A hundred people could *easily* sit at it and, as far as I knew, it was just my parents, Ella, and I together for breakfast. I made eye contact with Father and he smiled a huge smile.

"Ah! Rose! So glad you had time left after getting ready to join us! How was your night?"

Loaded question.

Rolling my neck, I said, "The bed was so comfy, but with the transition, I didn't sleep much. Maybe the tutor will be done with me a little early and I can take a little nap before the ball."

"Haha!" Father laughed, then turned to Mother. "See? That's our Rose. If I didn't know better, I would say the 'The Princess and the Pea' was based on her!"

Mother smiled as Ella laughed and I blushed. Just as this little exchange finished, the breakfast plates came in; there was one for each of us – and two more.

Ugh. Peter's *going to be joining us. It's a good thing he's seated across the way next to Ella and not me or I would be forced to stab him in the knee with my fork. But who is the other setting for?*

Beautiful presentations of food were set before us. Even if it tasted like garbage, I would be happy just looking at it. However, that wasn't a problem I was going to have. Bright red raspberries and deep purple blackberries, a scrambled egg, and a piece of toast with blackberry jam all helped create the chef's work of art.

Before the waitress who delivered my plate left, I touched her arm and said, "Tell the chef the presentation is outstanding."

She nodded, smiled, and almost skipped out of the room. When I turned back to my parents, they were looking at me like I had two heads.

"What?"

"You never spoke to the employees before," Mother said.

I took a plump blackberry and popped it in my mouth. After swallowing I said, "You know, Ella said the same thing when I asked the Guard for his name."

136

Father accidentally sprayed his water all over the Guards; it was a good thing he wasn't facing the table.

Tentatively, I asked, "Is it a faux pas or is it really so much unlike me?"

"No, dear." Mother answered with a smile. "It's just different. That's all."

"Well, maybe some changes in personality won't be *so* bad." I winked at Father, who quickly recovered and smiled back.

Just then, a small boy who looked just like Tom when he was little, but with brown eyes, came romping into the room.

"Mommy! Mommy! Mommy!"

"Thomas!" Ella responded. I grimaced when I heard the name, but tried to offer a small smile. I wondered at the similarities.

I miss Tom.

"Ella, I'm so sorry we're late. Tom was having a rough time getting out of bed," Peter said as he barged into the room. I made the connection with what Father had told me in the car.

Duke Peter and Duchess Elleouise.

Subconsciously, my eyes got wide. Father noticed and was about to say something, but I subtly shook my head with pleading eyes, to which he nodded and resumed his meal.

It's amazing how an entire conversation can be had without saying a word.

I stood up. "Oh! Look at the time! I'm afraid I really must get going to my tutoring lesson."

Peter and Ella both looked up at me simultaneously. "Oh. Okay. I can be done," Ella said.

"Nonsense, Ella, you continue your meal with your family. There are always a few extra minutes in my day for my daughter," Father rescued me.

She nodded as he walked over to me and linked his arm in mine. I felt like I was going to pass out. I had been wrong. Something *could* ruin my perfectly lovely day with my best friend.

Some best friend. Stealing my boyfriend while I'm frozen for saving the kingdom, if not the world? So tacky.

Father and I walked in silence, Louis and Father's guard close behind, all the way to my tutor's room. I would have tried to memorize the way, but I was too distracted by the betrayal of the both of them.

When we stopped, Father said, "Would you like to share with me what that was about in there? Did you remember him?"

Trying to keep myself from crying, I sniffled. "No. Not him. He's nearly identical to my David, except his eyes; David's eyes were blue."

"Ah. So it was difficult for you to see Peter and Ella together."

"Yes. And a little strange. Ella was David's mother in my false life."

"Ew."

I laughed, "I know, right?"

He laughed as he pulled me in for an embrace and kissed the top of my head. "Things will get better, Miriam. It's hard right now, but things will improve."

Pulling me out of the hug and looking me in the eye, he said, "I am here for you. No matter what is going on, please, come to me and let me know. I love you, sweetheart."

"I love you, too, Father."

"Oh, and Rose? I need to talk with you about something very important at some point before the ball this evening. Could you stop by after your tutoring, before you get ready?"

"Yes, Father."

At that, I walked into the room where my tutelage would begin. The tutor was not at all what I expected; I was thinking Albert Einstein or Doc Brown. This guy was more like an actor unrealistically cast as a teacher, professor, or doctor. Unrealistic because no one that smart can also be that handsome.

All that being said, he still appeared to be twice my age, so beyond appreciation for his handsomeness, I wasn't interested. When I came in he was sitting at a desk reading something, holding his head up with the heel of his hand on his forehead. His dark, side-parted hair fell over his face and he snored. I giggled to myself.

He's not reading! He's sleeping. Maybe this won't be such a snore fest after all, or maybe it will! Although, I must say sleeping with your eyes open is slightly disturbing.

As nonchalantly as I could, I cleared my throat to wake him up; he just about fell out of his seat when he startled awake.

"Princess! I'm so sorry! I didn't mean to fall asleep. I –"

I held up my hand and smiled. "No need to apologize. I would be sleeping right now if I could, too."

He smiled. "I am very excited to teach you again. Please, have a seat and we will figure out what you need to learn."

139

Again? He must have been my tutor before.

I sat in the chair across from him.

"Tea?" He asked as he sipped at his cup.

"No, thank you," I said.

"What is it that you *think* you need to learn?"

"I have an odd question before we begin."

"Alright." He drained his cup and set it on the edge of his desk before leaning back in his chair and crossing his arms.

"I've noticed Guards and employees around the palace all speak pretty formally, at least with me. Notably, there seems to be a lack of contractions to the point that it doesn't feel or sound natural. Is there a reason beyond my being the Princess?"

"Very observant. No, there is no other reason. Between each other, I can nearly guarantee they use contractions as much as you do. That being said, in a formal setting, like the ball this evening, you will be expected to speak in such a way to your guests."

"Oh, boy," I laughed breathlessly.

"You will do fine. You are bright. That much has not changed. What else do you think you need to learn?"

I sat back and crossed my legs. "Well, I think I'm alright with math, science, and grammar – although I suppose one could say you can never know everything, and certainly science has changed significantly from what I remember – but I think the most prudent topics to learn about are the history, culture, society, and literature of this time."

He clapped his hands once very loudly and I flinched in my seat. "Brilliant! My thinking was about the same!" He stood up and crossed the room. "However, today, we will mainly be focusing on etiquette, dancing, societal expectations, and names – lots of names."

"Right," I said leaning forward and folding my hands. "Because everyone thinks I know everyone."

"Not *everyone*," he said as he crossed back with a book, sat me up and balanced it on my head. "Do not slouch. You did not know everyone who will be there tonight before your freeze. So we will only do the names of the people you knew."

With a sigh of relief, the book fell off my head.

"Again," he said, indicating he wanted me to put it back by flicking his index finger in the air. I complied. "Do not get me wrong, Princess. There are still a lot of names to work on. We will get started on them this morning and move into etiquette and societal expectations before lunch. Do not worry. I will give you some study cards with names and faces to bring back to your room to look at while you get ready for the ball."

Carefully, so as to not let the book fall, I said, "That's a relief."

"Very good," he said, adding another book. "Our goal is five books today. By your birthday next year, it will be ten."

"*Five?!*" I asked, not carefully enough. Both books fell into my lap and he put one back on my head.

Oh. I get this game. If I drop them, I start over again. That's just lovely!

"While you balance the book, I want you to look at the flashcards," he said, handing them to me. After I accepted them, he walked away.

"Wait! Where are you going? You can't just leave me like this."

141

"Yes, I can," he said, not even turning around as he left the room.

My jaw dropped to the floor and I looked at the giant stack of cards in my hand. It was roughly the size of two decks of cards.

I certainly hope each of these is individuals and not couples.

I couldn't be that lucky. Two and a half hours passed as I sat there straight as a board chanting names to faces. Every so often, he came back, put another book on my head, and left. At around 11:00, while I balanced five books, the tutor returned.

"Very good!" He exclaimed. "How many times did you drop the book?"

"Once."

"Really? Only once?"

"Yes. And that was when it was still only one. You never introduced yourself to me."

"Leave the books on for a little longer." He flicked his index finger again. "You may call me Doctor Bartholomew."

"First name or last name?"

"Does it matter?"

Quirking a brow, I drawled, "I suppose not. You're a tough nut to crack, aren't you, Doctor Bartholomew?"

"Yes. That is what they all say. You can gently set down the books." This time he flicked his index finger down. I was about ready to chop it off.

Gingerly, I took the books off my head and set them on the small table in front of me.

He gave a crooked smile. "Very good."

The rest of the time before lunch was spent on etiquette and flashcards coming out of nowhere at random times. Mostly, etiquette was essentially the same as the time period of my false life, so there wasn't much to learn. Mainly, we worked on posture, gesturing, handling of silverware and other objects, and handshaking.

"Excellent," Doctor Bartholomew said. He put a soft expression on his face and spoke gently. "Princess, I know I am being hard and I want you to know – I will always be this way."

I groaned.

"Now, now. I will have none of that. I do it for your own good. Regardless of the fact that you saved the world and you are the Rose of Petrichoria, the world will give you no breaks. Eventually, the novelty will wear off and people will expect you to no longer be entertainment; they will expect you to be their Queen."

My gulp of air was a bit louder than I intended and he gave me his crooked smile again.

"You are a quick study. After lunch, we will work on your dancing."

I choked on my air again.

"Dancing?" I finally found words.

"Yes, dancing. It *is* a ball. It will be expected. No worries. My theory is that your muscle memory will kick in eventually and you will be fine."

I remembered how it felt when Ella and I interlocked arms and walked together down the hall. His theory could very likely be fact. I nodded.

"Very well," he said and wagged his index finger in the direction of the door. "Go on to have some lunch now. I'll see you in a bit."

When I stood up, I realized how sore my back was from sitting with good posture all morning. Not wanting to show Doctor Bartholomew that little fact, I strode out the door as if gliding on air. Then, I went across the hall into another room, which happened to be the library.

Letting out a quiet grunt, I eased my back a little and observed the library. Rich, dark wood bookshelves stretched from the floor to the ceiling, which I couldn't even try to estimate. A large desk made of the same wood sat facing the window with a gorgeous view of the forest. Two large trees looked almost like columns on either side of the room. Large, soft chairs were in a circle in the middle of the room.

I bent forward and touched my hands to my toes, then I arched my back and pressed into it with my hands. As I rolled my neck, I heard the door slide open and close gently behind me. I turned around only to see Peter marching angrily toward me.

When I tried to back away, he grabbed me by the arms and pushed me against the wall.

"Let me go! You're hurting me!"

I managed to free myself, but he only grabbed my flailing wrists, crossed them, and pressed them on my chest.

"Don't cry. Don't scream. And *stop* fighting me," he seethed, inches from my face.

Breathing heavily from fighting, I whispered, "What – what do you want?"

"I want to know what you told your father."

My eyes widened and I clenched my jaw with indignation. Through my teeth, I growled, "Are you freaking kidding me? What kind of a lunatic are you? You don't need to sneak up on me and assault me to get an answer like that!"

He pressed my wrists in harder and I whimpered, sure that there were going to be bruises from this. "*That* is not an answer to my question."

"All I told him was that you were nearly identical to David and it was difficult seeing you with Ella," I said as I stopped moving. Dropping my gaze and lowering my voice, I added, "Which wasn't a lie."

"That's *all?*"

"Yes," I hissed, looking at him again. "If I had told him what you did last night, do you honestly think you would have eaten at our table this morning after I left?"

He dropped my wrists and turned to leave. I examined them, seeing the bruises already forming.

"How am I supposed to explain these bruises at the ball tonight?" I asked holding up my wrists.

He stopped, turned around, and said callously, "Wear gloves."

Chapter 16

I stepped out into hallway to find Louis waiting outside the tutoring room. I was fuming angry.

"Where in the world have *you* been?" I seethed.

He blanched with shock that I had come out of the library.

"Princess, I –"

"No. Don't 'Princess' me." My body shook and I pointed at him. "You weren't here to protect me. That is your one job and you failed at it."

His eyes transferred from mine to my wrists, which were quickly turning black and blue in a hand pattern. He looked horrified.

"Miriam, what happened?" he asked with concern and held the hand that pointed so he could examine it.

I winced. "It's nothing."

"No, it is not. This is my fault and I would like to know who did this to you."

"It doesn't matter who it is. You won't be able to do anything about it."

He paused, then a look of terrible realization spread across his face. Quietly, he said, "It was Duke Peter, was it not?"

I didn't have to say anything for him to know it was true.

"Miriam, I am deeply sorry. This will never happen again."

With real fear in my voice, I said, "Give me a good reason not to have my father fire you. Give me a reason why I shouldn't request someone else. And don't you dare try to blackmail me with this."

He looked down, trying to come up with a reason. When he finally looked up, he said, "I have a family. A wife. A daughter. Should I be fired, especially for this, we would probably have to move down to lower-income housing and my family would be disgraced. No one would want to hire me."

Well, I asked for a good reason.

Carefully, I took my hand back. "Very well, I'll give you a second chance. But if this happens again, I will not be so merciful."

"Thank you. It will not. I will never leave my post again."

"Where did you go, anyway?"

With his face flushing with embarrassment, he said, "The restroom."

Chuckling quietly and shaking my head, I said, "Next time you need to do that, just get another Guard to stand in for you until you return."

He laughed.

"So. This is what we're going to do right now," I began. "Instead of taking me to lunch, I would like to be escorted to my room. After we arrive, I will take care of my schedule issue." It was already 12:15.

148

"Very well, Princess."

With my arms crossed so no one could see my wrists, we quietly went to my room. Along the way, I told a passing Guard to inform Father and Mother that I wouldn't be joining them for lunch because the morning session wore me out; I also told him to tell Doctor Bartholomew that I would be arriving at 1:00 rather than 12:30 because there were a couple things I needed to take care of.

Once we arrived to my room, Louis stood at attention to the side of my door. I could tell he was definitely going to take this job more seriously in the future and I was glad for it.

As I walked in, I looked around for Adele. She happened to be there sitting in one of my chairs.

"Do you just sit there all day waiting for me to come in here?" I asked.

Laughing, she replied, "Sweet trees, no. I just happened to be here right now. Shouldn't you be at your lessons?"

I nodded, took a seat across from her, and began recounting the whole ordeal. After I was done, I added, "Adele, I don't know what to do. I don't feel safe in my own home, but if I disgrace him, I disgrace Ella and her son as well."

"I would just never enter any room before having a guard clear it. Louis or Frank would stand outside the room with you and you would enter when the other guard returned."

"That sounds like a good plan, but wouldn't people wonder why I'm being so paranoid?"

She sighed. "Yeah, they probably would."

We both sat there for a while in silence – both trying to come up with a way to keep me safe; neither of us succeeded. What it came down to was that I would have to be as careful as possible around the palace.

With that conclusion, Adele stood up and walked to the closet. She came out with elbow-length ivory gloves without my asking for them.

"I'm going to lay down before I need to go to my lesson. Can you wake me at 12:45?"

"Of course, Miriam."

I am not exaggerating when I say the second my head hit my pillow, I fell asleep. What was only a few minutes felt like hours, and when Adele woke me up, I was ready to face the rest of my day.

I might not even have to see him again before the ball.

I stretched as I stood and thanked Adele for everything. Once in the hall, I told Louis to relax a little and asked him to escort me to my next lesson. When we arrived to the tutoring room, there was a note forwarding us to the small ballroom.

Again, when we arrived, Louis straightened himself into attention as I entered.

The ballroom was amazing – and not at all *small*. Three giant crystal chandeliers hung from the ceiling and beautiful golden leaves were engraved into the ballroom floor.

If this is the small ballroom, I can't wait to see the large one.

Over in the corner, I spotted my tutor; he did not look happy at all.

"Why, Princess. How lovely of you to join me – finally."

I arched a brow. "Did you not receive the message from the Guard?"

"I did."

"Then that should be enough."

He smiled. "Indeed. Now. While you are on time, your dance partner is not here yet, so I will go through what we are going to do this afternoon."

"Wait. I thought you were going to be my dance partner."

"Those who cannot do – teach," he said with a flourishing gesture.

I wondered who could possibly be my dance partner. I hoped it was Father, though I knew it probably wasn't; he had a very busy schedule.

A few minutes later, the door flew open and Peter made his way over. Before the door closed, Louis gave me an apologetic look and I nodded stiffly to him one time. I knew I could have had him thrown from the ballroom, even arrested, for what he had done earlier, but the thought of disgrace falling on Ella or her son kept me silent

"Ah. Peter. How lovely of you to join us – finally."

"Do you say that to anyone who is late?" I asked him.

"*Of course* I do, or something along those lines. What? Did you think you were special?"

I chuckled nervously and took a step back when I saw the fire burning in Peter's eyes. "No, *of course* not."

When Peter got over to us, he got in Doctor Bartholomew's face. "You will not speak to me like that again, Doctor. Do you understand me?"

My tutor blanched. "Yes, My Lord. I do appreciate you taking time out of your day to help us."

Quickly, I wiped the smile off my face and looked at my feet. Peter's volatile nature was quite a force to be reckoned with. Briefly, I wondered if he had always been that way; it was difficult for me to imagine being in love with someone like that.

Peter backed off with a sharp nod.

"This afternoon, we will work on a basic Waltz, the Foxtrot, and the traditional ballroom dance, The Rose, you will do to begin the dancing at the ball."

"Well, that doesn't sound *too* difficult," I said nervously.

Peter just stood there like a lump with his hands in his pockets. He certainly didn't look like he wanted to be here. I understood the feeling; I didn't want him there either.

"Do not be nervous, Princess," Doctor Bartholomew said, detecting the nervousness in my voice. "Remember what I said. Once you get going with these dances, your muscle memory will kick in and you'll pick it up right away."

Again, I thought of how it felt when Ella and I walked down the halls interlocking arms.

"Like riding a bike," I said.

"What?"

"Never mind." I waved away my comment with my hand; it was a phrase to add to my No-Longer-Used category in my brain.

"Can we just get started?" Peter asked impatiently.

Doctor Bartholomew nodded to him with deference. It was almost as if he was scared of Peter.

Maybe I'm not the only one he hurt. He'd better not lay a finger on Ella or that sweet little boy!

152

"Very well. My Lord, please help the Princess get into position for the Foxtrot."

We went to the center of the room. Peter placed one hand on the small of my back, put my hand on that side on his upper arm, then held our other hands straight out. With a smirk, he gently rubbed his thumb on the satin gloves as if he was telling me he liked that I did what he suggested and I pursed my lips. I scowled at him.

"Hold on!" Doctor Bartholomew said loudly from the side of the room. "Princess, you should remove your gloves. Women generally do not wear them to dance, much less to formal events anymore."

I blanched and looked down. "I would rather leave them on, thank you."

"Really, Princess, you should remove them."

I tilted my head back and looked up to the ceiling, exasperated. "Will someone be offended by my gloves?"

"Well, no, but –"

"Then I will leave them on." I gave him a pleading look to no longer push the subject. He seemed to take the hint.

"Alright, then."

When I brought my head back into proper position, Peter leaned forward and whispered into my ear. "Quick thinking, Princess."

"Shut-up," I whispered back nonchalantly.

He laughed and the song began. Doctor Bartholomew was right. After struggling a bit in the beginning, and gladly stepping on Peter's toes a few times, I picked it up. Though I hated to admit it, Peter and I were very graceful dancing together. Gliding across the golden leaves on the floor, we kept perfect time.

When the song ended, Doctor Bartholomew clapped once loudly. I was beginning to realize that was what he did when I did something that pleased him.

At some point during the song, I had closed my eyes. When I opened them, Peter was staring at me with a smug grin on his face. I looked away.

"Perfection!" I heard Doctor Bartholomew yell. "Now, the Waltz!" He began fidgeting with things trying to find the right song.

We didn't need to move much to get into position for this dance. We just had to relax the position we were already in. Unfortunately, that brought me closer to Peter, who was still staring at me.

"What?" I asked in a whisper.

"What what?" He responded likewise in a whisper.

I looked at his face, but not his eyes. "Why are you staring at me like that? I know you hate me; you made that quite clear in the library."

He brought his hand holding mine down to my wrist and stroked it gingerly with his fingers, but his eyes stayed on me, trying to get me to look into them.

"Rose, I could never hate you," he said. "It was an accident – me hurting you. It was never my intention. I would never hurt you on purpose."

A single tear leaked out of the corner of my eye and I looked up again desperately trying to rein in the rest of them. "Do you even know how hard all this is for me?" I took a deep breath. "Do you know how difficult it is to look at you and see David? To know I can never have you? That there is no possible way I can ever kiss that face again?"

When I looked back at him, he was still staring, but now there was a hint of pain on his face. "Every morning since I heard you were awake, I have been filled with regret," he whispered fervently. "I shouldn't have given up hope on you, on us." Now he looked down. "I wish I could go back in time and tell myself not to do it; not to marry Ella. Do you know why I chose Ella over all the women in our kingdom?"

I shook my head and glanced at Doctor Bartholomew, who was obliviously still trying to find a song in 3/3, then looked back to Peter.

"I chose her because she was a piece of you. I chose her because she was the closest I thought I would ever get to you again." His hand returned to mine from my wrist. "I'm sorry, Miriam. Not just for today, though I will now have to add that to the list of regrets I have concerning you, but for everything." A tear now escaped his eye and he quickly wiped it away. "I'm sorry," he pleaded.

"Ah! Here's one!" Doctor Bartholomew interrupted. "Now, the Waltz!"

It was a beautiful Waltz. For some reason, I didn't even struggle with it. The moment the music started playing, we rolled over the dance floor like a calm wave, ebbing and flowing with the beat. Maybe it was muscle memory. Maybe it was our conversation that brought back the connection we had so long ago; it probably was. Maybe it was because he so strongly resembled David. But it didn't change anything – he was still married and he still hurt me. However, that didn't seem to matter in the moment.

When the music stopped, there was complete silence; we were all stunned by the performance.

Doctor Bartholomew cleared his throat. "Alright. Onto the Rose."

"The Rose?" I asked him.

"Oh yes, Princess. You have traditionally started all royal balls with this dance since you were young. *You* invented it."

When he turned back to his music station, now attempting to locate the right song for the Rose, I looked down and whispered to Peter, "I forgive you." I looked up to his eyes, "But if you ever hurt me again, I don't care who you're married to, I will bring you down."

He laughed quietly, "I'm sure you will, Miriam."

Doctor Bartholomew put the music on without saying anything and, again, we went right into it. My body recognized the unique dance in 3/3 time and there was no issue with it at all. In my false life, the music was something I wrote; I wondered if I had written it in my real life. During the song, I kept my eyes closed because I knew Peter was looking at me – and not only for the sake of the dance.

When my tutor made his way over to us, he patted us both on the shoulders and smiled. "Beautiful. Simply beautiful. Duke Peter, you are free to go, as are you, Princess. Be sure to look at your flashcards."

"Of course, Doctor." I said.

He turned and left the room, muttering words of fascination about my muscle memory. He either pretended to, or actually did not, notice that Peter still hadn't let go of me and gazed in apparent wonder at me. When I heard the door close, I moved my eyes to stare into his. I saw what he was about to do in his expression. He was dangerous in more than one way. I knew I should go, but I missed David so very much, and that made me so very weak.

I should have walked away when his trembling hand left mine to trail its way down my arm to my upper back. I should have stopped him when he tilted my chin just a little higher so he could reach. I should have slapped him after he pressed his lips against mine fiercely. But I didn't. In fact, I relished in his kissed and pulled him closer. When we stopped, we clung to each other in a tight embrace. Turning my lips toward his head on my shoulder, I whispered into his ear, "Never again."

He pulled away and looked into my eyes and whispered, "Never."

Chapter 17

As if he thought Louis wouldn't notice, Peter let me leave first. I looked at my tall Guard with a trembling lower lip, then realized he was speaking with the blond man from the night before. Quickly reigning in my emotions, I said to the man, "Hello. Is there something I can help you with?"

The man frowned, but not in what appeared to be anger. He seemed concerned. Louis said, "I was just informing Prince Harrison that none of the Princes are to have an audience with you until tonight. He was wanting to speak with you."

"Oh. Is everything alright, Prince Harrison? I trust your stay here has been comfortable thus far."

"Yes, of course," Prince Harrison said in a Southern drawl. With a wicked grin, he said, "I have enjoyed the scenery especially. Quite beautiful." By the tone in his voice, I knew he wasn't talking about the trees. "We had crossed paths a couple times and I just wanted to introduce myself."

Louis pressed his lips together, clearly irritated with the arrogant Southerner. "Well, now you have."

"Indeed," Prince Harrison said. "I will let you go, Your Highness. Thank you for taking a moment for me." He furrowed his brow again and I could swear he was trying to read my mind. With a short bow, he kissed my hand and took his leave.

What an odd man.

Turning back to Louis, I told him we needed to head to Father's office; I didn't know how to get there and I needed him to lead me.

On the way there, I felt horrible, not knowing which was worse: Peter hating me or Peter loving me and being unable to do anything about it.

Except, I did. We did. And I cannot believe we did. Never again. Never.

I spent the way to my room taking deep breaths and telling myself how excited I was for the ball to try to get my mind off of what just happened.

It's bad when you have to convince yourself to be excited for a ball. *A* ball *for Pete's sake. Ugh – Pete. I'll never have Peter.*

Every time I tried to convince myself, everything went back to Peter. I felt like the spoiled child who had everything yet still complained because she can't have *that* toy.

I rang the door chime when I arrived to Father's office and he beeped me in. He gestured me to a seat across from his desk and had a look on his face that concerned me.

"Is everything alright, Father?" I asked.

"I don't know," he sighed and paused.

I tried to patiently wait as he gathered his thoughts, but the longer he waited to tell me, the more nervous I became. I cleared my throat.

"I have spent my whole morning trying to decide how to go about telling you this. I did some research on the twenty-first century to try to get some insight, but there wasn't any there."

"Please, just tell me. I hate it when things are fluffed up to make them sound better than they are."

"You are going to hate this; you hated it before – you know. I just don't want you to hate *me*. I have missed you."

"Will it make you feel better if I promise to not hate you because of it?"

He smiled. "It makes me feel better that you will *try* not to hate me." He took a deep breath. "Rose, in our culture, for every heir to the Crown, there is a trial for who will be his or her spouse. If the heir is a man, a Queen's Test is held. If the heir is a woman, a King's Test is held."

"Oh. I think I remember you saying something about Princes arriving for that. Wait – are you telling me that this King's Test is going to start *tonight*?!"

"Not officially. Officially, it won't begin until the day after your Crowning Coronation. Only your mother and I know what the events of the test are. This is the only one you will be informed about prior to the event. Tonight, you will have your Introduction Event with the ten foreign Princes participating in your generation's King's Test.

"Before you went into your freeze, there was a targeted biological weapon, fashioned after the Daze, that killed all the Noble families. People began dying shortly after your Introduction Event. Because we had to instate new Nobility to replace the old, there are no noblemen of Arboria within the eligible age limits to participate. This is why foreign Princes are participating."

161

"Uh-huh."

Holy carp! I am going to be getting engaged in months and meeting him tonight! Can I take any more stress?!

"Are you alright?"

"Uh-huh," I lied.

"We'll be doubling your Welcoming Ball as your Introduction Event. You will dance and converse with each Prince once."

That's not so bad...

"Then you will go to the sofa in your rose maze. Each Prince will need to find his way to you where you will have a more intimate discussion and a – um – well – this is the part I'm afraid to tell you."

I swallowed hard. "Go ahead."

"At some point during your discussion, you will share your first kiss with each Prince."

I jumped out of my seat. "What?! No!"

"You promised," Father said lamely.

"I – I – I don't hate you, but I'm *not* going to kiss ten different men tonight! What kind of a trollop was I before this that I would agree to it?"

"I'm not sure what a trollop is, but based on your tone, I assure you, you were not one. You agreed, begrudgingly, to it because it is tradition."

"You kissed ten women for your Queen's Test?" I asked accusingly.

"No. I kissed twelve, including a set of triplets."

"Oh," I said quietly. I took my seat again. "So, *every* heir had to do this?"

He nodded. "Yes. Ever since the first Princess of Arboria's King's Test. The reasoning is that a first kiss will tell you something about a person. Trust me, it was quite revealing your first time around. You will report to me in the morning and the test will continue the day after your Crowning Coronation."

Not at all pleased with the concept of kissing ten men in one evening, I bit the corner of my lower lip.

"Father? How are Peter and Ella still alive if all the Noble families were killed?"

He sighed. "We were never able to figure that out. We are just grateful they survived."

"Do you know anything about Peter and me before my freeze? Did he really love me?"

"Very much. He hated to give up on his future with you by marrying Ella. She knew he did and I'm sure she knows how hard this is on him. I could tell she saw your hurt this morning, too. She's your best friend, Rose. She will be there to assist you through the whole King's Test as your Crown Princess' Maid. Trust us, Rose. We won't steer you wrong."

Defeated, I muttered, "Very well. I'll do what I need to tonight, but I'm not happy about it."

"If it makes you feel any better, you weren't happy about it the first time around either. But this is the *only* time such physical connection will be required of you for the King's Test. After tonight, you can *choose* when, where, and who you kiss."

"Thank you, Father. I'm sorry that my memory has caused so much hassle."

163

"Don't apologize, dear. Now, go get yourself ready for your Welcoming Ball."

"Must look pretty for the Princes," I said sardonically as I stood.

"There's my sarcastic Rose," he laughed and walked around to hug me.

As I left Father's office, I told Louis it was time for me to go get ready for the ball and we went back to my room.

When I arrived to the room, Adele and two other stylists were already bustling around it. They were so into their work, they didn't even hear me come in until I closed the door behind me. Excitement lit their faces and that was all it took to snap me out of it. I couldn't let them suffer just because I spent some of my time smooching my best friend's husband and feeling bad about it after the fact.

I plastered a giant smile on my face and said, "Let's get started, shall we?"

Adele rushed forward, grabbed my hands, and pulled me toward the two new women. She first gestured to the tall woman with billowy red-orange hair. "This is Christine, your hair stylist for the evening, and this –" She gestured over to the slight woman with pixie-short white-blonde hair, "is Bell, your makeup artist for the evening."

The women were both similar in age to Adele and seemed to be good friends with one another. "Go ahead and bathe," Adele said shooing me into the bathroom. "We still have a few more things to get together. As I turned away, my smile quickly fell.

It's going to be a long night if I'm going to be forcing a smile all evening.

Once again, there was a rose bath prepared for me, which I climbed into after mindlessly undressing. Closing my eyes, I leaned my head on the soft bath edge and took a deep breath of rose scent. I had to shake out of this funk I'd fallen into. I was still going back to that kiss with Peter that would probably live on in infamy within my mind.

One last kiss. That's all it was. Never again. Never.

I let out the breath I held, willing the anxiety out of my lungs.

But what if I have to dance with him again tonight? Surely he'll know better than to ask. What if he does it anyway? He's arrogant; maybe he thinks he can seduce me into an illicit affair. Maybe –"

I took another deep breath.

No. I have to be strong. I am the Princess. *He is a* Duke. *I am of a higher position, so I can refuse a dance, right? Shoot. Why didn't I ask Doctor Bartholomew about that? Because I thought Peter hated me while I was in tutoring today, that's why. The thought never crossed my mind because it seemed so improbable at the time. But now –"*

Deep breath again.

Knowing that if I didn't calm down, I would to go insane, I silenced my mind and focused on breathing. On the scent of rose invading my senses. On the warm water soaking my tense muscles. I felt weightless and –

A gentle rapping on the bathroom door startled me awake. "Come in," I said, trying to not sound like I was just sleeping in the bath. As a giant yawn escaped my mouth, Adele opened the door and gave me a knowing smile.

Carp. She knows.

At least she had the decency to not say anything about my little nap. "We are ready for you, Miriam. Do you need help with your

165

towel?" She gestured toward the large bath sheet sitting on the counter across from the tub.

"No, thank you. I will dry off and make my way out there in a minute."

Adele started back into the bedroom. "Oh, wait!" I said. She peeked back in. "Thank you for calling me Miriam." She smiled and closed the door.

After pulling myself out of the tub, my body stretched involuntarily because of my nap. I grabbed the bath sheet and quickly shook my hair through it and dried off my body.

When I stepped into the room, the three young women squealed like girls getting ready for the Senior Prom. Maybe if I remembered being a Royal, their informality might have bothered me, but I didn't remember. Grateful that Adele had probably spoken to Christine and Bell about my desire to be treated normally, I responded to their glee with a squeal of my own.

Despite the pain and confusion I felt about Peter all day, I really was excited for the ball. A *ball*! I knew that I had been to many in my life, but I had no memory of those balls. This was a first in my new life and I wasn't going to let Peter ruin it.

With smiles the size of crescent moons, the squealing women stepped aside and gestured to a mannequin decked out in the gown I would be wearing.

Unsurprisingly, the sleeveless ball gown was a deep emerald green. Around the hem and neckline, intricate rose vines were stitched with gold thread. Stepping forward, I traced the delicate pattern along the neckline with my index finger. As I appreciated the beautiful design of the dress, my gaze fell to a small table sitting next to it. On the table in a small box lay a simple rose-gold necklace with an emerald cut into the shape of a rose as its pendant. Next to the box, a pair of elbow-length gold satin gloves crossed at the wrist. On the other side of the box lay my tiara on a small, golden pillow.

Awed that something so lovely could be made for *me*, my eyes began to fill with tears. Desperate to stop the tears, I fixed my gaze on the ceiling. The flow stopped, but not before a couple tears had escaped my eyes. I could feel the silence and anxiety behind me; they were waiting for my response. Bringing my hands to my cheeks to wipe the tears from them, I turned and gave them a grin worthy of the Cheshire Cat. "Beautiful," I gushed.

After a few more squeals, the preparation began. As much as I would have loved to get myself dressed, I knew it would be impossible. Not only because the dress simply wouldn't allow it, but also because Christine and Bell didn't know about my memory loss; it would be strange for me to get myself ready.

Though it took a couple hours to get ready, it felt more like a few minutes. The time sped quickly past the giggles and gossip between the three ladies. Their energy was contagious and by the time they finished, I was wide awake and ready to face a ballroom full of people. While slipping on my gloves, I glanced at the clock to see it was 6:45.

I looked in the mirror and appreciated the work my stylists had completed. The dress was fabulous, the green of my eyeshadow brought out the color of my eyes, and my long hair was brought up into a beautiful updo of curls and tiny red ruby roses.

Turning back to the ladies, I said, "Thank you *so* much for your help this evening. You've really outdone yourselves. Christine and Bell, I would like for you to assist in my preparation for all future balls and special engagements. I will speak to Father about writing up a contract for you. Is that agreeable?"

Christine and Bell blanched. Christine was the one to respond. "Milady, it would be an honor." Bell simply nodded in agreement.

"Good!" I took a deep breath. "Well, I guess it's time to face the music." I laughed at my pun, and the ladies gave me a courtesy laugh, clearly confused.

Another phrase to add to the list.

I made my way across the room to exit, then heard Adele yell, "Wait!" as she ran toward me. When she approached, she placed my simple rose gold tiara embedded with emeralds on my head. She smiled and I glided through my door.

Looking to my right, I saw Frank standing there; he and Louis must have switched while I was getting ready. I spun in a full circle, then faced him. In the shoes I was wearing, he and I were actually the same height. He was trying so hard to be professional, but a smile curved the side of his mouth. There was nothing personal about it, so I thought; he simply thought I looked pretty. I couldn't fault him for that.

Wiping the smile from his face, he asked, "Are you ready, Your Highness?"

I smiled and said, "Yes." As we made our way toward the ballroom, Frank following a few steps behind, I asked, "Where are my parents? Will they be entering the ball with me?"

"No, Your Highness. Your parents are already in the room. As is Duchess Elleouise. You will be heralded alone."

I stopped suddenly, causing Frank to run into me. Leaning forward and tilting back, I windmilled my arms, then held them straight out until I could stay balanced.

"I'm sorry, Your Highness. Are you alright?"

I turned and looked at him with fear-filled eyes. "No! I mean –
yes, I'm fine from the run-in – but no, I'm not alright about going in
alone! No one told me I would be going in alone! That's terrifying!"

Frank's eyes widened and my brain reeled.

There has to be a way I don't have to do this alone. Ah ha!

"Could *you* walk in with me? Please?"

Apologetically, shaking his head, Frank responded, "No,
Princess." He looked down. "I'm too below your station to escort
you into the ball. It's nothing to be ashamed of, going in alone.
Everyone knows you've only just awoken after ten years."

"I'm *scared*. I don't want to do this alone."

Closing my eyes, I took a deep breath.

I can do this. I can do *this.*

"I can do this. Alright. Let's go."

We walked the rest of the way in silence. I could feel my hands
becoming wet with sweat inside my satin gloves. I cursed Peter
under my breath for what he did to my wrists, even though I already
forgave him. I was still having to endure the consequences of his
bruising.

*No need to focus on this. I spent the last several hours calming
down; I have to keep my calm. Keep my calm. Keep my calm. I'm
going to kiss ten men tonight! Keep my calm.*

We approached the beautiful wooden doors that led into the
main ballroom. The frame was engraved with leaves, trees, and
flowers. Frank stepped aside.

Keep my calm. I can do this. Keep my calm. I can do this.

169

The two Guards at the doors slid them open and I stepped through.

Keep my calm.

"Ladies and Gentlemen," the herald began.

I can do this.

"Please acknowledge Her Royal Highness, Princess Miriam Petrichoria of Arboria!"

The room exploded with the sound of applause and I couldn't help but smile.

I really can do this. These people are pleasant enough.

As I made my way down the stairs into the main ballroom, I took in my surroundings. Easily holding around two hundred guests, the room was the largest I had ever seen. Like the small ballroom, there were gold leaves and vines engraved into the floor; they were on the stairs as well. Numerous, beautiful crystal chandeliers filled the ceiling and the light reflected off the ceiling-engraving of a forest in a storm. I could almost see the trees actually swaying in the wind.

In recognition of our flag's colors, the women in attendance wore green of some shade and the men wore suits of chocolate brown. At the bottom of the steps, I saw my regal father and mother. Rather than emerald or brown, they were both dressed in ivory, Father in a suit and Mother in a mermaid dress, with capes of emerald green draped around their necks. Their crowns were significantly larger than mine and I wondered if they were developing a headache from them.

Like the ladies who prepared me for the ball, they had big smiles on their faces – Unlike them, thankfully, they didn't squeal. However, Mother looked as though she was going to burst into tears at any moment. When I reached the bottom of the stairs, both of my parents gave me a hug and stepped to the side.

"Princes of this generation's King's Test, please step forward as I introduce you to the Princess," the herald said, and I noticed the line of ten men standing in front of me. Each one wore an ivory suit instead of the chocolate brown color every other man was wearing. I noted a small amount of muttering went around the rest of the attendees.

"Prince Phineas of Britainnia!" The herald announced and a dreadfully handsome man stepped forward. He was tall with long, black hair pulled back into a low ponytail. With an athletically slim frame and a pointed jaw, he reminded me of what I would imagine a fae man would look like. He had sterling grey eyes, perfect lips, and a straight nose. "It is my honor to participate in this momentous event, Miriam," he said in his British – no – Britainnian – accent as he kissed my hand and stepped back.

"Prince Mamoru of Japan!"

Huh. Japan is still around.

As he stepped forward, I noted his grace and wondered if he was a dancer like me. His side-parted black hair shone in the light of the ballroom and his dark eyes sparkled as he kissed my hand wordlessly before stepping back.

I hope he speaks English or this is going to be a long event. I wonder how long the King's Test will last...

"Prince Joshua of Pacifica!" A darkly tanned man with sun-bleached blond hair and brown eyes strode forward with confidence. "Good evening, Princess. I hope our time together will be fun."

Ah. Pacifica = Australia. Good to know.

He winked, kissed my hand, and then stepped back to rejoin the line.

"Prince Estevan of Amazonia!"

An olive-skinned man with short, dark hair and bright brown eyes stepped forward. "I look forward to getting to know you, Princess," he said in an indiscernible, but intelligible accent before he kissed my hand and rejoined the line.

"Prince Leonardo of Swiss-France!"

A man with light brown hair and charcoal grey eyes pompously walked forward. "We will rule with justice and grace together, Princess," he said with a thick French accent.

Well, I guess I know who conquered who. But who does this guy think he is? He hasn't won yet. Wait – how is the winner decided?

He stepped back into the line and the herald continued. "Prince Ilya of Northern Europia!"

A man the size of a bear with cropped blond hair and light blue eyes stepped forward. Bowing stiffly, he said in a thick Russian accent, "It will be my pleasure to know you, Princess Miriam." His kiss on my hand was a second too long and he stepped back into the line with a self-assurance I had never seen before.

"Prince Alexander of Scandinavia!"

Probably the happiest man in the bunch took a swift step forward. His medium length curls bounced with his step and his sea green eyes twinkled with excitement. "So happy to finally gaze upon the beauty of the Rose of Petrichoria," he said. And I truly believed he meant it. He kissed my hand and returned to the line as swiftly as he had left it.

"Prince Harrison of Southland!"

I had been so preoccupied with each man introduced that I hadn't even noticed him standing before me. He swaggered forward and gave me elevator eyes before saying, "Nice to see you again, Princess," in a Southern drawl. He took my hand and kissed it for *two* seconds too long. He stood and swaggered back. At least two of his competitors seemed appalled at his demeanor, which I found funny. However, I did not know what to make of him myself.

Glancing at the line, I noted there were only two men left. Both had olive skin tones, dark hair, and brown eyes, which made me wonder if they spoke English. I mentally slapped myself for the pre-judgment.

"Prince Liam of Atlantis!"

The man with the longer dark hair stepped forward. "I look forward to one day showing you the great kingdom of Atlantis as I hope you will show me your kingdom of Arboria." Kissing my hand, he smiled, and then stepped back.

Long-winded and an odd way to introduce yourself to possibly your future bride...

"Prince Ramses of Egypt!"

The final man stepped forward and kissed my hand after saying, "You are lovely this evening, Princess. I look forward to our evening together." Then, he stepped back into line.

What on earth did he mean by that? Sure, I heard the words, but his tone was – is my skin crawling?

"Ladies and gentlemen! The Princes of this generation's King's Test!" the herald declared. The room erupted in applause and shouts of jubilation. "Now, Princess Miriam and her partner will dance The Rose to officially begin our evening of celebration!"

That's when I saw Peter step forward from my right.

173

Chapter 18

"No!" I said a little too loudly and probably in the wrong tone for the evening as Peter tried to take my hand. He widened his eyes and I quickly tried to save myself. With less terror, I said, "I mean – No. I will choose my partner from among the Princes of the King's Test." I glanced at Father, who nodded approvingly.

Peter closed his hand and walked back to join Ella on the opposite side from where my parents stood.

"I assume, of course, the Princes know The Rose?"

The line of bobbing heads assured me they all knew the dance. I began to pace the line of Princes as I considered my options.

Who to choose? Phineas is very handsome. Ramses gives me bad vibes. Ah. Harrison. Let's find out some more about my mystery Prince.

I offered my hand to Prince Harrison, which he accepted with a smug grin. As we made our way to the center of the floor, I hoped I had made a good choice, especially knowing how close he would have to hold me.

When we brought ourselves into position, the crowd pushed aside to make a large circle around us. He rubbed his thumb on my knuckles again and randomly said, so quietly only I could hear, "I love that you wore gloves this evening. They're so elegant; I'm not sure why more ladies don't wear them. The satin feels exquisite in my hands."

I knew it was a line, and the word 'elegant' sounded a little weird coming out of his mouth, but I didn't care. The moment his eyes met mine, I realized I was looking into David's Kona-blue eyes, not just Prince Harrison's. I don't know how to explain it, but I felt like I saw his soul and I suddenly felt right.

Not even attempting to smother the blush overtaking my cheeks, I said, "Thank you. Your eyes are *so* blue."

Did I just say that out loud? Ugh. I might as well have asked him if the sun shines in Southland, which I think must be the Southern United States based on his accent.

Mortified, my eyes widened and the blush started giving way to the pale face of shock. He chuckled good-naturedly and said, "Thank *you*. Your eyes are *so* green."

I gave a breathy laugh, not feeling quite so embarrassed and the song began. This version was played using a string trio of a cello, violin, and viola. The Rose was a relaxed dance in which the dance partners stand very close to one another. The song was in 3/3 and the moves involved steps forward in a straight line, a few zig zags back, and a few circles. These steps were done repeatedly until the end of the song when the man steeply dips the woman.

Taking a deep breath, Prince Harrison and I began the dance. While dancing with Peter felt natural, dancing with Prince Harrison felt *right*. We looked into each other's eyes and I knew he felt it, too – the rightness. He pressed his hand at the small of my back a little harder than necessary, bringing me closer to him and smiled as I consented. In the last few measures, he pulled me into the steep dip.

Thunderous applause sounded all around us, but I barely heard it. All I could hear was the thumping of my heartbeat in my ears.

When the applause changed to shouts and screams, and people began running toward the exits, I snapped out of it. Prince Harrison lifted me back to standing and we looked around trying to figure out what was going on. Then I heard the gunshots. Ducking, Prince Harrison opened his suit jacket and brought me under him like a hen would do for her chicks and we rushed toward the exit.

As we got out the door, Frank grabbed me away from Prince Harrison, who looked like he was ready to fight him. I held my hand out to him and assured him that Frank was my personal Guard and would bring me to safety. Prince Harrison looked like he didn't want to give me over, but gave a taut nod, kissed me on the cheek and took off.

Knowing how absurd it was for me to be thinking about it at a time like this, I brought my hand to the kissed cheek and smiled. However, I didn't have too long to think about it; before I knew it, Frank had switched his grip to my wrist and was pulling me down the hallway in the opposite direction of the exits.

"Frank, where are we going? The exits are the other way!" I yelled over the chaos.

He turned his head and said, "Secret tunnels."

Frank ran at top speed and I had difficulty keeping up in my heels. At first, he was patient with me, but the more I stumbled over myself, the more frustrated he became. He suddenly stopped, turned around, pushed me to the floor – ouch – and yanked my shoes off my feet. Throwing them behind us furiously, he pulled me back up and continued down the hall.

I'll have to have a talk with him about his attitude during emergencies.

Even though I now had an aching backside, I was able to keep up with Frank better. He stopped at the end of the hallway and pushed a hidden button on the giant mirror frame in front of us. We were through the secret door before it even slid open all the way.

The tunnel was dark and had a stale smell as if no one had been there in ages.

"Frank, I can't see anything. Why is it so dark? I saw my parents get out the other way before me."

Frank didn't respond and picked up his already strenuous pace. Soon, the hard wood became rough and my feet were picking up splinters. Because of the needle sharp pain I began to feel in my feet, I had to slow down, but Frank refused to stop. The green light from the Space Needle slowly shifted to red and started seeping in ahead of us. Next thing I knew, I tripped over a crack in the wood and fell forward, catching myself with my free hand on the rough wood – which, of course, put splinters in it, too.

"Come on, Princess. We need to keep moving," Frank growled.

"Understood, but I can't go that fast anymore. I have splinters in my feet and now my hand."

I held up my gloved hand to show him the tiny specks of blood on the satin and the slivers of wood poking through into my flesh.

Frank let out an exasperated sigh and let go of my wrist. Bending down, he cradled me under my back and knees and carried me as he continued running.

"Where is the safe room?" I asked as we approached the end of the tunnel. I blanched. "Frank, where is the safe room? Why are we going outside?"

As we burst out into the night, cold rain pelted us hard; it nearly felt like hale and it definitely felt like something wasn't right. Frank was still not responding to me.

Putting on my best I'm-the-princess-so-listen-to-me face, I demanded, "Frank, turn around this instant! It isn't safe out here! Who knows if they were able to catch the shooters!"

Frank sharply turned his head and stopped running. He was breathing hard from the run and had an intense look in his eyes. I couldn't read his expression. He could have been feeling any number of things – all inappropriate. Love? Hate? Rage? The sky lit up with lightening as the summer storm raged on and thunder soon followed.

He brought his face within an inch of mine. My eyes widened and I tried to pull away in vain. He stared at me with the same intensity and for a moment, I was afraid he was going to kiss me.

"Princess," he began and looked at my lips. "If you don't shut your pretty little mouth, I will be forced to knock you unconscious."

"I – I don't – I don't understand," I whispered into his mouth, which was still breathing heavily into mine. I blinked fast as the rain ran my mascara through my eyes and I felt it run thickly down my cheeks.

He slowly brought his lips near my ear and said, "We're taking you hostage. If you don't stop talking on your own, I'll make you stop."

He lifted his head back up, but kept his stare on me. Though I shivered from the cold, and quite possibly fear, he was as still as a statue. It took me a moment to process what he had just said and when I did, I swiftly brought my good hand up and punched him square in the jaw.

He gave a surprised groan of pain and dropped me on the rain soaked ground. I scrambled through the mud to my injured feet and started running, even though I had no idea where I was going.

I only made it ten feet before he yelled, "Stop!" For some reason, I *did*.

He caught up with me and wrapped his arm around my waist from behind. Still screaming, I began to struggle against him again, trying to get away. His other arm came up with a cloth of some sort and it held it against my face.

Gradually, I began losing my strength and my breathing slowed. I stopped screaming, but tears and cosmetics mingled with the rain on my face. He turned me around and slung me over his shoulder as if I was a sack of potatoes. My eyes began to lose focus and the last thing I heard before I blacked out was Frank saying, "I told you that I'd make –"

Part III

Chapter 19

When I woke up, laying on my side, and opened my eyes, I saw a white wall. I turned my head to look up and saw a white ceiling. Flipping myself completely onto my back, I slapped my left palm to my forehead.

"Come on!" I muttered to myself. "What is with all the white every time I wake up in a strange place?"

Confusion swept through my mind like an eel through a seaweed jungle. I didn't know how I had ended up there – or if everything I had experienced over the last few days was another dream – or if my false life was actually my real life.

Closing my eyes and taking deep breaths, I tried to recall what happened right before I passed out. In my mind's eye, I saw golden leaves engraved into wood. Digging deeper, I saw David's Kona-blue eyes. Then I remembered a rushing crowd of fearful people and Frank grabbing my wrist to get me to safety.

My eyes flew open as my memory of the last few days came flooding back into my mind.

Frank. That dastardly devil. I should have trusted what I had seen in my false life. It's beginning to seem that maybe it was all more than a dream.

I lifted my right hand to check on my splinters. My golden satin gloves had been removed and my hand was wrapped in some kind of bandaging. The bruising on my wrists seemed to have disappeared, which left me wondering how long I had been out. Glancing down at my feet, I saw they were also wrapped up and that the wall on that side was white as well.

I examined my clothing. At some point, someone had changed me from my ball gown into a simple brown dress with long sleeves. Running my fingers through my hair, I also noted my hair had been brought down.

At least I'm not wearing *white this time.*

I tilted my head back to see a white wall there, too. But when I looked on my other side, there was a window that took up the whole wall.

Slowly, I sat up and turned so my feet draped off the side of the bed. As I did, several joints in my body popped and cracked from disuse. The other side of the window was dark, so I stood to my bandaged feet to get closer – my feet were no longer sore.

When I made it to the window, I saw a silhouette of a man. He seemed to be leaning on the opposite side of the hall with his arms crossed.

"Who's there?" I quietly asked.

The man stepped forward into the light from my room and I immediately recognized him as Frank. He had a smug grin on his face as he strolled closer; I instinctively backed away.

"Oh, Miriam. No point backing away. There's nowhere in there you can hide."

All I could do was gawk at him as he began pacing the length of the window.

Shaking his index finger at me, he said, "You almost ruined *everything* we had worked for when you recognized me somehow and demanded another Guard. Thank *goodness* your mother talked some sense into you."

Jerk. Just rub it in.

He paused and tilted his head like a curious cat, looking like he expected me to respond. I gulped loudly and sat on the edge of my bed. He kept walking and turned a corner. I sighed in relief, but it only lasted a moment. To my left, the wall opened and Frank came in. I jumped to my feet and ran to the other side.

"You stay away from me," I hissed.

Furrowing his brow, and ignoring me completely, he asked under his breath, "How *did* you recognize me? I was only thirteen years old when you went into the freeze. I had only ever met you that one time. Of course, you were our *beloved* Princess. The desire of every man and the envy of every woman. I knew who you were and was even among your admirers as a boy." He chuckled. "I was too young to understand government and policy and," he sneered, "aristocracy. You were the one to introduce me to that. Thank you, by the way."

What? What did I say to tick him off so badly?

He started to move closer again and I flinched. I pressed up against the opposite wall, but he was right … There was nowhere to hide in my cell.

When he was inches away, he ran his finger down my cheek, and I shivered as goosebumps trailed up my arms.

"*So* beautiful," he whispered, almost admiringly. His hand moved to hold on to a lock of my hair and he gazed into my eyes. "And *so* off limits to anyone beneath your position."

187

Despite the fact my mouth was desert-dry, I managed another gulp.

"What is going on, Frank?" I asked meekly. How I wished I could be fierce in that moment, but fear held me captive more than Frank.

He glanced down for a moment and let out a dry laugh before bringing his gaze back to me.

"This is, understandably, probably very confusing for you. I had you *so* convinced of my loyalty and you felt *so* safe with me. Maybe you'll listen to your instincts better next time."

He leaned forward more and whispered into my ear, "Don't worry, Miriam. I didn't tell anyone your little secret. It's safe with me."

Like I can trust you, now.

Leaning his other hand against the wall behind me, he pulled his head back, but remained close and smirked.

"'What is going on?' Huh?" He murmured. Speaking more clearly, he asked, "Have you even stopped to think for a moment about the people under your family's rule? What it's like to know that your society views you as beneath everyone?"

"Yes," I replied honestly. His eyes widened with shock. "Yes, I have. I've even questioned the monarchy with a few people."

Frank scoffed. "*Right*. You'd probably say just about anything right now to save your own skin."

My eyes widened. "Are you planning on killing me?"

"No. No, no, no. We're planning on *using* you to further our cause. It's not the monarchy that is the problem, here, Miriam. Your family is kind and just; there is no debating that. The *problem* is society. The *problem* is inequality among your people."

"What is my family supposed to do about that? We can't control people's prejudices."

Slapping his hand hard on the wall beside me, he shouted, "*Something, Miriam!* Your family should do *something* about it."

He pushed himself back and turned away from me. Placing his hand on one hip and massaging his temples with the other, he let out an exasperated sigh.

With him no longer looking at me, a pebble of bravery hit me all the way to my bones. "Do you honestly think *kidnapping* me is a good way to get what you want?" My voice grew louder and more confident as I spoke. "Did you *think* of something a little less drastic? You could have just talked to me about it! You could have petitioned! You could have done *any* number of things besides this, *Frank!*" I said his name as if it was a curse word.

I punched him on his shoulder, but it barely nudged him. He turned around to face me.

Poking him in his chest with tears welling in my eyes, I continued. "And what's with the intimidation, *Frank*? You don't think I'm afraid out of my mind as it is? Does it make you feel like a big man scaring and threatening a woman half your size and three inches shorter?"

Feeling betrayed and humiliated, I leaned back and rubbed my face with my hands, then looked down at them. I couldn't look at him anymore. Barely audible, I said, "I thought you were my friend. You fooled me into believing you were going to protect me. And I'm here nwo, feeling like a fool for believing everything you've ever told me. I thought I had already lost everything and you've managed to take even more."

I sank down to the floor and brought my knees to my chin. When I wrapped my arms around my knees, I saw him staring at me like I had sprouted another head. He opened his mouth like he wanted to say something else, but closed it again.

Pressing his lips tightly together, he turned and marched out of the room. Again, I was alone with my thoughts in a big white room.

~ ~ ~

It was a whole day before I saw anyone again. I stayed in the same spot I was in when Frank had left the evening before; slept there, woke there, stared at the wall there. A slit in the bottom of the door would open so Frank, or whoever, could push trays of food through. Three were lined up with the food untouched. Though I was hungry, I didn't feel like eating. Also, I thought if they valued me so much for their cause, maybe a hunger strike would work in my favor.

For the entire day, I stewed on everything Frank had said. Sure, he totally creeped me out getting so near me and touching me, but I figured he did it to make a point. To show me who was in charge. Also, I did understand his complaint.

Equality is something the human race has striven for as long as we have existed, but have never successfully obtained. Clearly, it was an issue that had been stirring in Frank for years; God only knew how long it had been an issue for whoever else Frank worked with.

During that time, I really began to realize how much my memory was necessary in this life. Not only did I need it personally, but I was expected to lead this kingdom someday and I had no experience or knowledge to do it. Frank said he hadn't told anyone else about my memory problem, but I knew I couldn't trust him anymore.

I wondered if Louis was a part of this deceit as well, though he did seem genuine when he left his post the other day. That was another thing; I still had no clue how long I had been here. Obviously, it had been long enough for my wounds to nearly heal at the very least. My hunger also indicated it had been longer than a day since I had eaten.

I laid down on the floor and turned to face the wall for another night of sleep. I'm not sure why I didn't want to sleep in the bed or why I felt safer against the wall. Maybe it was because I gained a little courage in that spot when Frank tried to intimidate me.

The lights were never off, so I settled my arm over my eyes to give myself the illusion that it was dark and resigned myself to another day gone, away from my family and friends.

Just as I was about to fall asleep, I heard the door open on the opposite wall. Because I didn't want whoever it was to have the satisfaction of knowing they disturbed me, I stayed still. I didn't even flinch when I heard Frank's distinctive footsteps. My arm stayed over my eyes when he squatted down to the balls of his feet. I felt like I was trying to convince a T-Rex I wasn't there by being still, but, really, it was fear that froze me.

When he brought his arm against the wall and leaned forward, the hair on the back of my neck rose instinctively. I hated how he terrified me so severely. Gently, he removed my arm from masking my face and I was left to fake asleep without it. Desperately, I tried to maintain steady breaths and not squish my eyes tighter together.

Did I make him really angry with what I said? Is he here for his retribution?

Not certain if he could tell that I was awake, I could feel him watching me and goosebumps traveled up my arms. He brushed a stray lock of hair away from my face and tucked it behind my ear

191

with the hand not leaning against the wall. Then he start playing with my hair, entangling his fingers in it and pulling them through to the ends.

He's insane! One minute he's knocking me unconscious and yelling in my face. The next, he's creeping in my room and watching me sleep. He is so going to be punished somehow for all of this when I get home – if I get home.

Unable to control it any longer, my breathing increased with my raising trepidation. I felt him bring his hands back to himself and he shifted to his knees; I knew because they were against the middle of my back.

For quite some time, there was no movement from him or me. It was long enough that my breathing steadied and I began surrendering myself to sleep even though I was being watched by a creeper.

Just before I dozed off, I let out a deep sigh through my nose and cuddled myself against the wall. If he wasn't going to leave, I would just make myself comfortable.

I'm not sure how long I was asleep, but I woke up on my back with Frank leaning over me. I started and my eyes shot open, but he didn't move. Caressing my face, he brushed his lips against mine. I couldn't take it anymore. I slapped him, hard, and tried to scramble away from him. Frank laughed at me.

Of course, as he had so aptly put it, there was nowhere for me to hide, so I just ended up cornering myself between the wall and the foot of my bed.

"Good evening to you, too, Princess," he said, rubbing his cheek.

"I told you not to touch me."

"No. You told me to stay away from you."

"I'm pretty sure kissing me is not staying away from me."

He shrugged and started scooting over to me. "I thought I made it pretty clear that you were no longer the one making demands between us." He had made it to his destination, successfully blocking me into the corner.

"Whoever is in charge here has certainly given you ample autonomy," I muttered.

He chuckled and nodded. "Miriam, I *am* the one in charge. Not just between us, but over everyone here."

"Well – you've made your point. You don't have to continue cornering me. I'm plenty scared."

He frowned. "I'm not trying to make you scared, Miriam."

"Then – you're – failing to do – whatever it is you're trying," I stammered.

That darned same lock of hair had fallen in front of my face again and he brushed it back with his trailing fingers.

"I'm *trying* to make you feel safer now. To let you know that I'm not your enemy here, despite how the circumstances indicate the opposite. I know things were – intense yesterday and I'm sorry I shouted at you."

"Are you sorry for pushing me to my rear end, dragging me through splintered floors barefoot, and knocking me out?"

"Yes, yes, and no. I needed you to be quiet so I could get you here to my base."

"Lovely," I muttered.

"In the beginning, you were just the first step in our overall mission, but ever since the moment you told me to call you 'Miriam' and not 'Your Highness,' it became something more to me."

I scoffed and looked down. "You have a funny way of showing it."

He grabbed my chin and forced me to look at him. It wasn't in anger, though. It seemed more like desperation. "It's true! At first, it was all about the cause; that you may be sympathetic to us, but as the time passed, I became enraptured by everything about you! Your voice, your laugh, your walk." He paused and became less intense. "Your face. Your hair. Your shape."

I dropped my jaw. "You've only been my Guard for two nights! And you really failed the last one!"

He let out a dry laugh. "I realize that. But it doesn't change how I feel – that I love you."

"You're insane!" I whispered it and meant it literally. How could Frank think he was in love with me? He didn't even really *know* me. I didn't even know myself.

He patted my cheek. "That may be true, as well." He pulled my face to his and really kissed me this time; it wasn't just a brush of his lips. I struggled to get out of his grasp, but he just pulled me closer.

When he ended the kiss, he kept holding me to him and spoke breathlessly to me. As he trailed his hand on my face down my neck and shoulder, he said, "I'm trying to make it so we can be together. You'll see. It will happen."

Not whispering, I responded, "You're delusional."

He laughed and stood up. "We'll see, Miriam. We'll see."

As he left, I crawled into the bed, under the thin blanket and facing the wall. I thought I had been kidnapped with people who wanted to make life better for everyone, but I was wrong.

The man in charge was a predator and he had made me his prey; he made all those people his personal hunters by convincing them to rally behind his cause, but who knew if he ever intended to give them the equality they desired or if he was just going to get what he wanted.

I closed my eyes and wept.

Please, someone save me. I don't care who it is. Father, Louis, Peter, Prince Harrison. Anyone. I don't know how much longer I can take this.

Chapter 20

No one came. Days passed and I began to doubt anyone would be coming for me at all. I had no idea what demands Frank was making of my parents or if he had even made demands yet. Each day, a different woman came to tend to me. She would bring my food, which I didn't touch, take me to the restroom when I needed to relieve myself, and bring me to a small bathroom with a standing shower so I could clean up with scent-free soap, brush my hair, and change my dress into an identical replica of the one I had been wearing before my shower.

I didn't wonder why it was never the same woman. Based on the mad ramblings of Frank, I already figured it out. He had said once that I could turn anyone to myself because of my charm. I didn't even realize I *had* charm until he mentioned it.

Escape wasn't an option. One time, Frank brought me out of my cell, I refused to consider it my "room," to view the outside, probably trying to endear himself to me. When I saw what was out there, my heart ached. Out of any window, there was a pebble beach, then water. I was on an island.

Oh my goodness. It's like the island from my dream.

Even if I did manage to escape, there was no way I could swim to shore or even know where the right direction would be to swim. Even if I did manage to make it to shore, I didn't know where we were or how to get back to Petrichoria from here. I'd probably die of hypothermia from the cold water and insane weather the Northwest was known for. It bothered me that it was so cold and it was only September.

Every evening, Frank came to my cell and tried to convince me to love him. I would end up against one wall or the other, or cornered. He would talk about his movement or how I wasn't eating anything. He would touch my face and hair and kiss me at least once every time. Each time, I was more scared because each time he became braver with his affection. He never touched me in an inappropriate place, but, he was now confident with cradling my head in his hand or pulling me to him by my hips when he forced his kisses on me.

The night always ended with me weeping into my pillow and praying to be rescued before falling asleep.

I knew my birthday and Crowning Coronation Day had come and gone. By the tally I had going next to my pillow, I had been awake here for two weeks, assuming I woke up around three days after being captured. Every three trays of food, I counted as a day.

My hunger strike started to affect my energy level. Instead of thinking and stewing on the terrible hand life held for me, I spent most of the time sleeping.

On my last night in my cell, I had become so weak, I just planted myself in the corner, so I wouldn't have to jump up and run when Frank arrived. When the dinner tray came through the door, I made a mental note to add another day to my tally and fell asleep with my head tilted back into the corner and my legs curled beneath me.

A little while later, I heard the door open and close. Opening my eyes slowly and raising my brows, I greeted Frank with a pathetic scoff. I could tell by the look on his face he was surprised to see me in the corner and not showing fear at his entrance.

Truthfully, I was no longer afraid of him. Yes, he was crazy. Yes, he was delusional (which I did separate from crazy in my mind). Yes, I knew he would kiss me at some point during his visit. However, I also knew he meant me no harm; he wasn't going to hurt me.

I closed my eyes again and started to drift back into sleep. He came over and sat next to me, facing me, aka pinning me between the wall and my bed. He placed his palm on my cheek and turned my head to face him, which I didn't fight. I was tired of fighting. I was tired of everything.

"Miriam, you *have* to eat something," he said as his thumb stroked my cheek.

Breathlessly, I said, "I'll eat when I'm home."

"You're going to become ill if you don't eat."

I gave him a dry laugh. "Too late. I think I arrived at 'ill' a few days ago."

"Come on, love. When are you going to stop fighting me?"

"Never – at least, never in my mind. I no longer have the strength to fight you physically."

"Quite brave of you to say that."

I shrugged docilely. "Not really. You haven't hurt me since the kidnapping and it's not like it's a big secret I can keep at this point. As I said before, I'm ill."

He scrunched his face in concern. In his crazy mind, he loved me and didn't want to see me this way. That was the plan. Maybe if I starved myself, he would bring me home so I would eat. If he loved me, he would do anything for my survival.

I felt the traitor-lock of hair get brushed behind my ear and my head fell back and hit the wall. "Ow," I said meekly, not bothering to move my head or lift my hand to it. I hadn't realized I had fallen asleep again.

Opening my eyes, I licked my dry lips and whispered, "Listen. If you bring me home, I won't tell anyone it was you who took me. You can stay free out here and remain in charge of your people – or I would let you escort me back into the palace and declare you a hero for saving me and you can stay my Guard. Please, let me go home, Frank."

He leaned forward and kissed my forehead. "You know I can't do that, Miriam. It would be selfish. Besides, I don't want to be just your Guard anymore."

"Frank, you will never be more than my Guard."

"We'll see. Bringing you back would also likely destroy any chance these people have for equality."

"No. I would talk to my parents and the Delegates for each province. I would meet the equality demands you have, whatever they are."

"There's no guarantee they would listen to you. In fact, they probably wouldn't, given your memory loss and traumatic experience here."

Frank laid me down on my bed and sat on the edge with his head in his hands. I didn't realize I had fallen asleep yet again.

"I don't know what I'm doing wrong," Frank vocalized his thoughts; he probably thought I was asleep. "I've been patient and gentle, yet you still refuse me."

I opened my eyes again and said as incredulously as I could, "Are you serious?"

He started and looked at me with wide eyes, horrified that I had heard him.

"You seriously don't know what you've done wrong?"

He nodded with ridiculous hope in his eyes.

"Frank, you kidnapped me. You knocked me unconscious. You put me in a cell; as pretty and clean as it is, it's still a cell. You intimidated me. You have touched me and stolen kisses from me every night I've been here. I'm begging you to let me go home and you're refusing me. I can't see how you can possibly think I could fall in love with you after all of that." I said all that breathlessly, becoming lightheaded with each word.

He grabbed my hand, placed it palm up on his cheek, and held it there. "I'm your equal. There's no reason to be afraid of me or of falling in love with me. I would do anything for you –"

"– except bring me home."

"Yes. Eventually, you'll go home – with me. I can be your family. I can protect you from Peter and his undesired attentions."

I gave a dry laugh. "You can't even stop *yourself* from giving me undesired attentions."

Frank just nodded and looked at me with patience. "You'll change your mind. We just need to spend more time together."

"You're delusional." I said it at least once an evening to him. "You're hoping I get Stockholm syndrome and literally fall madly in love with you? That's not love, Frank. That's insanity."

"We'll see." He dropped my hand and leaned over me to kiss my forehead. I hated not being able to fight him; his touch made snakes slither through my veins.

Hoping he would take his leave, I closed my eyes and easily faked asleep. I felt the bed lift where he had been sitting and heard the door open and close.

I turned to the wall and scratched another tally mark with my fingernail. Sighing with frustration, I quickly fell asleep.

~ ~ ~

David and I are dancing.

We flow across the dance floor of the main ballroom like it is the most natural thing in the world. There is no music; we move to our own rhythm. There is no one else there to watch us.

When we stop in the middle of the room, I throw myself into his arms and he holds me tightly. Letting out my hopelessness and frustration, I sob into his chest and he strokes my hair.

"Please don't make me wake up, David. My life is horrible right now."

"I know, honey. I know." He brings his hand down and places it on my back and leans his cheek on the top of my head.

"I don't know how it's possible, but I'm on that island from my previous dream. It's horrible."

"I figured it would be."

"I wish I had never woken up in the first place. I wish I could have stayed with you. If I knew it was a dream, I wouldn't have let you or Tom die. I would have protected you."

"Don't concern yourself with that right now. That was your false life; this is your false life. I'm just a figment of imagination your brain created to help you cope with your situation."

I chuckle. "I know, but I feel safer here in my false life than I do out in my real one." I look up at him. "He's crazy, David. There is no reasoning or negotiating with a mad man. The only thing he wants is my love and I refuse to give it to him."

"He isn't deserving of your love. Save it for the right man."

I nod. "Do you think someone will come for me? Will I be saved or am I going to be stuck here until I die of starvation?"

He looks pensive as he considers my question. "I think your parents are doing everything they can to get you back."

"Yeah. You're probably right."

"I'm always *right."*

I laugh. I can't remember the last time I laughed. Oh, right. At the ball, when I was dancing with Prince Harrison.

"Miriam, I want you to be careful at the palace. Not everyone is as they seem. Not everyone is to be trusted."

I roll my eyes. "Now you *tell me. I think I should first focus on getting out of this prison and away from Frank, then I can concern myself with politics and espionage."*

"You'll be okay. I know you will."

He smiles and kisses me. This is *right. This* is *what love feels like. Not the insanity Frank brings to me every night.*

He pulls away and brushes away the lock of hair that is constantly getting in my face. Where the same touch from Frank felt like slime to my soul, David's touch feels like safety.

"You'll be okay. I know you will."

Chapter 21

I woke up dazed and with my eyes closed. I had a breathing tube in my nose and an IV pumping water and some other fluids into my body. The sound of beeping, in rhythm with the pounding of my heartbeat, sounded loud in my ears. Opening my eyes, I saw a pale blue ceiling. I was in a different room and hope filled my soul.

Did someone come for me? Am I at the hospital with Doctor Quincy?

The door opened and a woman in scrubs, who I didn't recognize, came in to check my stats. She looked at the monitor and made sure the IV was working properly. Finally, she looked at my face and she gaped at me.

"Where am I?" I moaned.

She rushed out of the room. I could tell she was going to retrieve someone, but she didn't give me a sense of where I was or who she was getting.

I sighed and looked around. This room had a window. Though I couldn't feel it, I relished the sight of sunlight bursting through the overcast sky and reflecting off the crashing waves of water. I smiled and pretended I could feel its warmth on my face, erasing the cold and melting the devastation that had built up inside me.

205

The door opened and I turned my head quickly to see my guest. My smile faded and the warmth left my body when I saw who it was. Of course, it made sense. There was no ocean outside the windows of Doctor Quincy's hospital.

Frank rushed to my side and gripped my hand in his. Depression crashed over me and a tear escaped from the corner of my eye. The sun no longer shone and a light rain began to fall. It was as if the weather was sympathizing with me.

He brought my hand to his lips and kissed it over and over again, then pressed my closed fist against his cheek. My stomach turned; I bent over the opposite side of the bed and vomited.

No. No, no, no.

Maddeningly, he held my hair back with his free hand, so vomit wouldn't get in it. I despised him for it; for everything he had put me through. I threw up some more.

"The doctor said you might vomit when you woke up. Something about your body taking in nutrition so quickly after two weeks of starving yourself," Frank rationalized.

No, stupid head. You're *the reason I'm vomiting.*

I fell back onto my pillow, ripped my hand from his, and put my hands on my face as I wept. I couldn't believe it. I was stupid to get my hopes up. How did they even have a doctor with them?

"I thought I was home," I sobbed. "I thought I was finally free."

He frowned at me. "You're lucky to be alive, Miriam. You were completely unresponsive when your assistant came in to take you to the restroom in the morning. We had you rushed upstairs to our medical floor as quickly as possible and began oxygen and fluids."

I turned my head away from him and didn't stop crying.

"Miriam, you scared me to death. I thought I was going to lose you." His voice was slightly louder and a bit more forceful.

I faced him with fury, my voice still croaking from the dry air being blown in my nose. "Lose me?! You would have to *have* me to begin with in order to *lose* me."

He grabbed my face with both hands rougher than he usually did. "Whether you like it or not, I *do* have you. You are here in *my* home base. You are under *my* thumb!" Now he was yelling and spittle began flying into my face. I blinked quickly to avoid it getting in my eyes. "*I* am in charge! *I* command *you!*"

He grabbed my shoulders and pulled me up so I was sitting, yanking the IVs from my arm and spilling the medical fluids all over his lap and the floor. He shook me. "I will *not* stand for this disrespect anymore, *Princess*." He slapped me and I fell back again to my pillow. Mortified, I raised my hand to my surely reddened cheek. I had finally cut the last thread of sanity in his brain and I knew I was going to die.

He tried to grab my shoulders again and I rolled off the bed, separating myself from the breathing machine, crawling through my vomit, and scrambling to the wall. Reaching up to the window, I searched for the opening in vain. I turned around and saw he slowly approached me with his hands out in front of him, palms up. He reminded me of a small child who approached a cat that he fully intended to swing around by the tail, but tried to make it feel safe so he could get it.

My breathing was ragged and I pushed myself into the corner. Stupid corners. There was never an escape. Even though I knew it would make no difference, I stood up and pressed myself against the wall. I tried to wipe the sweat from my forehead, but only smeared the blood on my wrist from the IV across it.

When Frank was right in front of me, I closed my eyes. As I turned my head away from his direction, a whimper involuntarily squeaked from my mouth. My lower lip trembled as my muscles tensed, preparing myself for the next strike.

"I – Miriam, I'm –," he stuttered his gentle words. He was horrified with himself, as he should have been. When he placed his palm on my cheek, I tried to push myself further into the wall, but it wasn't possible. All I could do was gasp and hold my breath, waiting for the impending slap, but it didn't come.

Slowly opening one eye, I let out the shaky breath and looked at him just in time to see a tear running down *his* cheek. Have I mentioned that Frank was crazy?

I turned my head fully to face him and his hand traced a pattern on my injured face. After a moment, I realized he was tracing his handprint.

He sighed and tucked my hair back behind my ears; it had all fallen forward onto my face in my frenzy. He kept his hand cradling the back of my head and a dull throb started building where he placed his hand.

Putting his forehead against my bloody forehead, he said, "There is no good reason for what I just did. None. There are lots of bad excuses."

I stood perfectly still, not wanting to incite any further outburst of emotion, regardless of what it would be.

He circled his other hand around my waist. Starting to become lightheaded, I realized I held my breath again and released it. Though I'm sure it smelled horrible after my being out for God only knows how long, Frank didn't move away, but did remove his forehead from mine. His face was still an inch from mine.

"I just – I just can't take it anymore, Miriam. Your constant rejection and fighting. I *need* you to accept me now. Be done with your deadly hunger strike and pouting, and be with me."

I didn't want to be slapped again. I hated myself for my weakness. If I couldn't stay strong in this situation, how was I going to stay strong for my kingdom in the face of tribulation? Naturally, that was assuming I ever made it out of there alive.

Then the gears of my brain started turning and creaking like a machine that hadn't been working for a while.

I am going about this all wrong. I said it in my dream with David, there is no reasoning or negotiating with a mad man. This isn't a battle of strength, but a battle of wits. My mind is clearly stronger than his; I can do this. Perhaps I can –

The plan formulated so quickly in my mind I barely kept up with myself. I would fool him; I would give him what he wanted. He was so insane, he wouldn't question the sudden turnaround. I would gain his trust, then run away when the time came. That time had to come; it was my only hope.

We were still staring at each other; he pleading and I petrified. I took a deep breath.

Keep my calm. I can do this.

With a shaking hand, I lightly touch his chest. It was *so* difficult to fight my instinct to push him away, but I didn't. *This* was my strength. *This* was how I would lead my kingdom against any adversity that may come.

I placed the palm of my other hand on his cheek and he closed his eyes.

He's already buying it and I haven't even begun to sell it.

"You're right," I whispered. His eyes flew open and stared into mine. I cleared my throat, which was still dry from the breathing apparatus. Though my voice was hoarse, I continued with my charade. "You're right. You've been nothing but kind to me since I woke up here – and – and – and I've given you nothing but disrespect."

His jaw dropped and a look of blissful confusion spread across his face.

"I – I – I'll start eating. I won't fight you anymore. I'll give you a chance."

A stupid grin appeared on his stupid face.

"Really?"

I nodded. Only when I felt dripping on my foot did I realize my wrist bled profusely. I looked down at it and he followed my gaze.

"No! Here, let me help you back to the bed. I'll get someone in here to clean you and your bed up, and get your wound taken care of."

Before I could start walking, he rushed me up into his arms and placed me on the bed.

What does he think he is? Some kind of hero from a romance novel?

Those were my thoughts, but my face showed a grateful smile. All those years of acting in high school and college were paying off – despite the fact those years didn't really happen.

Frank wiped my forehead clean with a wet cloth that sat next to the bed on a tray, and kissed it before rushing out to find someone.

When he left and the door closed, I took a few cleansing breaths and rolled my eyes up into the back of my head. A smile I couldn't resist spread across my face as I realized I had just taken the first steps toward going home.

It'll be worth it. I can do this.

Moments later, the nurse who had cared for me before came in with another nurse. One pressed some gauze on my wrist, helped me stand, and walked me away from the bed to get me into the small bathroom so I could shower. The other began cleaning the vomit and blood off the floor; I had destroyed the room.

I took off the soiled hospital gown, cautiously removed the gauze, and turned the water on. Just as I was about to step in, I heard a knock on the door. Peeking my head around the edge of the door, I sought out my intruder. It was the nurse again.

"I almost forgot to give you these," she said as she handed me a basket.

"Oh. Thanks," I murmured, accepting it and closing the door again. Inside, there was rose-scented soap, shampoo, and conditioner with a note.

Miriam,

I know how much you like this scent and I love it on you. Enjoy.

-F

Wondering how long he had this stuff ready to go, I popped the top off the shampoo and breathed in the lovely aroma.

Bonus. I get to smell like something besides antibacterial garbage now. Thanks, Fabio!

I put the three bottles onto the shelf in the shower and pulled the glass door shut when I stepped in. Unlike the lukewarm showers I had when I was in my cell, this water was nice and hot. I washed up and let the water soak my skin until it was red. Though I hated to do it, I shut off the water and stepped out of the shower to towel-dry. I noted that the IV hole had stopped bleeding and was grateful for it.

I peeked out the door again and saw that the bed had been made up and the floor had been cleaned to a spotless shine. The first nurse was patiently waiting in the chair by the bed.

"Are you ready for your clean clothes, Princess?" the nurse asked me.

"Yes, please and thank you."

I wrapped the white towel around myself and stepped into the room. The cool air felt nice against my red hot skin. The nurse gave me a smile and set a brown dress, like I had been wearing before, with some undergarments on the bed. She nodded to me and left me to my clothes.

Yes. I can do this. I'll be okay.

Chapter 22

Rather than take me back to my cell, the nurse guided me to a *real* room. It was still pretty small with only a navy blue bed and sofa, and a dark wood vanity with a mirror attached and a small bench that was stored beneath it. The walls, a dark ivory color, contrasted with the dark hardwood of the floor, which was a nice change from the tile I had before.

Upon entering, I saw a tray with food on it sitting on the vanity. There was still no clock to keep time, but I had a window. It was dark out. There was a delicious scent of herbs and spices rubbed into chicken. And when I lifted off the lid, a pat of butter was melting over a scoop of steamed broccoli. Water and an empty wineglass sat in the upper right corner of the tray. I sighed.

Empty wineglass probably means lover boy will be arriving soon.

Wanting to be done eating before Frank showed up, I ate the food pretty quickly. I still didn't feel like eating, but I needed to in order to demonstrate my willingness to be cooperative.

When I finished, I wrinkled my nose and yawned. I still felt weak from my hunger strike and the events of the day. Gently collecting the wineglass, I made my way over to the sofa and sat down. It was much softer than it appeared, which was a good thing because it looked rather stiff.

I curled my legs beneath me and leaned myself back and into the arm of the couch. Raising the glass so that it was between my eyes and the overhead light, I examined how the light bent in the imperceptible waves of the smooth glass.

I was still twirling the stem when Frank knocked on the door and entered without any acknowledgement from me. Closing the door behind him, he searched the room for me until he found me. He leaned himself sideways against the door and put his hands in his pockets. This wasn't a surprise for me; he usually tried to make himself seem approachable and smooth, as if I didn't know better. He was a wolf in sheep's clothing.

I turned my head away from the mesmerizing glass and light, and gave him a relaxed smile. Relaxed was much easier to pull off than bright. Bright was difficult to fake realistically; it always looked forced to me, so I decided I wouldn't be using that one, at least not tonight.

Feeling assured by my smile, he made his way over to me and his eyes landed on the glass raised in my hand.

"Rotting roots. I forgot," he muttered to himself as he turned and left the room for a few moments. I rolled my eyes when he left and summoned the smile by the time he returned.

With a bottle of White Zinfandel in one hand and a wineglass that matched mine in the other, he closed the door and came to sit by me.

He ended up very close to me, nearly sitting on my feet, and gave me that stupid grin again. I laughed. He chuckled nervously.

"It's nice to see you happy, Miriam," he said sincerely. "It's been a long time since I've heard your laugh."

Still smiling, I shrugged. "Well, this room is certainly nicer than my cell and I actually feel clean after using the soaps you sent me. Thank you for that."

"You're welcome." He handed me his glass and pulled a bottle opener from his back pocket. The top shot off across the room and he chuckled at that, too. He seemed to be a person who chuckled a lot, but rarely let out a full laugh. He was more nervous than a teenager on his first date.

He poured into both glasses and set the bottle off to the side. Taking his glass back from me, he brushed his fingers against mine.

Real smooth, buddy.

I shyly looked down to my glass and put on a smile I hoped read as "sweet" and not "I want to rip your hand off your arm and feed it to the orcas off shore."

Frank turned to face me and put his arm around my shoulder. Lifting his glass, he said, "To second chances."

"To second chances," I repeated and clanged my glass gently into his.

To a second chance for escape from this God-forsaken island.

I sipped at my sweet wine while he took a big gulp. Frank held out his glass to see how much was left, finished it off, and set his glass next to the bottle. The only thing missing was a huge belch.

Do I really have to do this? Yes. I do. I can do this.

I took another sip of my wine, stood up and set it on the tray on my vanity. When I sat back down I curled myself the other way, so my head rested on his shoulder.

Nice touch, Miriam. Maybe now that he has you, he won't feel pressured into kissing you tonight. All you need to do is prove you're comfortable with him.

Thankfully, he didn't kiss me right then. He just wrapped his arm tightly around me and laid his head on mine. The hand around my shoulder began tracing patterns between my arm and clavicle. I closed my eyes and took a deep breath.

I hope I don't have to do this for long. My skin is crawling and I already feel dirty after my hot shower only a little while ago.

"Miriam?" He said, still tracing patterns.

"Hmm?" I responded dreamily.

"Do you remember when we walked to the ball together?"

"Of course."

"I had to walk behind you because my position was so much lower than yours. I knew I was supposed to be guarding you, but all I could think of was the little twirl you did to show off your gown and beauty to me when you left your room."

I sighed. "It was a lovely dress."

That you destroyed when you kidnapped me.

I felt him smile and breathe in the aroma of roses in my hair. "I watched you sashay your way to the ballroom and my heart beat to the rhythm of your steps."

I didn't think this kind of mush really existed.

"Yeah?"

"Then there was the abrupt stop you made when you realized you were going to have to go in alone. I ran into you and you almost fell."

"Mm hmm." I sighed. "I was pretty terrified."

As he continued recounting the story I already knew, the tracing became a little faster and began going between my neck and clavicle, abandoning my arm.

Keep my calm. I can do this. I have to get home.

"You begged me to escort you in and I had to say no because of our stations."

"I remember, though I don't know that I *begged*."

He chuckled. "Semantics. Anyway, it was in that moment I *knew* I was doing the right thing, even though I knew you would hate me for it at first. I couldn't stay platonic with you anymore and there was no way for us to be together as it was."

He paused, but I didn't respond. I wanted to, but couldn't. It *was* true. I *did* hate him for it. However, the "at first" part wasn't right. I still despised him for it.

"I followed you in shortly after you were announced and stood by the doors at attention. I admired you from a distance, noting your dainty hands graciously accepting a polite kiss from each *Prince*." At this, he brought one of my hands up to his lips and kissed my fingers lightly.

The tracing stopped and he rearranged us so that we were looking at each other.

Seriously. I feel like I'm trapped in a sappy chick flick.

Smiling, he tucked my traitor-lock of hair behind my ear and gave me a pained expression. "Then, the Princes who had arrived

217

for the King's Test were introduced and I could barely handle the way they looked at you. I saw you gasp when you saw Peter approaching; I could see the fear in your eyes and I wanted to sweep you off your feet and dance the Rose with you to save you. Again, I couldn't."

He looked down at our interlocking fingers, then looked back at me. "Then that *Prince* stepped in, literally saving the Damsel-in-Distress, and I loathed him even more than Peter. Peter couldn't have you, but this Prince, he was eligible. He could take you away from me forever if I let it happen. He could have won your heart, too. I could see him already working his way into your eyes, your mind."

"Oh," I breathed, looking down.

"The distraction of gunshots rang around the ballroom and he almost got away with you. I was afraid I wouldn't be able to catch you in time or that you wouldn't come with me."

He tilted my head back up so I looked at him and cupped the bruised side of my face in his hand. I closed my eyes and nuzzled into it.

It's not Frank's hand. It's David's hand. I miss David.

When I opened my eyes, his head was tilted with mine and he brought me closer.

Well, darn. I guess he's going to kiss me after all. Breathe. I can do this.

"I *am* sorry about how rough I was with you that night. There was no other way to get you to come with me when you started to struggle."

Perhaps waiting for an utterance of forgiveness from me, he stopped speaking for a moment and cradled my head in his hand. I didn't say a word. I could barely concentrate on what was about to happen and I didn't want to vomit again. Though the idea of seeing him covered in vomit didn't bother me, I knew I couldn't for the sake of my role.

"The first time I kissed you, it was so heady for me. Even through your struggle, I knew we were meant to be. I just have to succeed with the mission for equality. Then, we can marry and I can be by your side as a support during your rule. You should be able to wed anyone you desire. You shouldn't be limited to Royalty. You deserve more than that."

By the end of his monologue, he was hardly speaking. His gaze dropped to my lips and I knew it was coming. I only hoped it wouldn't be any more intense than the others. Knowing I would just have to go along with whatever he was going to do, I closed my eyes as his other hand dropped to the small of my back.

I can do this. Keep my calm. I can do this. Just think of home and all the people who need me. This will all be over soon and it will be nothing but a terrible memory.

Unfortunately, it was like slow-motion; I just wanted it to be over and done with.

A moment after closing my eyes, he pulled me against him with the hand on my back and lifted my mouth to his with the hand cradling my head. He was gentle, not like he'd been with his forced kisses.

Now. This is the selling moment. This is the moment that will set you free.

Gradually, I lifted my hand to his neck and softly pulled him a little closer. He quietly let out a short groan.

How do actresses do this and look so sincere? I'm not sure how much longer I can persevere.

A tear rose out of the corner of my eye when he tilted his head and deepened the kiss. He brought his other hand to my waist and tried to pull me closer, but we were already pressed against each other; his pull only tightened his hold on me. When I brought my other hand behind his back, he quietly groaned again.

Is the groaning really necessary? Keep my calm. I'm an actress. This is just the romance scene of an epic film. I can do this.

His mouth left my lips and traced a path down my jaw to my neck. I let out a breathy sigh and he brought his mouth to my ear.

After the tiniest of nibbles and a convincing gasp from me, he spoke with a light, shaky voice into my ear. "I knew you loved me, too. You just had to give yourself permission."

Pulling back so our faces were inches apart and we were gazing into each other eyes. Frank wiped the stray tear from my cheek without ever releasing eye contact with me until I closed my eyes.

He cupped my face and said, "Tell me."

I bit my lower lip. "Hmm?"

"Tell me what you've been fighting this whole time. We could have been like this long ago."

"Mm hmm."

"Miriam, look at me." I opened my eyes. "Tell me you love me."

Don't panic. It's just a scene. I'm just an actress. I can do this.

I tilted my bruised cheek into his hand because I wanted him to both feel like the monster he was and that I was putty in his hands.

I furrowed my brows to show sincerity and gave him a short, soft kiss. This time when we pulled apart, *his* eyes were closed and I knew I had him hook, line, and sinker.

"I love you, Frank."

I knew the risk I took in giving him what he wanted. The moment could go anywhere; I just hoped it wouldn't go *there*.

His eyes flew open and he scanned my face, looking for any sign of dishonesty, but I was convincing and he was insane. Rather than smothering me with kisses like I expected, he gripped me in a tight embrace and began crying. No. He wasn't crying; he was bawling – and whispering utterances of love and gratefulness.

God, please tell me this is almost over for tonight.

He stopped crying and separated from me completely, laying back on the other side of the sofa. I mimicked his action and leaned against my arm of the sofa and watched him covering his face with his hands and panting.

Boom! That's how it's done.

Sliding his hands down his face, he looked at me in earnest. "Tomorrow, Miriam."

I tilted my head to show him I had no idea what he was talking about. "What's tomorrow?"

"We'll go back to Petrichoria."

"You're going to bring me home?" I asked excitedly.

He nodded with a giant, stupid grin on his face. "Yes. I'm going to take you home. And we will lead my army to victory. Tomorrow, Miriam. Tomorrow, we're going to conquer the kingdom of Arboria."

Chapter 23

As difficult as it was, I did not to respond in horror to the notion of overthrowing my parents and crowing Frank King – though he would technically be King Francis Miller II, he informed me shortly after the revelation of his end goal. Instead, I kept a smile plastered on my face.

I was wrong when I began the evening thinking I wouldn't be using the bright smile. For the rest of the time he was in my room, it was the only way I could continue smiling. He couldn't tell the difference, anyway. Crazy is as crazy does.

When he stood to leave, I joined him and walked him to my door. He grabbed at me and gave me a long, emotion-filled kiss, then left, muttering something about a speech and actual invasion plans.

After he closed the door behind him, I ran to my pillow and screamed into it. I screamed my frustrations and hopelessness into the giant fluff of cotton. Throwing the pillow at the bed, I began to pace the room. My plan had backfired and I wondered if he thought *he* had been playing *me* the whole time.

I massaged my temples with my fingers.

No. No, no, no. How could I be so idiotic*? Of* course *he only wants to be King. Equality?! How could I fall for that bologna? He* *doesn't want equality; he just wants a different aristocracy where he is in charge.*

I stormed into my small bathroom and stripped off my dress. I felt dirty and used and stupid. The idea that he had fallen for me so quickly *was* insane because it wasn't true. Turning the shower on hot, I stepped in and wept. Tears mingled with water and my emotions danced with the heat.

I saw the same type of rose soap, shampoo, and conditioner had been put in this shower, too, so I used it. I turned around and pressed my forehead on the smooth wall, letting the water pound a gentle massage on my back.

When I had finished crying and brought my breathing back to a normal pace, I washed my face one more time and stepped out of the shower. It was only after I towel-dried that I realized I didn't have a change of clothes – and it was cold.

Crossing my arms, I tilted my head back in frustration, hoping there weren't security cameras in the room. The thought had never crossed my mind before. When Frank said "movement," I was thinking a few dozen people in a rundown warehouse. Never did it ever occur to me that he would have an *army* of people. With an army, he could have any number of resources I had never thought of before.

Exhausted and not wanting to deal with the clothing issue at the moment, I pulled back the thick blankets on the bed and climbed in. The bed and pillow were much softer than the one in my cell. It was a double bed with two pillows, so I laid my head on one and cuddled with the other one in fetal position, facing the window. All I could see was pitch black and millions of stars.

This problem is much smaller than the whole of creation. The right path will show itself.

I closed my eyes and started dissecting my time at the palace. It was a little difficult; I had spent more time as Frank's prisoner/sick obsession than as the Rose of Petrichoria.

Were there other people in the palace sympathetic to his cause? Who would want Frank *to be King? Why did he want to be King? What will he do if or when he succeeds?*

Aside from all the questions about the palace, I was nervous about my true standing with Frank. No longer confident in my plan, I wondered what devastation I had just set in motion; if he really did love me or if he was trying to make me swoon for his own end goal.

Flipping over, I waved my hand over the light panel and the lights turned off. Snuggling back into the blankets and my pillow, I despaired. When I made it into the room earlier, I thought I would maybe fall asleep without crying for once. However, I once again found myself closing my wet eyes and feeling the tears drench my pillow.

Did I just pave Frank's path to the Crown?

~ ~ ~

The door burst open and Frank's incessant mad ramblings were already running out of his mouth at super human speed. Jerking myself awake, I shot up, subconsciously making sure I wrapped the blanket around my naked body. Noticing it was still dark outside, I figured it was probably early morning. I gawked at him with wide eyes and a dropped jaw as he paced around in his Royal Arborian Guard uniform as if he was in a war room.

Still sitting up straight, my bare arms held the blanket in place and a leg hung out off the side of the bed. I was too in shock to do anything, but sit there and watch him pace and mumble through biting his thumb nail.

225

Dropping his hand from his face, he finally turned to acknowledge my existence. He stammered himself silent and widened his eyes.

"Miriam, what are you *doing*?!" Frank asked me in shock.

"What am *I* doing? I was sleeping, Frank! What did you think I would be doing when you waltzed in here while it's still dark out?" I responded incredulously, more horrified and tugging my blankets tighter against me.

"But you – *you're* – why?" He stammered. He gestured with his arm straight out and palm up whilst moving it up and down.

I grunted and threw myself back on my pillow, pulling my leg up with me. Confident that I was decent enough, I slapped my palm to my forehead. When I looked back at him, he had pressed himself against the door.

I smirked. "My, how the tables have turned." I waggled my eyebrows at him, knowing it would make him even more anxious.

Frank chuckled nervously, clearly uncomfortable with the situation he had thrown himself into.

Raising an eyebrow, I calmly explained. "After you left last night, I took another shower because it's been so long since hot water has been made available to me. I was so emotional from everything that happened, I didn't think about the fact there was nothing clean for me to put on once I got out. I knew the guard outside my door was probably a man, so I figured I would just go to bed and put on the clean dress that would come in the morning."

Frank scratched the back of his neck. "I guess you weren't expecting me."

"Nope. I don't normally see you until the evening."

"But you knew we were leaving today."

"I didn't know that would be this early in the morning or that I wouldn't be getting a change of clothes."

He let out a single laugh and left the room.

If I had known it was that easy to get rid of him, I would have gone to sleep naked a long time ago.

A few minutes later, he returned with clean clothes, but they were different than what I had mentally dubbed my prison uniform. When I sat up and looked down, I saw that there were normal undergarments, but instead of a dress, at the end of my bed lay a green beret, tight-looking forest green pants, a brown tank top, a matching green leather jacket and brown knee boots.

The star of the outfit was the leather bomber jacket. Though there was a zipper that ran diagonally from the left shoulder to the bottom-center of the jacket, there was also the option of leaving it partially open with a beautiful collar. On each side, two faux zippers ran horizontally near the middle of the jacket; one ending at the side of the back and the bottom connecting to the zipper on the opposite side. There were two vertical zipper pockets on the front.

I looked from the clothing back to Frank. "This is new," I drawled.

He chuckled. "I didn't think you'd be very comfortable in that brown dress during our journey today."

We stared at each other for a few moments as he just stood there with his stupid grin on his stupid face.

I pursed my lips and looked down at my blankets pointedly. He followed my gaze and said, "Oh. Right," turned around and left the room.

227

I rolled my eyes and stood up. Quickly, I put on my new clothes, did a couple stretches, brushed my hair with my fingers, and braided it over my shoulder (tying the end in a knot, since there was no hair tie either).

Leave it to a man to not consider giving a woman with waist-length hair a brush.

When I felt confident with my reflection and prepared to play my role, I went out the door to meet up with Frank. I had decided that even if he *did* think he played me, it wouldn't be so bad. It would mean he had grossly underestimated me and I could roll with that.

Putting my best timid face on, I slowly opened the door and stepped out. Frank was leaning against the wall across from me, legs and arms crossed like he was the Fonz, and gave me obvious elevator eyes. I felt my cheeks redden from my anger, but I was sure he read it as a timid appreciation.

Looking down at my twiddling fingers, I mildly said, "Um – Frank, can I talk to you for a moment – about last night?" I raised my eyes, but not my head, to meet his and a sudden expression of shock and concern spread across his face.

"Sure. Of course. Yes." Frank stuttered and gestured back to the room. Reopening the door, he led me in by the small of my back. I turned to face him.

Closing the door behind him, he scratched the back of his neck with his hand. Approaching me, he asked, "What's the matter, Miriam? I hope you're not having second thoughts about – what you said –"

I widened my eyes in feigned shock as he closed the gap between us and I ended up sitting on the edge of my bed. "No! Of course not!"

Frank slapped his hands to his face and slid them down in relief. "Beautiful blossoms," he muttered and smiled. Taking hold of both my hands in his and looking down at them, he questioned, "If not that, then what is it?"

When he made eye contact with me again, I tilted my head and gave a slight shrug. "It's just – when – oh. Never mind. It's probably just my own paranoia and vulnerability from my confession. Just forget about it. We can go where we need to."

Knowing he would stop me, I started to stand up. He gently placed his hands on my shoulders and pushed me back down to sitting as he brought himself to his knees. "No," he drawled. "I just got you. I'm not going to allow doubts to already start snaking their way between us. Please, ask me."

I took a deep breath. "When I told you I loved you, you hugged me, pulled away and immediately began talking about your mission of conquest and desire for the Crown." I looked down at his thumbs rubbing my hands, trying to not shiver with disgust. "You fooled me once into trusting you as a friend. Do you *actually* love me or have you simply been trying to fool me again so you can rightfully become King?"

As difficult as it was, I didn't look back at his face when his thumbs stopped moving at my words. I desperately wanted to see his reaction to determine the truth of what he was about to say or do, but I knew that the sincerity of the moment dictated a shy posture unless he turned my face back up to him.

I heard him sniffle and he released my hands. He stood, but didn't leave his spot. Tenderly, he brought me to standing and embraced me, one hand pulling my head into the crook of his neck. I felt a few tears drip into my hair and I had my answer. He really was as insane as I originally thought him to be – more so, now that I knew he also wanted to become King of Arboria.

He pulled away and tilted my head with a finger so I gazed up at him. After circling my waist with his arms, he said, "There is no one I have ever loved more than I love you, especially right now. Over the last few weeks, I have seen and admired your fierce ability to be independent and loyal to your kingdom. But last night, and right now, I'm seeing a whole new side of you. One that's gentle and willing to express your concerns and desires to me."

He paused and I forced a tear from one of my eyes, once again thanking my lucky stars for those fake years of acting.

"I'll be honest with you, Miriam. You deserve that. At the beginning of our movement, I was selected to be leader and somehow get you to marry me so I would become King. I joined the Royal Arborian Guard shortly after finishing my education and worked hard to quickly earn high rankings. I had decided the best route would be to earn the trust of your parents enough that they would put your safety in my hands when you woke from your deep sleep. It didn't hurt to have my own father's recommendations. In accordance with the plan, your parents did put me there. But that first night, everything about my mission changed."

He cupped my face in one hand and I laid my head against it. "I told you about it last night, but I'll elaborate. When you came out of your room in the middle of the night in your robe and asked me to call you Miriam, I felt the change happen. Following you and guarding you outside of the rose garden, I fought it, hard. I had nearly succeeded when I saw Peter come out and faltered. After you came out, clearly upset, I failed. I felt so many things. Ashamed, angry, confused, but mostly, I desired to pull you into my arms and comfort you."

"It was that fast for you, huh?"

He chuckled. "Yes. From then on, every little thing you did made me fall deeper in love with you. Even when you fought me."

He shook his head. "Thank goodness you're done with that – Miriam, my original goal was to become King and your love makes that victory even sweeter."

I smiled.

Don't count your chickens before they hatch.

Frank gave me a short, soft kiss. "Is that a satisfactory answer for you?"

I nodded and bit the corner of my bottom lip.

As he pulled away, he smiled, took one hand and tugged me toward the door. "Good. Now, let's go introduce you to our army. Don't worry. I'll do all the speaking. All you need to do is stand by my side and look beautiful."

Trying not to feel slightly offended by the comment, I allowed him to escort me out of the room.

Chapter 24

Frank held me by the waist as we walked through his home base. Even though I already knew escape wasn't possible, it became clearer just *how* impossible it would have been to try. Aside from the place being a giant maze, there were, indeed, security cameras everywhere I looked, the elevator was secured by a fingerprint scanner, and it wouldn't move once you were inside until it did an optical scan.

Seeing all this, and noting that there were over twenty stories in the building, made me nervous; this was no ragtag army. My mind reeled on how expensive everything appeared and the implication of the size of the movement it made.

There was also plenty of time to consider everything Frank had told me since I became his captive and it didn't add up. When I was first awoke on his base, he told me his movement was all about equality, but just a few moments ago, he said the original goal had been to put the Crown on someone new and he had been chosen.

If they wanted equality, why were they alright with a monarchy at all? Why did it matter that they had me to officially make someone else King? If they really wanted equality, wouldn't they be asking for a new government with elected leaders and officials? It made no sense for them to keep the nation a kingdom. Though I had some answers, I had more questions, but they would wait until we were on our way back to Petrichoria.

Finally, we arrived at the second level of the complex and made our way down a short hallway. Initially, I wondered why we had only gone to the second floor rather than the first, but when Frank opened the door at the end of the hall to a balcony, I promptly understood. I actually stopped and it made Frank fall back a little.

He turned to look at me and I couldn't hide my shock. My face was pale, eyes wide, mouth agape. Frank furrowed his brow and walked back to me; his people had already exploded in applause and shouts of admiration and victory.

"Love," he drawled. "Is everything alright?"

I tried to clear my throat, but I was completely dry. "Um – yes. There are just – a lot more people than I thought there would be. You've certainly amassed quite an army."

He smirked; it wasn't the stupid love grin he normally gave me, but a smirk of pride and arrogance. There was easily a thousand men and women in the large hanger. They weren't the average person, as I had expected. They were soldiers, dressed in uniforms that mimicked those of the Royal Arborian Guard, and obviously trained.

"Come on, love. Like I said, you don't have to say anything. I wouldn't expect that of you now. Just come stand with me and give them your beautiful smile."

Bright smile it is.

I could only offer my forced smile, but he seemed happy with it and offered me his arm. I took it and we both made our way forward to the railing of the balcony made for two. Although I didn't think it possible, the roaring of the crowd increased in volume and fervor when I joined him. He circled his arm around my waist and raised a hand to wave to his people. I put a delicate hand up in the proper wave Doctor Bartholomew had taught me and they went even crazier.

Through the noise, I was gradually able to make out phrases the people nearest to us were saying. "Long Live King Francis and Queen Miriam!" "It's time for new blood!" "Now is the time!" "Miriam, we love you!" "Miriam, you're beautiful!" "The Rose of Petrichoria is with us!" "Kiss her!" "Kiss her!" "Kiss her!"

Pretty soon, the entire crowd begged for Frank to kiss me and he obliged without warning. He turned me to face him, pulled me close and gave me a long, deep kiss. Goosebumps trailed my arms and a chill ran down my spine. For the first time since I had been there, true fear wrapped itself around my soul. Perhaps this was something that could not be fought after all. Perhaps I was doomed to live my life as King Francis' Queen.

He slowly separated from me and gazed into my eyes with fierce love and excitement for the coming invasion. I tried my best to offer a timid smile, which he bought and gave me the stupid grin I had become accustomed to seeing.

Pulling me back into a straight posture, he circled his arm around my waist again and I turned back to the crowd. This time when he raised his arm, he didn't wave, but signaled for silence, which fell unnaturally fast. The faces of the men and women before me were still beaming and they were entranced by the charisma he exuded.

This was a Frank I had never seen before. Sure, he was a very professional Guard and had even fooled me into accepting him as a loyal and subservient Guard, but the Frank I had seen over the last few weeks had been bumbling and emotion-ruled.

The Frank next to me now stood straighter. His shoulders were more squared. His head lifted higher. One arm held me strongly and close to him while the other set his hand firmly on the steel railing before us. He looked his part in his posture and stature; he looked nearly regal.

When the army had stopped their cheers and claps, there was a long, deafening silence that followed. All I could do was stare at Frank as he scanned the people and deliberately made eye contact with many of them. I glanced out at the crowd with the corner of my eye and it was clear they read my stare as a look of admiration. Good.

Finally, King Francis II spoke.

"People of Arboria!" His voice echoed through the room; he had no need of any amplifying device. "Today, the Rose of Petrichoria has joined us and has agreed to become my Queen!"

"Our King Declares The Truth!"

The crowd's shout in unison was enormous and an obvious sign that none of these people would be joining me to defeat the mission of King Francis II; they were all *his* to command. I really was there to just look pretty; I was his trophy Queen.

"Today, we journey to the outskirts of Petrichoria! Today, we will prepare to fight! Prepare to conquer! Prepare to protect our people from one who would come into *our* kingdom to wed *our* Princess and become *our* King! Today, we prepare for victory!"

"Our King Declares The Truth!"

A pregnant pause hung in the air.

"Tomorrow, we will march the streets of Petrichoria to the gates of Evergreen Palace! Tomorrow, we will speak for those in our movement unable to come with us! Tomorrow we will fight for them

236

if need be! Tomorrow, we will overthrow King Aaron and Queen Amoura! Tomorrow, we will bring back honor and dignity to the Crown of Arboria!"

"The King Declares The Truth!"

Good God. "We will speak for those in our movement unable to come with us"? There are more followers besides what I see here?

"Men and women of Arboria, march to your ships! We make our way to victory *now*!"

"The King Declares The Truth!"

After the last shout from the crowd, I redirected my attention back to the army. The only sound in the room was the synchronous clanks of boots on concrete as the army marched toward the large doors leading to the docks. Rain poured at a slant because of the stormy winds, and waves crashed against the sides of the boats.

I didn't move; I didn't dare. This changed everything for me. The arrogance and confidence I felt in my deceit melted away to hopelessness. There was no longer any bravery to mock King Francis in my mind. Or to even call him "Frank" anymore; it no longer fit.

I looked back to him and he was still in the stature of leadership, head high. Watching his army march to his orders. Relishing their undying commitment to bring his justice to reality. Confident that there would be victory tomorrow.

Finally, he turned his head to look at me. Sparks were in his eyes, igniting a fire in his soul that could not be squelched by any means. He was different. He was determined. He was undaunted by the task that lay before him.

His gaze pierced mine and I felt the power he attempted to show me. It was a power I could not defeat alone and it was one I doubted

237

could be defeated unannounced. If my family stood a chance against him, they would need to be warned. I had to find a way to warn them he was coming to their doorstep with an army; that Frank was coming.

No. He wasn't Frank, Royal Arborian Guard of Princess Miriam, anymore. He was King Francis II, conqueror of Arboria.

Chapter 25

Frank let go of my waist to take my hand. I gave him a small smile, but he didn't smile back; he gave my hand a light squeeze of acknowledgement, then led me out the door towards the elevator. As we walked, he kept his regal posture and I tried to seem demure and not frightened.

By the time we arrived on the first floor, everyone had already made it to their assigned boats. We briskly made our way across the massive, empty room to the storm outside. As we stepped out, he brought his arm over my shoulder and held me tight. Because the wind was strong, I was actually grateful for his arm steadying me as we walked all the way to the end of the dock to the large ship that would lead the fleet to shore.

The boats along the docks were in no way military vessels, though I was sure that was the point. That many fishing vessels wouldn't be as big a red flag as a fleet of battleships on anyone's radar.

Frank stepped on board our ship first, then took my hand to guide me from the dock to the deck. There were three floors on the boat. There was the one we were on, then one above and one below us. Though I had no idea where we were going or what was going on, I followed Frank without question about wherever he was taking me. This was definitely not the time to ask the questions running through my mind.

Finally, we came to a door at the end of the long hall. Frank shuffled through his pockets, brought out an old-fashioned key – the first I had seen since waking up from my false life – and unlocked the door. It opened out and he held the door for me as I went in first.

For a ship's quarters, it was pretty big. There was plenty of walking space, a small bed on one side, and a sitting window with a cushion on the other. Everything was colored with dark blues and light greens and the woods were all light. Across from the door stood a small desk and chair with a portrait of me hanging over it. On the wall beside the door, there was a rack with four hooks on it.

Frank immediately went to it and hung his beret and coat on it. He then walked over to me, unzipped my green leather jacket and took it off to hang next to his. I hadn't really stopped having an expression of shock since we had gotten on the elevator again. Blinking a few times to rest my face, I walked over to the window and sat down cross-legged on the cushion.

I sat there in silence, staring out the window, for a few minutes before I heard Frank clear his throat. I looked back at him; he stood with his arms crossed and a smug grin on his face. I smiled back at him softly.

"Well, love, what do you think?" he asked me.

I took a deep breath. "It's all so much."

"What is?" He came over and sat on the opposite side of the cushion from me, leaning against the wall with one knee bent up and the other draped over the side.

I bent my elbows on my ankles and placed my chin on my interlocking fingers. "The uniforms. The ships. The people. And the knowledge that there are more following you that aren't even here."

"Hmm." He looked out of the window at the storm and there were another few moments of silence between us.

I shifted my head so my cheek was on my hands. "Does anyone actually call you 'Frank?'"

He laughed a little. "No. Actually not. I tend to go by Francis among family and friends. I enlisted under the name 'Frank' because I didn't think I would last long among other men with a name like 'Francis'."

I let out a breathy laugh. "Why didn't you have me start calling you 'Francis' when you brought me here?"

"I like that you call me 'Frank,' Miriam. It's something different – for us."

"Hmm." I smiled. "So, your people clearly call you 'Francis,' then, too?"

"No – They call me 'Sir,' 'King Francis,' or 'Your Majesty'."

I leaned back against my wall and hugged my knees against my chest. Looking down, I said. "Darling, do you remember this morning, when you said I deserve your honesty?" I looked back up at him.

One of his eyebrows raised. "Of course."

I sighed and slightly shook my head. "I don't feel like I have the full truth about what is going on here. I'm missing something and I'd like to know what it is."

"How do you mean?"

241

"When I first got here, you told me that you were fighting for equality. Now, I'm hearing you want to be King and your people even refer to you as such already. I can't see how those things jive."

"Jive?"

"Ugh!"

He widened his eyes.

Another word to add to my list.

"Sorry. It's an old word that I used sometimes in my false life. When I say 'jive,' I mean two things that work together – that complement each other. Like you and me." I smiled and his eyes went back to normal as he smiled back. "Equality and the aristocracy you are building don't complement each other. So, please. Enlighten me. Tell me the whole story."

"You're very observant, Miriam."

"Thank you."

He crossed his legs, sighed, and folded his hands. "Alright. You're right and I'm sorry that I tried to deceive you. It was wrong. I should have trusted you with the truth after you told me the truth about your feelings."

I nodded, but didn't say anything.

"This isn't totally about equality. It *did* start that way, in a sense, but it isn't anymore." He paused. "When you went into your freeze, you remained the same; you stayed young and beautiful – and unmarried. There were new Nobility who were all young and married. No one knew how long you would sleep.

"I held out hope for you and Peter, believe it or not. I remembered you saying that it was never an option for you to fall in love and the story of Peter and your romance spread like wildfire while you were asleep. After a few years, though, the people became restless and nervous at Peter's age and that he had no heirs. So, the last of the eligible Arborian Nobility married."

"Peter and Ella," I drawled.

"Yes. Peter and Ella. Personally, that was when I began hating him. How could he give up on you like that? When he became engaged, your people began discussing what would become of the Crown. Unless you stayed under for another fifteen years, there would be no one among the aristocracy eligible to marry you and become King.

"After a couple months, King Aaron announced that should you awaken before there were men of marrying age among the Nobility of Arboria, the King's Test would be taken among Princes of other nations. Admittedly, most people were alright with this arrangement; some even rejoiced that there would be a merging of kingdoms. However, others, about a quarter of the population, were not comfortable with a foreigner taking the Crown – or with the fact that you had *no* say in the matter.

"As far as we were concerned, it's bad enough you don't get a say once the King's Test begins, you should have at least had a say about its participants."

"Wait – what? What do you mean I have no choice once the King's Test begins?"

Frank blanched. "No one told you?! I figured with the Introduction Event taking place you had been told."

"Told what, Frank?" I was on the verge of panic with wide eyes and a shrill voice. Frank shifted me so my legs were over the side of the window seat, pulled me to him and kissed the top of my head.

"I'm so sorry. I would have told you if I had known... Ultimately, King and Queen get the final say, regardless of how the heir feels, once there are only two participants left."

It was my turn to blanch. "What you're saying is that I never would have been able to marry for love?"

"It would have been unlikely." He reached down and lifted my legs up and wrapped me in a tight embrace.

Outraged, but trying to keep my calm, I said with and intense quiet, "And you think what you're doing is for equality? You removed more choice than I originally had before this movement."

He turned my head so I looked at him and matched my tone. "No, not equality. Nationality. As I said, some people were opposed to the idea of some *foreigner* ruling next to our beloved Princess Rose. Multiple petitions were sent in to our Delegates to demonstrate the number of people against the idea; there were protests and rallies at the Noble houses. There were even those presenting the idea of still having the King's Test, but with one eligible man per province. Still, the Province Delegates and your parents would hear nothing of it."

I breathed heavily now, feeling lightheaded from the revelation. I placed my face in my hands and began to weep and Frank put his cheek on my head.

Freedom has never been mine. I just didn't know it. I am doomed to marry either without being truly loved by a Prince or being this mad man's obsession.

A loud knocking came from the door and Frank gently released me so he could go answer it. I didn't look up; I just continued to silently weep out my helplessness into my palms.

"Your Majesty, I am sorry to disturb you and our Queen, but we will be docking within the next ten minutes."

"I see. We will join you above in a few minutes. Please return to your station, soldier." Frank responded with authority.

The door closed and I was at last able to lift my face from my hands. Frank was already on his knees on the floor in front of me so that we were at eye level with each other. He used both of his hands to wipe the tears from my face.

"Miriam, I'm sorry the decision was made for you, but I am *glad* that neither one of us is going to have to marry without love. It was destiny for us to come together for such a time as this. We will rule this kingdom with order and live our lives with love."

I nodded slowly, though my heart was heavy. Despite the fact the choice of my future husband was narrowed down to ten men I knew nothing about, I knew I had to choose that route rather than let Frank take the Crown. He had shown himself to be unpredictable and that could not be a characteristic in the King of my kingdom.

It had also occurred to me that had Peter just been patient, none of this would have happened. Though I knew it was unfair of me to blame him for everything, it gave me yet another good reason to distance myself from him when all of this was over.

"Now, my beloved, are you ready to join me as our army begins our journey home?" Frank asked me.

"Will it be a lot of walking?"

He chuckled and took my hands as he stood up. "It would be if we were walking."

My eyes widened. "Please don't tell me we're riding horses!" I was terrified of the beasts.

245

He laughed heartily at that.

So glad my fear can entertain you, my dear.

"Miriam, did no one use vehicular transportation back in your day?" He smirked and I couldn't help but smile and blush from embarrassment.

"We'll be taking hovers and driving through the forests to keep cover from the satellites. We'll be sitting the whole time." He finally explained.

"Oh. Good. Is it very far?"

"A few hours. We won't be going all the way into the city tonight. We'll camp out a few miles south of Petrichoria and go in tomorrow morning."

He pulled me to my feet and helped me into my jacket, then put on his coat and beret. I accepted the elbow he offered.

Frank softly smiled at me as we headed back to the upper level and said. "Let's go take what is rightfully ours, Miriam."

Part IV

Chapter 26

It is dark and stormy like the sea had been earlier. I walk alone through a cemetery, not knowing what, or rather who, I am looking for, but it feels important.

My long grey dress trails behind me as I make my way barefoot down the path. I jump to the left, when I see lightning strike on the hill to my right. The thunder roars ominously, then the strong winds start blowing in that direction, whipping my soaked hair in my face as it does.

"Miriam."

I hear my name and look around for the source, but find none.

"Miriam."

It is the wind. My name carries through it like a tangible thing and I feel beckoned to follow.

"Miriam."

Afraid, but unable to resist the urge to climb the hill, I abandon the path and feel the wet grass between my toes.

When I reach the foot of the hill, lightning strikes again with thunder roaring in sync with the flash. In the light, I see a shadow standing between the tombstones.

"Miriam."

My heart beats fast and unsteady. I freeze and stare. In the darkness, I can still see him, his hand outstretched as he calls me to him as a whisper in the wind.

"Miriam. Come. See."

He bends his fingers in a manner to indicate his desire for me to come closer.

"Who are you?" I shout past the wind.

"Miriam. Come. See."

I gulp. Curiosity overwhelms me and I continue toward the strange man. There is no part of me dry and I can feel rivulets running down my face. I blink to try to get the rain out of my eyes in vain.

"Miriam."

I am finally standing in front of the graves and him. Though he is directly in front of me, all I can see is his undefined form.

"What do you want?" I cry with my hoarse voice.

"See."

His voice is never above a whisper. I shake my head, then understanding comes to me. He wants me to look at the graves.

I sink to my knees and wipe my eyes with my wet sleeve.

"See."

"Alright. I'm trying."

I lean forward, but it is meaningless. I can see nothing in the dark.

"It's too dark," I mutter to myself.

Just as I say it, lightning strikes again, this time striking the silhouette of the man. The thunder is deafening and I squint to use the light to see the graves.

"No." I say.

The graves are for Elleouise of Maple, loving mother and wife; and for Thomas of Maple, sweet son.

No dates are engraved. There are only names.

"NO!"

"Miriam. Miriam. Wake up!"

"No, no, no," I heard myself whimpering and slowly opened my eyes.

"Miriam, are you alright? You were screaming." It was Frank hovering over me and patting my sweat-soaked face.

"Huh?" I dumbly responded.

"Were you having a nightmare?"

"Yeah – Yes. I think I was," I said, blinking my eyes quickly to wake up.

There was no thinking about it. It was definitely a nightmare. However, lately, a sinking feeling started coming to me about these dreams and my false life. They were *so* real when I had them; it was like I was really there. I could use all my senses. I could feel everything like I was there.

I could still feel the rain and hear the deafening thunder from only a few moments ago. I could remember everything from the past dreams I had like this, but could not remember anything from nights of sleep without them.

How did I recognize Frank or Doctor Quincy or any number of the other people I had never met when I woke up? How did I know Frank was up to no good without having any clue who he was?

Are these dreams actually some kind of visions? No. That's ridiculous.

Or was it? Was John Quincy suspect since he was a villain at the end of my false life? Were Ella and her son in danger? Who was that man showing me their graves?

"Miriam?"

I realized I was dazed, gazing out the window of the hover we were in.

"Yes, I think I'm alright. Just a horrible dream," I said, still slightly distracted.

"Do you want to talk about it?"

"No, not really."

Frank sat back into his seat and pulled me up to his side, wrapping an arm around my shoulders and pressing my head to his chest with his hand. I was so disturbed by my thoughts, I didn't even mind when he began soothingly running his fingers through my hair. It wasn't like I could fight it anyway.

It does no good to focus on this now. I need to figure out a plan to warn my family about this invasion. I'll see if I can get a message to Peter to tell him to keep an extra eye open for Ella and Thomas.

"Are we nearly there, darling?" I asked.

"Yes. Nearly. We've let the other hovers go ahead to their locations. Some of the soldiers assigned to our location are getting our tent set up so it will be ready when we arrive."

I whispered, "Hmm. Good." I snuggled into him. It was becoming easier to act this part. I got through everything by continuing the charade in my mind that I was just an actress and he was an actor and we were playing our parts for a film.

Though, my instincts were smarter than that. I couldn't help but feel the occasional tremor in my hand or shiver down my spine. The most common instinctual reaction was the trail of goosebumps up my arm. Even then, as he stroked my hair, my neck stiffened just slightly.

After a few minutes, Frank tapped my arm to let me know we were arriving. Looking out the window, I saw a multitude of brown and green tents. People were starting fires, cleaning their weapons, and talking in small groups. As we passed by, the men and women would stop what they were doing and salute or wave. Even though I knew they couldn't see me through the tinted windows, I smiled and waved back to them; it made Frank happy.

I can't wait until I no longer have to concern myself with his happiness and will only need to determine his sentence for treason.

Now knowing the full explanation of the movement, I felt a bit torn about the people in this army. I understood their concern about Arboria having a foreign ruler, but this protest had crossed the line. I was a little disappointed that my parents couldn't see reason and negotiate with these people. Would it really have been so bad to allow some men from our own kingdom to participate in the King's Test even though they didn't come from Noble families?

No. I wasn't torn. No matter how upset they were, this was going too far – and both sides of the conflict were behaving selfishly.

255

Not only were they unyielding for each other, but the whole thing was a giant argument about who *I* was going to marry. If anyone should have a say in how this King's Test was run, it should be *me*. Just because something is traditionally done a certain way, it doesn't mean it should continue being done that way.

However, that was neither here nor there. It was clear that *someone* was going to have to make a sacrifice at some point and I had an idea for a peaceful solution to this problem. The answer hinged on whether or not I could find a way to contact the palace; I had a plan for that, too.

Finally, we pulled up to the tent. When I placed my hand on the door handle to leave the car, Frank reached over and put his hand on top of mine to stop me.

I turned to look back at him and he smiled. "Let the driver get the door, my Queen."

Begrudgingly, I withdrew my hand and waited. When the door was finally opened, it was on Frank's side. He stepped out first and I heard the thunk of boots slamming together to stand at attention. Slightly, he ducked under the doorway and offered me his hand. I delicately placed mine in his and he helped me out of the hover. As I stepped out, the soldiers brought their arms up in a salute. Not knowing what the proper protocol was for the moment, I looked at Frank.

"At ease," Frank said, guiding me toward the tent. The men and women dropped their hands behind their backs and spread their legs shoulder-width apart. I gave each person a smiling nod as we made our way and they smirked back at me.

Regardless of all this insanity, these are still my people. They've just been misguided by a psychopath.

Pulling the door-flap back, Frank let me in first. To my left, there was a closet rack on wheels with a spare men's uniform and an identical outfit to the one I was wearing. There was a soft rug in the middle of the floor to prevent the sticks and rocks of the ground from digging into one's feet. At the back of the tent, there was a small table with two chairs. On my right, I saw a double bed. My heart stopped and I felt my face pale.

Tree blossoms. He's expecting me to share a room with him tonight. He said "our tent" before and I didn't even hear it because of my stupor.

"Are you going to let me in, too, Miriam?" Frank's chin rested on my shoulder as he spoke into my ear.

You can do this. Just stick with the plan.

I giggled. "Oh, of course. I'm just a bit weary from the long day. Sorry." I went the rest of the way in.

"No need to apologize, love." He followed me in and zipped the door shut.

"Um." I cleared my throat. "Is this my tent?"

Frank came up behind me, wrapped his arms around my waist, and put his chin back on my shoulder. "Yes. And mine."

I looked and gestured to the bed. "There's only one bed."

"My observant Miriam." He turned his head and breathed in before placing a kiss on my bare neck and moving his hands to my hips.

I stepped forward out of his arms and turned to sit on the edge of the table. Folding my arms over my chest, I tilted my head and looked at him.

"What?" He did the stupid grin, knowing *exactly* what I was thinking and stepped forward.

"You know what. I think I've been pretty understanding today, but I have to put my foot down somewhere."

He chuckled and stepped closer until he was right in front of me again. Pulling me against him by the small of my back, he pouted, "Come on, Miriam." He bent his head so he could place some rolling kisses under my ear.

"You couldn't even look at me covered with a blanket this morning and now you're ready to – *this*?" I asked gesturing at the bed with disgust.

He smiled and nibbled my ear lobe and I gulped.

Can't make this sacrifice. I won't do it.

I looked away. "No. I won't budge on this, Frank. I will share the tent, if you wish, but we won't be having sex until after the wedding."

He lifted his head and raised a brow. "Are you a – "

"How am I supposed to know? I have no memory, remember?" I snapped and interrupted his uncomfortable question. I gentled my voice, gazed into his eyes and cupped his face in my hands. "I love you, Frank, but I'm not going to sleep with you until after we're married. I've gone with everything else. Can you please just – honor me with this?"

The smirk left his face and for a moment, I was afraid I was going to be slapped again; the bruise on my face was still green from the last one. But, he didn't slap me. He kept his eyes on mine and nodded.

"Let's compromise on this, alright?"

"There isn't much negotiation room here, darling."

He chuckled. "I don't think you'll find this disagreeable."

"Alright," I drawled. "Go on."

"We won't *sleep* together, but we'll sleep together tonight. Just sleep. I swear I won't try anything."

I thought on it. As crazy as he had been over the last few weeks, since confessing my love, he seemed to have become more open to my concerns.

He won't try anything. If he does, I don't care what he thinks; He'll get an elbow in the gut and I'll run away.

"Alright. I think that's agreeable."

"Good." Frank kissed my forehead and separated from me. "Now, why don't you go ahead and lay down for a rest. We have quite a long day tomorrow. I need to head down to meet with our commanders about tomorrow's march."

This is my chance.

I wrapped my arms around his waist and he did likewise. "Oh, I don't think I'm ready to go to sleep quite yet. My back is actually pretty sore from all that riding today. I was thinking about taking a short walk in the trees. I need a little time to myself to digest everything I've learned today, too."

"Hmm." Frank considered. "I don't know, Miriam. It's already dark out. Maybe you should bring a guard with you or, if you can wait a couple of hours, I'll go out with you. I promise to stay quiet while you – digest."

I sighed and looked straight ahead at his chest. "I just know this is going to be the last time for a while I can get some peace and quiet, you know. I'm finally feeling secure with this life and it's

259

about to be turned upside-down again." I lifted my eyes, eyelashes first, to look back into his.

"Please, Frank. I'll only be gone for a little while. I'll be in bed by the time you return."

His gaze softened.

"*Please*, darling."

Nice touch.

He sighed. "Alright, love. But take this with you, just to be safe. I don't know what kinds of animals are out here at this time."

Frank walked over to the small table, reached under, and held out a handgun for me to take.

Taking it with shaky hands, I swallowed, though my mouth was dry. "You really trust me, don't you, Frank?" I looked at him, feeling only slightly guilty for my deceit for the first time.

"Of course I do. I love you." He came back to me and gave me a hug while kissing my forehead. "Be safe, love." Next thing I knew he was gone.

I hope this plan works. I know we're south of Petrichoria, so I just have to find north and walk.

I knew I took a huge risk with what I was about to do. If I wasn't back in time, Frank would freak out. Not because he would think I had betrayed him, but because he would think a bear or coyote or something got me.

When I stepped out of the tent, I took a deep breath and did some quick stretches for my arms and legs. Just before I was about to head into the woods, I heard Frank shouting for me.

When he made it to me, he bent over, putting his weight on his knees with his hands, and huffing.

"Is everything alright, darling? I was just getting ready to go for my walk. You barely caught me in time."

Still panting, Frank said, "Yes. – Everything is – fine. I just – wanted to give you – this light stick. So you don't – have to walk in the dark." He stood up with his stupid grin on his face.

Smiling, I accepted the stick and gave him a quick peck on the cheek. "Thank you. That was very thoughtful. Now, no more worries for me. You just go and solidify the plans, hmm?"

"I will worry about you until I see you laying in the tent upon my return." He returned the cheek-peck, turned around and walked away, inspiring salutes all along his path.

Here we go, feet.

I turned back to face the forest and turned on the light stick. I figured I would keep it on as I entered and turn it off after a time.

Even though, I was on my own personal mission, it was a nice reprieve to get away from people. I hadn't been alone since the moment I woke up from the freeze; I was always with someone or being monitored.

I took in a deep breath of rain-soaked ground and dragged my fingers along the bark of the trees. After a while, I turned off the light stick and examined the stars in the sky to find north. The moon was full and it lit the forest floor enough for me to see where I was going without the light stick anyway.

The amount of sky the trees revealed was not enough for me to determine direction, so I fixed my gaze forward and started walking again. Fifteen minutes into the walk, I stopped again and looked up.

261

As I examined the sky, I felt someone grab my arm and pull me. Instinctively, I bent over and bit the hand holding my arm and it let go. In my last observation of the sky, I was able to determine north, so I ran in that direction.

Running through the forest at full speed, I heard the footsteps of whoever it was that followed me. Based on the heavy sound of the steps, I figured it was a man.

I turned my head back to see how close he was getting and ran straight into the arms of another man. Struggling, I tried to fight my way out of his arms, but soon gave up when I was circled.

The man who was chasing me finally caught up. "Trees, Rose. Why did you have to go and bite me?"

I gasped and the man holding me captive released me. I turned around and couldn't believe my eyes. I wasn't going to have to go any further. The man I bit was Peter. I turned back to the other man and saw it was Father.

I was surrounded by the Royal Arborian Guard.

Chapter 27

"Daddy!" I yelled and threw my arms around him. I didn't care to try to figure out if I still called him that – or ever called him that at all. Immediately, we were weeping and hugging. "How did you find me?"

"We saw the mass number of ships and the hovers they were drifting toward. Once we got a lock on the head hover, all we had to do was trace it."

I squeezed a little tighter, then pulled away and looked at Father in the eyes. "I don't have much time. I have to go back."

"What? Are you insane?" Peter asked.

"No. Frank is." I replied, turning to face him. "And I was coming to warn you that he and an army of a thousand men and women, give or take, are going to march the streets of Petrichoria and attempt to take the Crown."

"What?!" Peter yelled. "Who the rotting roots is *Frank*?!"

I frowned at him and hissed, "Peter, shut up! We are not far from the camp and there are not enough people with you to win a fight with them right now." Peter snapped his mouth shut.

I turned back to Father. "In a nutshell, this is a group of people who are outraged at the fact there are only foreigners participating in the King's Test. Frank told me they requested it be only men of our kingdom, even though they are not Nobility, and they were refused numerous times. Frank joined the Royal Arborian Guard and weaseled his way into the position of protection for me so he could kidnap me and convince me to marry him."

"That's insanity," Father said simply.

"Yes, it is. Listen, Father. I don't know the story from your side, but there isn't the time to go back and forth. I don't know by what means they intend to remove the Crown from you and Mother, but I am certain they will succeed. There are more people aside from Frank's army in the kingdom sympathetic to their cause."

Father looked to the sky. "Sweet tree blossoms."

"I have an idea. It would involve compromise on both sides."

"Have you spoken to Frank of it?"

"No. Life has been much easier for me since I have been pretending to be in love with him. I can't go against him; not yet. He's volatile."

"What?!" A chorus of three men yelled. I looked over and glared at Peter, Prince Phineas, and Prince Harrison – it was only then I realized the Princes were there.

I snapped my fingers and pointed at the trio. "Listen. I'm glad you all came for me. Truly. I'm moved. But if you don't shut your mouths, I will personally shove pinecones in each of yours. Understood?"

All three nodded in compliance with wide eyes.

"What is your idea, sweetheart?" Father said quietly – probably also not wanting a pinecone in his mouth.

"The King's Test should have both Arborians and foreign Princes as participants."

"There aren't any more Noble Arborians, Rose."

"I understand that, Father."

"You're suggesting I give in to their demands?"

"No, Sir. I'm suggesting that both you and he compromise. You both get what you want in this. If it sells it, I would even allow for Frank to participate, though I would never choose him in a million years – not that *I* get a choice."

Father blushed. "Rose, I was going to tell you – "

"I don't want to hear it right now.

"If I may, Your Majesty." The Britannian voice that came from my right was familiar; it was Prince Phineas. "For what it's worth, if it would prevent civil war among your people, I would not fight such an agreement and I'm sure I could convince the other Princes to go along with it as well."

Prince Harrison piped in, "We both could. I would have no issue with it, though if you allow that Frank guy to participate, I might need to straighten him out as far as his unwarranted affections towards our Princess here."

I looked at them both and said graciously, "Thank you, Prince Phineas and Prince Harrison." They both had just a moment of shock, probably that I remembered their names after only one meeting, but then recovered. I was pleasantly surprised by their very different statements of support.

"Of course, Princess Miriam," Prince Phineas said. Prince Harrison just gave me a stupid, but loveable, grin.

Father stroked his bearded chin in thought. "I shall have to call an emergency meeting of the Council to vote on this."

I rolled my eyes. "Then get on it quickly." I looked at the stars. "I have to get back or Frank will suspect something. I love you, Father. I will see you tomorrow. Please, get you and the Guard back to Evergreen Palace. It is not safe for all of you out here."

We embraced, then he signaled for his Guard to follow. Prince Harrison approached me, gave me a bow and said as he rose, "Princess Miriam, I haven't been able to stop thinking that if I hadn't let you leave with that Guard two months ago, none of this would have happened."

Two months?! I didn't realize how long I was unconscious during my captivity.

I furrowed my brow and looked him in the eyes. "Prince Harrison, none of this is your fault. This is the fault of a mad man who convinced a lot of people to commit treason. You had no way of knowing that Frank was going to kidnap me."

Prince Harrison shook his head and looked down. "Even so, hearing that you forgive me would set my mind at ease. I would hate for this to make a negative impression of my kingdom and myself before the King's Test even begins."

I nodded and, as platonically as possible, tilted his head back up slightly to face me. Smiling, I said, "Very well. I forgive you. I would also add that you have made a very *positive* impression on me. You didn't only rescue me from – " I tilted my head toward Peter, who was talking with Prince Phineas, and Prince Harrison smiled back – "at the ball. I looked around tonight and made note that you were among the only two of ten Princes who ventured out here to find me. Thank you."

"I've been praying for your safety, Princess, and will continue to do so until you return to your home." He lifted my hand and kissed my knuckles.

"Thank you, Prince Harrison. I hope to see you soon."

As Prince Harrison walked away, Prince Phineas approached. When he took my hands, I thought he was going to kiss one, like Prince Harrison did, but instead, he pulled me in for a hug. "We have all been so very worried for you, Princess. I am glad to see that you are well. Stay that way." He separated from me, bowed, and walked away leaving me dumbstruck.

After Prince Phineas followed Father and the rest of the Guard, and made it several yards away, Peter approached me. I turned away quickly. "Not now, Peter. I can't handle anything from you at the moment."

"I've been worried out of my head for you, Miriam."

I turned back to him. "I understand. I have been, too. But we can't do this, especially not now." I looked down and bit the corner of my bottom lip. "Listen, Peter. I know this is going to sound crazy, but I think I had a vision today while I slept in the hover on the way to the camp. I think Ella and Thomas may be in mortal danger." I looked up at him and he paled. "Please, keep them extra safe. Get them out of the city tonight, if you can. I can't lose Ella. Please – please, promise me you'll keep them safe."

He hesitated. "You're right. It *does* sound crazy. But I know you've been through a lot these past couple months and I swear I will keep them safe tomorrow. Alright?"

I nodded. "Yes. Now, please, go. You need to be safe, too."

He grinned. "I *knew* you cared."

"Shut up. Go away."

Before he could say any other idiotic thing I turned around and began my walk back to camp. I couldn't be certain of how much time had passed, but I knew it was somewhere near an hour. When I could no longer hear the retreating footsteps behind me, I turned my light stick back on.

Unbelievable. Peter is absolutely unbelievable. I can't believe he was going to start something out here when everyone is in danger. It's his own stupid fault we can't be together and I'm stuck with King Francis II *right now.*

Taking deep breaths of the musty forest air, I worked toward a normal breathing pattern and heart rate. Sincerely, I hadn't been ready for sleep earlier when I told Frank that. Now, however, I definitely was. Though I knew I had to have one more chat with Frank before I was out for the night, I was greatly looking forward to the bed. I only hoped Frank would keep his word and not try anything on me.

I really hope this plan works. If not, then I'll have to come up with a different way to stop Frank.

I knew love would most likely not be in the equation when it came to my future marriage. However, I felt that sacrifice was worth it. If Father *did* end up choosing someone from another kingdom for my husband, we would have to figure something else out to keep the people opposed to the idea happy. This way, though, at least the men of Arboria would be getting a chance.

Ahead of me, I caught sight of another light stick moving towards me. As it got closer, I was able to see Frank's face lit up with it. I smiled at him and walked briskly to close the gap.

"Is it very late?" I asked. "It didn't feel like I was gone too long."

"No. It's only been around an hour. We just took a break and I thought I would walk out here to find you and escort you back." He smiled and shut off his light stick. Taking my hand, he instinctively interlocked his fingers in mine and we began the trek back to camp.

"Do you know what I learned about this night in this forest since I've been out here?" I asked him.

He quirked an eyebrow at me. "No. What did you learn?"

I shut my light stick off, let go of his hand, and planted myself on the ground. He looked at me like I had two heads.

Pointing at the wide gap in the trees above me, I said. "It's a full moon tonight and the stars are bright as well. I haven't really needed to use the light stick most of the time I've been out here." I folded my hands behind my head and lay down.

Frank laughed. "Miriam, you're lying in mud."

"It's not soaking mud, Frank. Just damp dirt. Plus, I saw a change of clothes for both of us in the tent." I patted the earth next to me. "Come now, look at the sky with me."

Still laughing, and actually rolling his eyes at me, he lowered himself to the ground and mimicked my position. I scooted closer to him and he wrapped his arm around me.

"Well?" I asked. "Isn't it beautiful?"

"Yes. You were right. The sky is lovely. Now let's get back to camp."

"Breathe, Frank. Tomorrow will bring a whole new level of stress to both our lives. Let's just relax with nature for a few moments."

He sighed, slightly frustrated, but nevertheless relenting to my wish.

"Are you scared, darling?" I asked. "I'm a little scared."

"I would have to be crazy *not* to be scared, love."

I let there be a short pause, biting back the insult on the tip of my tongue. "Would you be open to an idea I have? I think it may be a good compromise and it would prevent certain civil war."

"I'm open to anything you have to suggest – even laying in mud and looking at the sky."

I laughed, then let another pregnant pause occur. Propping myself up with an elbow and looking at him, I asked, "Would you like to hear it now or wait until you come back to the tent after your meetings are over?"

He glanced at me, then looked back to the stars. "To be honest, Miriam, I would like to wait until after my meetings. I won't have as much on my mind and I'll be able to give you my full attention."

I kissed him on the cheek. "Alright. Let's go back. I know you're eager to return."

I sat up first, but he jumped to his feet and helped me up the rest of the way. He interlocked our fingers again and I leaned my head against his arm. We walked the rest of the way like that, in silence.

Frank was a dolt, yes, and definitely out of his mind, but he had treated me well for most of the time I had been in his care – with the exception of him pushing me and knocking me unconscious at the beginning, keeping me prisoner and touching me when I didn't want him to, and the slap in my face only yesterday – Alright, maybe he *hadn't* been the most gracious host. Nevertheless, the churning of guilt in my stomach made me sick; there was no reason to feel guilty for my deceit. I was doing what I needed to survive and for the good of my people.

When we made it to the tent, he opened the door-flap and let me in. Before zipping it closed, Frank gave me a peck on the cheek and said, "I shouldn't be gone much longer. Go ahead and try to get some sleep. I'll wake you when I get back so you can talk to me. I promise. Alright, love?"

"Alright. I'll do that."

As I walked in, he zipped the door shut and I heard his retreating footsteps. Looking at the bed, I saw the plain brown dress I was familiar with folded on the bed next to some folded workout pants and t-shirt. Wishing there was some way for me to shower, I shrugged out of my clothing and changed into the dress.

I was grateful that it had long sleeves. It was very cold, which made sense now that I knew I had been gone for a couple months; that meant we were well into autumn now. The only article of clothing there was no change for was the green leather jacket. I unzipped the tent to brush off the dirt from laying in the mud and the guard outside bowed.

I nodded in acknowledgement so he could stand. I was so tired, I didn't feel up to a discussion about how much such gestures made me uncomfortable. Besides, I supposed I needed to get used to it, seeing as though someday, I wouldn't only be Princess, I would be Queen. In fact, *these* people already viewed me as their Queen.

I began to beat the back of the jacket with my hand.

"Your Majesty, I would be happy to do that for you," the guard offered.

I smiled at him. "Thank you for your kind offer, but I can do it. You just keep doing what you're doing."

I bent back over and beat the jacket some more.

"May I be frank with you, Your Majesty?"

"No. He's over in the planning tent."

He chuckled at my lame joke, probably out of courtesy.

"But, seriously. Yes, you may speak freely."

I stood straight and held the jacket with both hands in front of me so he could look me in the eye. I was done with it anyway.

"I wish there wasn't this divide within our kingdom. I fear that if we overthrow the King and Queen, civil war will break out."

I nodded. "Yes, I have that concern, as well."

"Do you have plans for maintaining peace when you and King Francis begin your rule?"

"I have some ideas. Really, though, the future cannot be planned until after tomorrow. The results of the invasion will directly affect our plans."

He nodded, then returned to attention. "Thank you for your time, Queen Miriam."

"You're very welcome. I'm going to turn off the light stick in here and try to get some rest. Please don't let anyone disturb me. Only King Francis may enter for the rest of the evening."

"Yes, Ma'am."

With that, I went back into the tent, zipped it closed again, and did exactly what I told the guard I was going to do. Even with the light stick out, there was still enough light to make my way around because of the fire still burning at the center of the campsite.

I took the knot out of my hair and brushed the braid out with my fingers. As I pulled myself onto the bed and under the blankets, I groaned with the instant relief on my muscles. Truly, my backside was sore from the sitting and my legs were now tense after the exertion of my miniature expedition.

I curled up facing the wall of the tent and let my thoughts finally run. For the moment, I was alone without anyone or anything to fear.

Really, I had no intention of falling asleep, but it just happened.

Chapter 28

I sit in a rocking chair in the blue nursery we have prepared for our baby boy, clutching the small bear that should have been his.

David has gone to work; his grievance leave has ended, so I am home alone.

I curl my legs beneath me and weep, letting the tears soak the bear's head.

When I finally stop, I take a few deep breaths and sing; singing always helps me feel better. I wrote a song in 3/3 when I lost my first baby and now seemed a good time to sing it again. Rocking the chair in time, I sing:

> *Why so downcast, my soul?*
> *Why so disturbed within me?*
> *I am not alone*
> *Though the storm rages on*
>
>
> *Oh I...I've tried so hard*
> *Oh I...can't do this on my own*

You
You are my Petrichor
My Beauty within the rain

I look up to the clouds
Grey is all I see
Does the sun still exist?
Is there light at the end of this?

Oh I...I've tried so hard
Oh I...can't do this on my own

You
You are my Petrichor
My Beauty within the rain

The downpour comes
The thunder roars
the lightening blindly flares
I look as You
Come shining through
Upon my rain-stained face

You
You are my Petrichor

I woke up still humming the tune, realizing that the melody was the same as the Rose Waltz. I felt the bed sink behind me and Frank wrapped an arm around me.

"You were humming the Rose Waltz," he whispered into my ear.

"My dream was a memory from my false life; when I lost my second baby. I was in a rocking chair holding the bear I bought for him and crying. The song was something I wrote when I lost my first babe."

I don't know why I shared something so personal with Frank. He had put me in a situation where I could sing the song again with meaning. I felt like the film I was acting in would never end; I would always have to feel the slithery hands of Frank.

He tightened his embrace. "I'm sorry, love. What a horrible dream."

"Yes. A dream."

Despair had been building in me since I was taken and at that moment, I thought there was no way out. All this acting and acquiescence was for naught.

"Is it very late?" I croaked.

He kissed my clothed shoulder. "Yes. Well past midnight. I'm sorry. The planning went longer than I thought it would."

As I turned over to face him, he pulled away. I was glad for it because even though we were sharing a bed, he was a couple feet away, rather than pressing himself against me.

"What made it so long?"

He sighed. "Some of my commanders are having second thoughts about the invasion. We had a long discussion about how there really isn't another choice before we continued with the plans."

"Hmm." *Perfect opening.* "What if there was?"

"Was what? Another way? I would be open to hearing the idea. I don't know what else we could do, though. We've tried all the diplomatic means of negotiations and they didn't work."

I propped myself up on an elbow and placed the side of my face in my palm. "However, when you tried to negotiate before, you didn't have *me*."

Frank slowly mimicked my position and furrowed his brow as he considered this. "This is what you wanted to talk to me about, isn't it?"

"Yes."

He licked his lips and pressed them lightly together. It looked like he was trying to control an outburst of fury, so I gave him a moment to collect himself. I exuded no fear or force; I simply stayed up on my elbow and looked at him calmly.

"I did promise I would listen, didn't I?" He asked in a calm voice, masking his impatience. It was unfortunate for my case that he had already been through people's doubts that night.

I sat up and curled my legs beneath me, facing him. "Yes, you did."

He groaned as he sat up and crossed his legs. "Alright, Miriam. I'm listening." He shot and held a dark gaze straight into my eyes.

I took one of his hands in both of mine, but maintained eye contact. "Darling, I know it's been a long day for you and I'm sorry our people are having doubts. I want to begin by saying I don't doubt your plan. I'm sure it would work."

He nodded and stroked my hand on top of his with his thumb.

"I want to try to negotiate. Before I put out the terms for you, I want you to remember what we were talking about earlier when we were discussing the King's Test. Sometimes, as a ruler, one must set aside one's desires and do what is best for one's kingdom. Do you agree?"

He simply nodded. His dark gaze slowly morphed into one of pain.

"The Royalty and Nobility insist on having only men in some form of aristocracy participating, yes? That's why there are only Princes right now."

"Correct."

"This movement originated because the people wanted only men of Arboria to participate in the King's Test because giving a foreigner the Crown troubled them, right?"

"Right."

I took a deep breath. "My idea involves compromise on both sides and a willingness to accept the future King regardless of nationality or position. Here it is: The ten Princes who have already arrived for the King's Test will still participate, in order to avoid any conflict with another kingdom. There will also be ten men of Arboria participating. Nine of these men will be elected by the people; you will be the unelected one."

Frank had an expression of thoughtfulness and frustration.

"Frank, this would prevent a certain civil war. I'm willing to make the sacrifice for that. It doesn't feel right for people to die for me to marry for love. I want it; I do. But don't you agree? Could you really live with yourself if our people died for our selfishness?"

Frank pursed his lips, stood up, and began pacing the room. "No. I don't think I could. Honestly, I haven't even thought of it like that. But now that you mention it, that's exactly what we're doing here."

I stood up and took his hand to stop his pacing and have him stand still in front of me. He made a pained expression and traced the green fingertip bruises still on my face. "I can't believe I did this. Our time together has been marred by it."

"Forget about it, darling. I have."

He nodded. "You're asking me to sacrifice my love for you; to give other men a chance to take what is already mine."

"Yes, I am. And I'm also suggesting that I sacrifice my right to decide who I marry when I have already done that."

He wrapped his arms around my waist and pulled me to him. I placed my hands on his shoulders.

He let out a deep sigh. "It's the right thing to do. You're right." He chuckled. "For someone who can't remember her training to lead a kingdom, you certainly have wisdom when it comes to negotiations."

I shrugged. "We have yet to see if Father and Mother will accept the terms. I think the most difficult thing to accomplish will be convincing them to allow you to participate when you kidnapped me and planned to overthrow them."

"Yes. There is the risk of them charging me with high treason as well."

"I'll try to get pardons for you and everyone in this movement. Your grievances are understandable and the way they were received by our government is inexcusable."

Frank nodded and gave me a soft kiss. "Let's not wait on this." He turned and walked toward his clean uniform.

"What do you mean?"

"Let us, you and I, go and talk with them now. Let's try to stop a civil war from occurring."

Without warning, facing the wall of the tent, he started to strip out of the sleeping clothes he wore. I quickly turned around so I didn't see anything and waited patiently for him to finish.

I could tell when he turned around because he laughed. "Didn't want to watch?" He joked.

"Very funny, Frank." I muttered.

"Come on. Get changed into your clothes."

I turned around, put my hands on my hips, and looked at him in disbelief. "Not with you watching!"

He held up both hands in surrender. "Okay, okay!"

"Why don't you go see if you can track down a brush or comb for me while I change? I haven't had a chance to do it since before I was on the hospital floor. Then, there won't be any temptations for you."

Laughing, he came over to me and kissed my forehead. "Alright, love. I'll go do that. Be quick." Saying that, he left the tent to go on his mission.

Having a feeling he would be quick, I yanked the dress off and immediately started pulling the clothes on in record time. Just as I was finished pulling on my second boot, Frank burst into the tent with the stupid grin on his face and a hair brush in his hand.

I laughed. "I'm too quick for you, Frank."

He laughed. "I have *no* idea what you mean." He held out the hair brush for me to take.

As I accepted it, I rolled my eyes and shook my head. I sat on the edge of the bed and began brushing. Frank was out of breath from his sprint around the camp, so he threw himself into one of the chairs at the small table and watched me brush my hair.

I glanced over at him and saw his face was no longer full of humor, but solemnity. As I carefully worked out my knots, I asked. "What are you thinking, darling? You seem so sad."

"I'm afraid."

"Don't worry. I won't let them execute you. I'll help you escape before I let that happen."

"I would rather be executed than face the fear I'm having."

I furrowed my brow and stopped brushing for a moment. Setting my hands in my lap, and knowing what he was probably talking about, I questioned, "What could be worse than public execution?"

He walked over and sat next to me. Taking my empty hand, he said, "Losing you would be worse than dying a thousand deaths."

He does *realize no one actually talks like that, right?*

But no, after weeks of listening to him, I knew that his poetic speech was completely natural for him. He never said anything without flourishing it in some way.

I looked at my brush and said, "That may not happen. Maybe you'll be in the running at the end of the King's Test and Father will select you."

"You know that won't happen." He pulled our interlocking fingers to his lips and gazed at me.

I set the brush down, genuinely feeling bad for him. As crazy as he was, he *did* love me, and I knew he was right. No way would Father ever select him even if he *was* still around at the end of the King's Test.

Turning to join in his gaze, I put my palm on his cheek. "Remember, Frank, you're not the only one making a sacrifice here.

There's a fairly good chance I'll be marrying someone who loves my Crown more than he loves me, if he loves me at all."

He nodded and let his head rest in my hand. "Are you sure you want to do this?"

I sighed. "No, but it needs to be done. It's the right thing to do. We'll be saving *so* many lives."

He pursed his lips together and lifted his head. "I imagine that was your line of thought when you refused the assistance of your Guards when Doctor Watson was attacking you."

I let out a breathy laugh. "Probably. We see how well that worked out for me."

After a moment of silence, Frank mused, "It's not fair. That you always do the responsible thing and never get what you want."

"It is what it is. Anyone who ever thought running a kingdom was easy, didn't think it all the way through." I escaped his gaze and looked down. Laughing dryly, I said, "I've now been in love three times and have not been able to pursue it." I had to include Frank in the number for my role.

"Three? Who besides Peter and me?"

An unpremeditated tear began a flow that I couldn't stop. I pulled my hand from his and covered my face. As I wept, Frank pulled me into his shoulder.

When I pulled away, he wiped my face with the edge of his sleeve and waited for my answer.

"David."

He frowned. "Who?"

"My husband from my false life. I loved and lost him twice, essentially. He died with my son, Tom, in an accident. When I learned that he had never really existed, it was like he died all over again."

"You had a son?"

"Mm hmm. And a daughter. I lost everything when I woke up."

"I'm sorry. I guess I've never really thought about that aspect of it. Just because it wasn't real, it doesn't mean it wasn't real for you."

I sniffled and shrugged. "I think it's that way for everyone. I'm not upset about it. How could they understand? Not everyone lives an entire life, only to find out it never happened. On top of that, to lose all my memories from this life – it's all so confusing and I haven't really had a chance to figure things out."

"And now I've brought all this down on you," he said with regret.

I looked at him as I pulled my hair over my shoulder and began braiding it. "Don't fret, Frank. What's done is done and now I must do my duty as the Princess of Arboria. I don't have the luxury of having a lot of personal time. There are things that need to be accomplished."

He smiled. "Even if you don't have specific memories, your mind remembers who you are. The attitude you just displayed is why your people love you so much. You care more for them than yourself."

I knotted the end of my braid. "Let's hope that's true. You never know what's going on when the public isn't watching."

Chapter 29

I braced my hands on my knees and stood up with a stretch. "Let's get going. At least it's not raining right now."

Frank stood and held my hand as we exited. Before we could leave, he had to use his comm, a small band on his wrist, to notify the commanders about the change of plans.

As we headed for the tree line, we were bombarded by the commanders stationed at our camp. They had a million questions that Frank and I took turns answering.

"With all due respect, Your Majesty," a red-haired man said, "your people have been preparing for this day for a long time."

A blonde woman nodded. "I agree, Sir. Besides, we've tried negotiations before and they were fruitless."

Frank furrowed his brow and pinched the bridge of his nose. "I know we went through this earlier and I convinced you toward this way of thinking. However, it didn't occur to me then that we didn't have Queen Miriam with us then," he said using my own rationale. I could tell where the conversation was leading and it wasn't in my favor. Slowly, I began backing away toward the trees.

The woman countered, "It doesn't matter if Queen Miriam is with you, Your Majesty. The second you are seen you will be arrested. Nothing she would say or do could prevent that."

Frank nodded and turned to tell me something, but I was already several feet away.

He turned back to his commanders. "Give us a moment."

Leaning on the nearest tree, my mind machine was whirring at top speed developing a new plan.

Why didn't I have a Plan B?

Frank was too near for me to run without him catching me, so I waited for him to join me. Clearly, I wasn't going to get away without anyone noticing.

"What's going on, Miriam?" He asked when he got to me.

"We *can't* fight today. I won't let those people die for me."

He put his right hand on my shoulder. "My commanders are right, though. These people have spent the last three years preparing. I can't take victory away from them."

"Just because this has been going on for so long, it doesn't make it right."

He put his left hand on my other shoulder. "I think you had better just go back to the tent again and wait for me to finish up here. We march in the morning."

I nodded. "Alright. But let it be known that I am against this decision."

He nodded. "So noted." He turned and walked back to his commanders. When he got to them and they all became enthralled in their conversation, I continued backing up. When I was well into

286

the forest, I turned and began to run as fast as I could, which wasn't very fast at all. My body had become weak from the weeks of starvation and the months of inactivity and I could already see spots in my vision.

When I saw the green light of the Space Needle about a quarter mile away, I laughed.

I'm almost there!

"Miriam! Miriam! Stop!" I heard Frank yelling for me.

I turned my head to look behind me and saw a light stick.

Blossoms! That must be him!

I turned my head facing forward again and tried to pick up my pace. I was so close, but so was Frank. I could hear his footsteps nearing me and there was no way I could go any faster. When I was only a few yards away from the tree line, Frank dropped his light stick, jumped on me and tackled me to the ground.

"Let me go! Let me go!" I screamed.

He brought one hand around front and covered my mouth.

"Stop screaming, Miriam. You'll wake the closest neighborhood." Frank said with a deadly calm voice.

"Hmmph," I tried to say "good" into his hand, but it didn't work out.

He flipped me over onto my back, but continued to put all his weight on me to hold me down. To stop my squirming he pressed his elbow into my sternum. I yelled out under his hand and sobbed in pain and defeat. I finally moaned in surrender and stopped squirming, but he didn't move his elbow.

He leaned close. "What in the name of all that is green and good are you doing?"

I frowned at him and looked down to his hand over my mouth to let him know I couldn't answer.

Frank rolled his eyes. "If I remove my hand do you promise not to scream?"

I sighed and nodded.

Yes. I won't scream and I'll beat your head with the light stick when I regain your trust.

Gradually, he moved his hand off my face and wiped my saliva on his pants. My braid had come out during my run and now my hair was everywhere.

"Trees, I can't see your face," he said as he brushed it off my face with his free hand; his elbow was still on my sternum.

"Would you mind removing your elbow?" I hissed in pain.

"Are you going to squirm?"

I grunted. "I promise not to squirm."

He lifted his elbow and I took a deep breath. Still sitting on me, he said, "You haven't answered my question."

"I don't suppose I can convince you to get off me?"

"Miriam! We do not have time for this! Answer the rotting question!" He was yelling now, but I kept my voice calm.

"I'm scared out of my mind, Frank. I was running to the palace to try the negotiations on my own."

It was actually the truth.

288

Still panting from the run, he looked up to the sky. Dawn was breaking. It was almost time.

Looking back to me, he dropped his hands to either side of my head. "You promise that's what you were going to do?"

I quirked my eyebrow.

Is he going to let me go?

"I swear. I don't want to see a civil war."

He curled his neck forward until the top of his head landed on my chest, though not in a sensual way.

"Alright." He pushed himself up and off me.

"Alright?" I slowly sat up and rubbed my chest where his elbow had been.

He nodded. "Go. Try to make your parents listen. I will lead my army through the city as I planned. I'll meet you and your parents at the gates of Evergreen Palace." He pointed at me. "But know this, Miriam. If they do not listen and accept your compromise, we *will* overthrow them. You *will* be my wife. Understood?"

In shock, I slowly dipped my head to let him know I did. Without any demonstration of affection, he turned and began running back to camp.

Having difficulty comprehending what had just happened, I stared at him until I couldn't see him anymore. I couldn't believe he let me go.

I shook my head to get myself out of confusion and turned back toward the city. No longer being able to run, I simply began walking. I was so tired. As I walked, there was a slight, cold breeze and its music whispered through the trees. Leaves were rustling. Branches were slapping together. There was a quiet whistle in the wind itself.

"Miriam."

I remembered my strange dream and a chill ran up my spine. I hoped Peter had listened to me and got Ella and Thomas out of the city. So many questions were running through my mind.

Who was that man? Was he gloating over the graves or warning me?

But my thoughts went beyond just this most recent dream. My other dreams, including my false life, had real life implications as well.

My first dream of David was in a transforming Kona-to-Northwest-Coast beach and I ended up being trapped on an island. Both times, he assured me everything would be alright and things had begun working themselves out.

These comparisons brought a sense of dread to me. In the ballroom, David told me to not trust everyone in the palace. That meant that there were more people aside from Frank.

"Miriam."

Then there was the most recent dream. It was so dark and dreary – and realistic. I said a quick prayer for my friend and her son.

As the sun rose higher in the sky, people began leaving their homes for work. The further I went, the more people noticed me. By the time I made it to the gates of the palace, I was dragging my feet; I was exhausted.

The gates were closed and locked. It shouldn't have surprised me, but I couldn't take any more disappointments. I leaned my arm against the wall and started crying.

I felt a hand on my shoulder. "Princess Miriam?"

I turned around quickly, feeling startled. There was a Royal Guard behind me. No. Not just *a* Royal Guard; it was Louis.

I threw my arms around his shoulders and my sobbing got worse. Awkwardly, he patted my back.

"I want to go home," I cried. The crowd of people that had formed as I walked through town began to cheer at my arrival, but I couldn't acknowledge them. I needed to be home; I needed to stop a civil war.

Louis nodded. "Of course, Your Highness." I untangled myself from him and he looked grateful for it. Though the hug had made him feel awkward, he *did* let me lean against him as he opened and closed the gates and escorted me into the palace.

"I'm sorry," I muttered as we got to the stairs that led to the main doors.

"There's no need to apologize, Princess. I'm sure you've had a rough couple months."

"I'm so glad you were able to keep your job, but it sucks that you ended up working graveyard duty."

"What is graveyard duty?"

I sighed.

Another phrase to add.

"It just means 'night shift'."

"Oh. I didn't get assigned the night shift." He pushed open the door and began to lead me to the hallway that led to the palace offices.

"Then, what were you doing out there?"

"When King Aaron returned from the search, he called me in to help you when you arrived. He knew you would be grateful to see a familiar face."

"Thank you, Louis."

"You're welcome, Princess."

We walked the rest of the way in silence, for which I was appreciative. It was nice to rest my voice and pretend the world was normal – well, my new normal.

Louis opened the door to Father's office without knocking. I assumed he was told he didn't need to when he brought me to him. I stepped in and was immediately smothered with a tight embrace.

"Oh, Rose! I'm so glad to see you safe!" Mother was cutting off my air supply, her hug was so tight. When she pulled back, she kept her hands on my arms and examined me.

"Sweet Blossoms, Miriam! You're so thin! Did they starve you?"

I shrugged. "No. I starved myself on a hunger strike."

"I want to hear everything." She hugged me again. "I love you so much." She started to pet my hair.

"And I want to tell you everything, but there isn't time for that right now." I separated from Mother, only to be hugged by Father.

"Father, they have probably already started their march. We need to talk things through before they arrive."

He pulled back. "Was Frank not receptive to the idea?"

"He was, but his commanders weren't so keen on the idea. That's why he let me go ahead. He wanted me to discuss the compromise with you. We agreed to meet at the palace gates."

Father took a deep breath. "Well, I called an emergency session of the Council and presented the compromise and our current situation with them."

I waited for him to continue as he massaged both of his temples as if he had a massive headache.

"And?"

"And they all talked about how some of their people had been approaching them about this for a long time, but they never thought it necessary to bring up with me."

"Idiots."

"Now, Miriam."

"I'm so frustrated, Father! This could have been prevented in so many simple ways, but no one thought of them in time. And now, here we are." I huffed. "I'm sorry, Father. Please continue."

"They are open to the idea of including Arborian men of unaristocratic position. In fact, they were completely in favor of your idea and praised you for it."

"Excellent."

"However, there are two other things they requested. I don't think you're going to like them."

I frowned. "What?"

"There was a vote of eleven to nine in favor of pardoning Frank and everyone in his army."

"What?! How could they do such a thing when they have no idea what he has done?"

"They fear that should Frank be executed or imprisoned, it would only serve to make him a martyr. We don't know how far his reputation has traveled or how many people there are in his movement."

Suddenly feeling weak, I sank to my knees. Having no tears left, I couldn't cry about it.

There will be no retribution for my months of imprisonment and molestation. And he's going to think I asked for it because I told him I would. He'll think I love him. I'll never be rid of him.

I looked up into Father's eyes and I could see he understood how I felt. Even though he didn't know everything I had been through, he knew it had been a lot to bear.

"What of his job?"

"I *did* manage to convince them that he shouldn't be able remain in the Royal Arborian Guard at all. He will be honorably discharged."

I looked down and scoffed. "Honorable. At least it's something"

My parents both lowered themselves to the floor with me. "What is the other thing, Father?"

He hesitated. "There will be ten Arborian men, but only nine will be elected."

I looked at him with desperation. "Oh, please, Father. Don't tell me they *want* Frank to participate."

"Of course they don't. However, they feel the army won't surrender without their leader being able to participate. They have also voted to rig it so he lasts to the final two Arborian participants."

Now I'm really in trouble.

"I need to tell you something, Father." I swallowed. "Frank is insane. He has believed he's in love with me since the first night he was my Guard. Trying to find a better opportunity to escape, I convinced him I was in love with him, too. When I presented this idea to Frank, I told him I would ask for the pardons and his participation in the King's Test."

Mother's eyes widened with understanding. "He'll think *you* requested them. He'll continue to think you love him."

I looked at her. "I don't know what to do. Most of the time, he's kind, but if he gets angry – "

Mother traced the fading brown hand mark on my face like she hadn't noticed it before. The look on her face was one of mortification.

"You'll just have to keep up with the charade," Father said.

I turned back to him pale and mouth agape. "Are you serious?"

"Yes. When he fails, it will be a tragic thing for him, but at least he won't think it was planned. There will be less chance of retribution on his part."

Knowing he was right, I nodded. "Well, I suppose we should head out to the gates and wait for King Francis II and his army."

Chapter 30

When we made it outside, there were fifty Royal Arborian Guard soldiers waiting in straight rows and columns. The soldiers saluted my parents as we walked down the steps and Father saluted them in return. Frank's father, High General Miller looked ashamed. I would be ashamed, too, if my son was the biggest traitor in our kingdom's history. His curt nod to my father told me, though, that it was us he supported, not his son.

When we made it to the back of the group, they turned around and marched in sync behind us. It was odd that I had now been involved with two different armies. I always thought I wasn't made for the military, but here I was, next in line to be the Commander in Chief over the military for the entire kingdom.

The strange thing about it was that I wasn't uncomfortable with it. It felt natural.

Maybe Frank was right. Maybe my mind does remember who I am.

I felt my posture straightening and my chin lifting as we approached the gate. When we got there, Father took an extra couple of steps forward and the soldiers behind Mother and me marched in place for a count of six steps, then stopped.

A dead calm settled in the palace courtyard. Curious pedestrians began to crowd around the gate. That's when we started to hear the screams coming in from all sides.

"Please return to your homes for safety. There will be an announcement later concerning what will happen here today." Father shouted to the crowd, though once the screaming started, people were heading back anyway.

Father put a hand to one of his ears. "Good. Hold them for now." Turning back to face Mother and me, he said, "North portion of Frank's army have surrendered. They were surrounded before they knew what was going on and no one was killed or injured."

I nodded. When I looked at Mother, she was just standing firm, which Father must have read as agreement.

The sound of screaming approached the gates and we could now hear the faint sound of boots marching in unison. It didn't take long before a mass of people turned a corner and were running away from the army following them.

Local people in their homes opened their doors for their neighbors and I couldn't help but be proud. The fact that they would put their lives at risk for their fellow man said a lot about the values my parents used to lead our kingdom.

Eventually, the streets were emptied of civilians, who either fled down side streets or jumped inside the houses that opened to them. All we could hear then was the marching coming in from the left, right, and approaching the street in front of us.

The first person to turn the corner was Frank. When he became visible to us, his army began chanting.

"Our King Declares The Truth! Our King Declares The Truth!"

The chanting with the rhythmic marching reminded me of the drums and battle cries of the soldiers in historical movies. I always thought it was silly, but seeing it in real life made me afraid.

I hope this works.

When the three sides converged into one massive unit, it was overwhelming. Definitely more than when I stood on the balcony with Frank.

Head held high and flanked with guards to each side and behind him, Frank made his way to the gate. It was incredible to me how regal he could make himself appear, even though he was really nothing more than a self-involved, psychopathic control freak.

Father was already at the gate, which I thought was brilliant. Though Frank brought an army with him, *he* still had to approach the true King of Arboria.

The marching and chanting stopped. Silence fell over everyone present as the King and King Imposter glared at each other.

"Frank, it is – interesting to see you in these circumstances. Please state your business." Father addressed him as if he was any concerned citizen approaching him as their leader. He maintained his leadership over Frank in subtle, yet significant, ways.

"Aaron, I have come to tell you that your rule as King is over. I will take Miriam as my bride and we will begin to rule today."

I blanched at his bluntness with Father and the way he made marrying me sound like a task on his to-do list.

Not responding to the obvious disrespect of Frank calling him by only his name, Father said, "I am afraid that is not going to be what happens here today, Frank. As I am sure you are aware, the next King of Arboria must participate in the King's Test."

Frank gritted his teeth as he said, "I am aware of that tradition. However, despite the concerns raised by some of the citizens of your kingdom, you have allowed ten *foreigners* to participate when your kingdom is filled with good men, though they happen to not be of a Noble position."

Father nodded. "Yes. I only recently learned about the concerns from the Delegates and Nobles. I assure you, negotiations would have been different had I been informed about the issue."

Frank scoffed, clearly not believing the truth Father had put forth. "I am not interested in 'ifs' in this situation, Aaron. I am interested in keeping the Crown on an Arborian, even if that means removing the Crown you."

Father put on a pensive face and stroked his chin with his hand. "Would you be open to a compromise, Frank?"

For the first time, Frank's gaze left Father and landed on me. I gave him a slight smile and he nodded tersely in response. "What would you propose?"

"The Council wishes for there to be Royalty or Nobility as King, but you and your people wish to give an Arborian the Crown regardless of their position, yes?"

"Yes."

"I propose we keep the ten Princes who have arrived for the King's Test. It could cause conflict with another nation, should we send them back. However, I am open to the idea of also having ten elected Arborian men participate as well." I noted that he didn't include Frank's participation or the pardons; he was keeping his cards close to his chest.

Frank's eye twitched; he noticed. "Aaron, as brilliant as the idea is, my people have been preparing to crown me for years. How could I deny them that?"

"What if you were to participate? Evidently, you have already been elected by a good number of people, so I do not see how your participation could be argued. Would your people be amenable to that?"

Frank looked behind him at his nearest commanders, who nodded. He must have prepared them for this possibility. "They would be agreeable. How do I know that we will not all be charged with high treason before the King's Test even begins?"

Father's fingers twitched a little at this. I could tell he really hated to offer the pardons, but it had been voted on and approved, so his hands were tied. "I would be willing to offer full pardons to you and those who follow you."

Frank extended his hand to shake on the deal. Though there was a moment of hesitation from Father, he took Frank's hand and shook it.

"Princess Miriam, please step forward," Father ordered.

I ended up standing next to him. Staring at an old, tall tree behind everyone, I kept my head held high as Father asked, "Have you heard the conversation in its entirety, Princess?"

I swallowed. "Yes, Sir. I have."

"And is it agreeable to you?"

Not at all.

"Yes, Sir. It is."

"May I make a request, Aaron?"

"You are pushing my kindness and generosity, Frank. If you are going to be allowed to participate in an event as important as the King's Test, it would be good to continue referring to me as 'King Aaron'. Despite rank, you should always address someone by their title while in public. You will note I even called my own daughter by her title."

Frank clenched his jaw. "Yes, Your Majesty." It made my heart happy to see him struggle with letting go of his control.

"Go ahead and make your request, Frank. Though I cannot promise you any more compromise than you have already received."

"I would have Princess Miriam demonstrate her agreement, as well, given the circumstances she has been in over the last couple of months. Her willingness to proceed with the King's Test with the proposed changes is of the utmost importance to me."

Father looked at me as if to say it was up to me. I had to take an extra step forward – my arms were much shorter than Father's – and offered a delicate hand. Frank took it, and kissed my knuckles.

Frank turned around to face his army.

Great. I'm going to have to endure another one of Frank's speeches.

"Men and women of this army, I thank you for your commitment to our cause over the last several years. As you know, our movement began because we felt the need to have an Arborian crowned King. I am pleased to announce that King Aaron has finally agreed to allow ten of our men, regardless of position, to participate alongside the ten Princes of the foreign nations. We have succeeded with this victory!"

"Our King Declares The Truth!"

How do they all know when to say that?

"Though I have been granted one of those positions, there is a chance that neither I nor any Arborian man may be chosen in the end. Should this happen, I expect no rioting or rebelling. At that point, we will have had our chance and failed. Return to your homes. Embrace your families. Celebrate our victory and the coming Crowning Coronation of the Rose of Petrichoria. She will be your Queen regardless of the results of the King's Test and deserves your highest respect!"

"Our King Declares The Truth!"

Frank's speech was interrupted by the random sound of a single gunshot. Frantically, I searched around both armies, but none looked guilty.

"Miriam!" Frank shouted from the other side of the gate and reached through to bring me close, much to my chagrin. His people were beginning to march forward to force the gates open.

Staying in character, I said, "Don't be afraid. I don't think another shot will happen. It was only one."

Feeling lightheaded, I staggered.

"Miriam!" Frank shouted as I slumped in his arms and he lowered me to my knees, his body pressed against the gate.

I felt a sharp pain and wetness in my abdomen and finally looked down at myself. I had been shot.

"Oh," I said weakly.

The Guards rushed my parents out of harm's way and another shot rang out. This time, the force of the bullet hitting my shoulder was too much to bear and I fell forward into the gate.

Frank sobbed as a Guard lifted me into his cradling arms and I could hear accusations being thrown around on both sides of the gate.

I looked at Frank, seeing my blood covering him. "Get somewhere safe." I don't know why I said it or if it really mattered to me. All I knew was that I didn't want anyone else to die.

With great reluctance, he turned toward his army. I thought he was yelling, but all I could hear was a shrill ringing. The guard turned around to rush me inside.

I could feel and see the chaos surrounding me, but couldn't feel anything emotionally at that moment. No. I could feel something. I could feel the blood rushing from my shoulder.

In my delirium, I thought of the most insignificant thing at the moment.

I really liked this jacket.

At that thought, my world blurred and darkness surrounded me.

Chapter 31

I am standing at the top of the stairs in the ballroom wearing a red satin mermaid dress and a beautiful new tiara made from rose gold and encrusted with emeralds.

Hands folded in front of me and posture straight, I look at the men standing before me. A line of identical green silhouettes stand before me, but one is different.

One is pitch black with shining stars interspersed all over his body. Tilting my head, I try to figure out who he could be. It is then that I realize he is the same man from the graveyard.

I start to move forward, but I am stopped by someone taking my hand. When I turn around David is standing there.

"Don't go near him."

"Who?"

"The Man of Night. He means to commit great acts of treachery and will only bring darkness into your life."

I look back at the man. "But he's so beautiful. How could someone so lovely do anything so wrong?"

"Miriam, you should know better than anyone that appearances aren't always what they seem."

"Why can't I see his face or the faces of the other men?"

"I don't know, honey."

I look back to David. "Does it hurt?"

He furrows his brow. "Does what hurt?"

"Seeing me here like this. Knowing that when I awaken, I'll be coronated Crown Princess and the twenty men before us will all be vying for my hand in marriage."

His face softens. "No, it doesn't bother me."

"I mean, aside from you being a figment of my imagination. How would David really feel about all this?"

"I am David. I've always been a figment of your imagination, so anything I say to you is what I would have said when I was living in your personal world."

"Oh. I suppose that makes sense."

There is a pause in our conversation.

"It doesn't bother me because I know you're living your real life now. I wish happiness for you. I wish for you to fall so madly in love that I don't enter your dreams anymore."

Tears begin falling down my face. "I'm scared, David."

He brings me in for a hug like he has done a million times before. "I know. You'll be okay. Just be wary of the Man of Night."

"How will I know who he is?"

He sighs. "I don't know. Hopefully it will be clear to you."

"I don't want to wake up."

"But it's time now, Miriam."

"Beware the Man of Night," I mumbled as I woke up. I opened my eyes to see the dark red ceiling of my own room and immediately began crying.

I'm home. I'm finally home.

I was vaguely aware of the heart monitor, breathing apparatus, and IV's in my arm. It felt similar to waking up in Frank's hospital, except I knew I was safe. At least for the moment, even though I was tired of going unconscious and not knowing where I was when I woke up.

Beware the Man of Night.

I had no idea what it meant. My dreams were becoming more and more confusing. At first, they were comforting, like when David and I were on the beach together. However, the latest ones were foreboding. My life was about to become complicated and dangerous.

I had decided that my dreams, were, in fact, visions. Not that I would tell anyone about them. They would blame it on the Daze or claim I was crazy. I didn't believe in magic, so I knew it wasn't that. It left religion or science; both were viable options as far as my personal reasoning went.

Would anyone even believe me if I told them? Peter looked at me as if I was the Mad Hatter when I told him about Ella and Thomas and the vision. I hope he heeded my warning, regardless.

Even though I knew before I passed out that no one besides me had been hurt, I worried about the chaos in the aftermath of it. Everyone blamed the opposite army from them and I knew threats were being thrown around.

Though I wasn't a big fan of Frank, I hoped he was able to get his people under control. I had a feeling that if one side could be calmed, the other would follow suit, no longer viewing them as a threat.

I turned my head to my left and saw Ella fast asleep in a chair.

She wore simple brown trousers with a seafoam green sweater. Her blonde hair was down and a bit ragged. I wondered what time it was.

Quirking an eyebrow, I asked, "How long have you been here?" My voice was scratchy and it hurt when I spoke.

Ella's head shot up and she looked at me with wide eyes. She scurried over to sit next to me on my bed. Taking my hand, she said, "It doesn't matter how long I've been here. I'm glad you're awake."

I smacked my parched tongue with the top of my mouth and she brought a glass with a straw in it to my lips. After drinking, I said, "Of course it matters. You should be home with your husband and son." My voice was less scratchy now that I had wet my tongue.

Ella smiled and looked down at our hands. "But I've almost lost you three times now. I couldn't do anything the first or second time. This time, I could sit with you and take care of you. I've been letting the nurse know when your fluids were out."

"Thank you, Ella. You really are a gem."

Ella smiled sadly. "You always used to say that to me."

"Really?"

"Yes. Every time I made fun of your title, the Rose of Petrichoria, you would say, 'Gee, thanks, Ella. You're a real gem.'"

"It *is* a pretty weird title."

We both laughed about it, but the laughter quickly died down. For me, it was because it *really* hurt. For Ella, she wasn't done being serious yet.

"Rose, I'm sorry that I married Peter."

An unintentional tear streamed out of the corner of my left eye. "Oh, Ella. I understand. You both needed to secure your family lines. Plus, if I didn't wake up before my parents died, you would have had to rule and you shouldn't have had to do that alone."

"There are many excuses. But it runs deeper than that for me. I gave up on you and so did he. I never thought you would wake up in my lifetime, to be honest, and I felt so terrible for Peter. He was heartbroken. Did you know he called the hospital every day to check in on your condition – even after we were married?"

I shook my head. "No, I didn't know that."

After a pregnant pause, Ella said quietly, "I *know*, Rose."

I tilted my head up slightly. "What do you know?"

"And I don't blame you. It's Peter's fault. I'm not angry with you."

"I don't understand." Then it dawned on me and I'm sure Ella saw understanding spread across my face.

"Ella, I'm so sorry. It should have never happened. I was just so confused having just learned the truth and – "

Ella put a gentle finger to my lips to silence me. "Like I said, I don't blame you. Peter actually told me the day after you were kidnapped. He blamed himself because he thought if he hadn't taken advantage of your confusion and given into his heartbreak, he could have protected you while you danced with him."

"Well, you can tell him I don't blame anyone but Frank. I'm glad he confessed to you. I felt terrible and I'm not sure if I would have done it."

She smiled. "I understand." Looking at her hands again, she said, "Don't almost die again, okay?"

I smiled. "I don't intend to. I think I've been in enough dangerous situations in my lifetime. One is even too many, but now I've had three."

"Four."

"Four?"

She nodded. "Doctor Quincy was able to figure out what went wrong during your time in deep sleep. During your time in the freeze, someone opened the hatch for a moment to look at you. They closed it back up and turned everything back on, so no one noticed the anomaly. Doctor Quincy thinks that the Daze was able to seep into your mind deeper than they thought and begin an episode while the tank was open."

"I'm not sure if that's more terrifying or creepy. Who was it that opened it?"

"They were never able to identify him."

"Great. So stalker-guy is still out there somewhere."

She giggled. "I'm sure security will be at least doubled now."

"And hopefully background checking will be a little more thorough."

"About that, how do you feel about the Council demanding he be allowed to participate in the King's Test?"

I knew by "he" she meant Frank. How did I feel about it? I rolled my eyes. "Horrified, terrified, disgusted, disappointed in humanity." I sighed. "There's no justice in it at all."

Ella tilted her head as she looked at me. "What happened while you were his captive?"

I closed my eyes and took a deep breath. Looking back at her, I told her. "I was lead out of the palace through a tunnel with splintered floors barefoot, knocked unconscious and carried around like a potato sack, intimidated, was wooed by a mad man who thought he was in love with me after two nights, I starved myself in a hunger strike, I was slapped across the face, kissed and touched unwantedly, and chased through a forest."

Ella was clearly mortified, her mouth agape and her eyebrows arched. "And they *want* him to participate?!"

"Apparently. Though, in all fairness, they made the decision without knowing what I had been through. In fact, you're the only one who knows anything about it. After he slapped me, I changed tactics and began pretending I was in love with him, too. That was how I ultimately escaped, but it took more than words to convince him."

"You didn't – "

"No! Trees, no! I would rather die!"

Ella paused. "What if he wins?"

"I thought Father gets the final decision."

Ella shook her head. "Under normal circumstances, he would. For this test, whoever scores best in the end wins. Because of the uprising, Council decided it was fairer for the King's Test to be performed objectively, rather than subjectively."

My mouth dropped open. "Fairer for who? So I *have* to marry the person most qualified for the job? What if I fall in love with someone? Or if the most qualified person is a total jerk? What if *Frank* ends up finishing first?"

"All good arguments that Uncle Aaron brought up when it was being discussed yesterday. They still believe it is the fairest way to do things this time." I began to cry. "Oh, Rose, Frank won't be first. There's no way. The Princes are more qualified than he is and we have yet to see who the other nine Arborians will be."

"I hope you're right, Ella. Because if you aren't, we'll be crowning a monster."

Epilogue

"You missed, you idiot!" The Man of Night shouted at his sniper. "You were not supposed to hit the Rose of Petrichoria! You could have ruined everything!"

"I am sorry, Sir. Something seemed to jam in my light gun and it caused my aim to be off," the sniper excused himself while fidgeting with his hands.

"Give me the light gun," the Man of Night said, holding out his hand to receive it. "Let me check it."

Nervously, the sniper began to sweat. "Sir, I will check it myself later, if it is all the same to you." He knew it was disrespectful, but the Man of Night was not a man to be messed with.

"It is. Give it to me," the Man of Night commanded.

The sniper stilled as he felt the mind control begin. "Please, Sir. I know I missed. I – I have a family." The sniper watched his hands as he involuntarily gave the Man of Night the light gun, but could say no more since the Man of Night held his lips closed.

The Man of Night examined the gun as he multitasked with keeping the sniper still and silent. Without hesitation, he pointed the light gun at the sniper's head and pulled the trigger, creating a burrowing tunnel through the man's forehead.

"Seems fine to me," the Man of Night muttered as he tucked the gun into the back of his pants. Now he had to head back to his room to come up with a new plan to meet his ends. At least he had one less incompetent person working for him.

Acknowledgements

First, and foremost, I would like to thank God for everything He has done for me. Most specifically, I thank Him for His inspiration and gift of writing.

I would not have been able to write this first novel, or the rest of the Rose of Petrichoria series, without the support of my family at The Barn. Thank you for all your encouragement and love! My husband, Nick, was gracious enough to let me use his idea of the Daze for the pandemic in this series. Be looking forward to a couple prequels where it plays a more prominent role.

Several people read through and critiqued Forgotten and I am appreciative for all of you, too: Julie Hauenstein, Philip Gosvener, Lynnette Bonner, Becky Luna, Blaine Bradshaw, Steve Mathisen, Courtney Evans, Sheri Mast, Deborah Wyatt, Cara Koch, Allison Grindley, and Kei Jager.

Note From The Author

Forgetting your life, or knowing someone who has, is a horrible experience. In 2007, my mother suffered strokes while recovering from quadruple bypass heart surgery. One of the debilitating consequences was a loss of short-term memory. Over time, her vascular dementia has progressed to the point that she most often doesn't remember most long-term memories either.

If you have a loved one who is living with dementia, it is understandable that it would be difficult to see them go through it, or even to experience the heartbreak when they don't recognize you. People with dementia don't have the luxury of remembering your last visit. They live in the here and now. While it may be hard for you to see them, give them the love and respect they continue to deserve because they are still human beings with human feelings.

They have forgotten, do not forget them.